Return to Grace

Return to Grace

MARLENE CHASE

Dedicated to Diane, my friend and colleague for thirty years, whose careful critique and artistic support are invaluable. A professional photographer and colleague in Salvation Army ministry, Diane's stunning photograph of "Pinehill" graces the cover.

Chapter 1

Anne Westin turned to study her restored 19th-century house and sensed it studying her in the brooding light. Surrounded by a lush lawn and a private wood, the stone structure seemed impenetrable, an iron maiden for whom time held no threat. The porch ran the length of the southern exposure and wrapped around the eastern side where hydrangea bushes had blanched to a dull brown. A gust of wind sent burnished leaves flying from the stately maples whose denuded branches appealed to a sky plotting winter—her first at Grace Arbor. According to the locals in the small Wisconsin community she'd adopted, summer's trapeze act often ended with a descent into snowy arms as early as October.

A shudder that had little to do with the chilling wind rippled through her. She turned up the collar of her fleece jacket—a long-ago gift from Richard, whose arms could no longer hold her. A sudden heart attack had brought an end to their thirty-year marriage. Still, she'd gone ahead with the renovation of Grace Arbor, determined to live there with purpose and peace. But the latter had been in short supply. How long did it take before you were welcome on your own land—in your own house?

"Why move so far north where winter comes early and stays late?" her friends had wanted to know. "Whoever heard of Ladystone anyway?" Peter, ever the pragmatist, had said it sounded like a variety of granite. The son had nonetheless championed the mother's resolve and, during his first summer visit, had found that Ladystone yielded something unexpected— a neighbor with shining amber hair and eyes who viewed the world from a different perspective.

Anne had loved Grace Arbor from the first moment she'd seen it. Situated six or seven hours away from her native Chicago, Ladystone had been just the getaway she and Richard had dreamed of. It would be a place for their children and grandchildren to visit, a haven for their expanding dreams. Here, pioneer Harlan Stone had carved out a lumber empire in the midst of raw wilderness. He named the town that grew up around it for his wife, Lady Lillian. It had flourished for nearly a century and held its own through the good times and bad with uncommon grit and tenacity, but Ladystone had never been a major player. Instead, it had become an idyllic refuge for hunters, fishermen, and perhaps for those with something to hide.

Richard was gone, and it had become her refuge. She steeled herself against the bittersweet ache that still smoldered like an unquenchable flame. She cast her eyes over the vast ten-acre estate spreading beneath the leaden sky. Here, she would listen to the secrets that whispered in the wind and to the voices of Ladystone friends and neighbors. They were a hardy lot, but she had learned they embraced strangers with reluctance.

It was foolhardy enough, some conjectured, to retire at 52 to the north woods. But when a dead man was found on her property the day she'd moved in, a sensible woman would have looked for other options, wouldn't she? Anne smiled wryly. Had it really been only six months since her arrival and the frightening days that followed?

The mystery of her neighbor's death had been solved, and the age-old treasure buried on Grace Arbor's land had been exhumed; surely, now she could really enjoy her new home without history intruding. She surveyed the uncultivated part of the estate—acres of forest whose colors shifted and changed with the seasons. In the green bounty of early summer, death had visited there. The skies were pregnant now with rain or snow, and a blast of warning wind blew across the rust-colored meadow. She quickened her steps. There was much to be done before the snow came.

She drew back the latch on the small stone shed, which once might have been a gatehouse. Now, it bore a cache of rakes and mowers and summer's leftovers—birdseed, gardening catalogs, rakes, and hoes. It was high time to bring a bucket of ice melt up to Grace Arbor's redwood deck.

She glanced over the hedge that bordered her property and felt her pulse quicken. Her neighbor's house was little more than a shack, which had once been part of Anne's property—a kind of servants' quarters. Vera Popov and her brother Alexei had lived there after fleeing Eastern Europe with a formidable elderly dowager whose past was the stuff of legends. After Alexei's body was found in Grace Arbor's woods, the story revived. It had sent Ladystone tongues wagging and brought curious history buffs to the obscure little town. Vera had welcomed neither and openly showed her disdain for her new neighbor.

Vera Popov wasn't watching her today—at least, not that Annie could tell. "Deluded old Ruskie," a neighbor had said of the woman now alone in the little house adjacent to Grace Arbor.

Who would have guessed that she and her brother were connected as children to the historic Romanov Dynasty and the Bolshevik Revolution? Who would have imagined that their mistress had been a child into whose garments precious jewels had been hidden—jewels that had been buried for decades on Anne's property? The treasure had been sold and the money

3

turned over to its rightful heir, young Tess Popov of the amber hair and shining eyes—Tess, the lovely Deaf girl who might just have stolen Peter's heart.

Tess had lived with the old servants, even taken their name, for two decades. Anne paused at the line of lilac bushes to view the run-down house where Vera lived—alone now that her brother was dead and 21-year-old Tess had moved into town. In summer, generous purple blooms obscured the old shack, but the season's barren march laid all things bare. There was no hiding the torn shutters and smudged windows and the collection of junk around the tumble-down place. Two chicken coops near the house were little more than rotting boards held together with rusting wire. More than once, the shattering cries of Vera's prized cocks had split the morning air. Occasionally, Anne found a straying Popov hen or two roosting atop her shed.

She paused, fingers on the latch. Something caught her eye at the south end of her shed. She moved closer to the boundary line. What on earth? Soggy straw hung off the shed roof. Egg shells, feathers, bird droppings, and a host of unidentifiable detritus mingled and spilled onto the ground in noxious clumps. A discarded aluminum pail and bits of broken crockery added to the mess.

It looked like someone had cleaned a barn and hefted the garbage over the lilac hedge onto her property. She stared in dismay. The stuff had to have come from Vera Popov's chicken coops just beyond the long row of bushes. It wouldn't be the first time her neighbor had expressed her disdain. From the day Anne arrived, she had been treated as an outsider and anything but welcome.

Anne felt her Irish blood rising as she pictured Vera's heavy arms bulging in an ancient house dress, eyes like black pebbles in the withered pool of her face. Her hair was still black at 60 or more—not even the slightest intrusion of gray—but age and bitterness had worked deep crevices into the broad, sloping forehead and around the grim mouth. Her Russian accent, though not as pronounced as Alexei's had been, underscored her formidable rants.

Anne clasped her arms at the elbows of her jacket and marveled at the oddities, the inequities of life. To Vera, Tess, the lovely Deaf girl she and her brother had raised, was an accident of birth. It was no wonder that Tess had viewed herself that way for so long, misunderstanding the hearing as thoroughly as they misunderstood her. Only Alexei loved her and did his best to care for her, even in his later years when he had grown senile and become the talk of the town. "Crazy old coot," they called him when he began digging up the ground in search of a buried treasure.

Somehow, Tess had developed into a sensitive and intelligent young woman. Who would care about her now that Alexei was gone? She could hardly depend on Vera's inscrutable whims. And though she had inherited her grandmother's wealth—perhaps because of it—she was vulnerable.

Anne Westin, a Midwestern romantic with a penchant for small-town friendships, had championed the girl Alexei had loved. Tess had made her way into a new world, moving with Anne's help into her own apartment close to the hospital's data processing department where she worked. She was out from under the nose of her caustic Aunt Vera.

Championing the young girl had been Anne's unforgivable sin. Vera blamed her not only for Alexei's death (after all, he'd been found in Grace Arbor's woods) but for Tess moving out on her own. Who could blame Tess for wanting to escape the bitterness that hung over Vera like a shroud? Still, hadn't Vera always resented caring for the granddaughter of her former mistress, the woman who, as a child, had escaped the famed Romanov massacre?

As a young woman, she came to the East Coast of America and brought Alexei and Vera with her. She had married and had one daughter who died shortly after her little Deaf baby was born. The woman fled north and built the graceful mansion in Ladystone that years later would become Anne's. She lived only a few months after moving into her northern refuge. As she lay dying, she begged Alexei to take care of her granddaughter, entrusting the special child and the jewels to his keeping. The old woman had known to keep the inheritance secret from Vera—not so much because she was greedy or selfish but because she was childlike and simple. Vera might well have spent the fortune on her beloved chickens.

Anne contemplated the mess of smelly straw, feathers, and eggshells. This was her punishment for buying Grace Arbor, for befriending Tess, for being who she was. Perplexed and fuming over the absurdity of her neighbor's behavior, she flung back the shed door and hauled out a rake and broom. She'd need a barrel to collect the trash and debris. Didn't she have enough to do without cleaning up her neighbor's messes? What had she done to deserve this unreasonable treatment?

Anne sighed. She had really tried to be a good neighbor, offering friendship. After Alexei died, she had taken Vera and Tess a home-cooked meal and flowers from her garden. The gifts had been received in stoic silence, and none of the containers returned. So much for her welcome to the neighborhood. Well, that was water under the bridge. *Or trash over the roof,* she thought grimly.

Anne removed her jacket, leaving only her cotton-weave sweater. She had to get the stuff off the roof. It would take hours to rake up the debris and restore order. She pulled on her gardening boots and paused, one foot in the air. Why should she have to do this? She would just march through the hedge and demand that Vera clean up the mess she'd made.

Steady, she told herself as the timeless words intruded with contemporary meddlesomeness: "A soft answer turns away anger." God's prescription for anger could be downright annoying when you want to give someone a piece of your mind. Still, withholding anger didn't mean becoming a doormat.

She strode through the hedge and knocked at her neighbor's sagging door. The house was a disgrace. Why hadn't the woman fixed up the place? She had more than enough money now to live comfortably, thanks to Tess, who had graciously shared her inheritance. No one would have blamed Tess if she never stepped foot in that house again. But Tess wasn't likely to abandon Vera, even though there were no blood ties between them.

"Vera! Are you there?" Anne called. "I want to talk to you."

Silence. If Vera were inside the house, she was obviously not going to respond, or perhaps she was in one of the coops tending the chickens.

"She talks to them like they were her babies," Tess had said, eyes wistful. "She never talked to me like that."

Poor Tess. Bereaved of her birth mother and her grandmother, she had been denied even the slightest tenderness from the woman who'd taken her in by default. Alexei was dead, and Margaret Morris, the elderly school teacher who may have been her only friend growing up might not recover after a serious bout with pneumonia. From Grace Arbor, Anne could see Margaret's house, a small square on the distant hill with no smoke rising from its chimney. Margaret had been in a nursing home for several months.

Anne frowned, saddened over Margaret, who had become her friend too in the short time she'd known her. *Onward to the task ahead!* She sighed and pushed through the door of the first coop, sending a draft of cold air into the damp interior. Chickens squawked at the intrusion, and a few dirty white biddies shook their feathers and muttered their bird warnings. But there was no sign of Vera.

Anne let the door flap shut and whirled around, her mind racing. This had to stop. How could she live next door to someone who refused to abide by even the most basic rules of civility?

The whole thing had been like a soap opera. Vera had unwittingly conspired to steal the inheritance that Alexei had hidden for Tess—hidden and, as dementia set in, forgot. Reporting on the girl's movements, Vera had played into the hands of a young man determined to grab the jewels for himself. Authorities had taken into consideration Vera's diminished capacity. Since she'd not participated in the kidnapping or the actual theft, charges hadn't been filed. The man had held Anne and Margaret Morris at gunpoint, thinking they knew where the money was.

Anne had no wish to punish Vera Popov. She simply wanted peace with her neighbors and a clear title to Grace Arbor. One would think the woman would be grateful to have escaped legal recompense and would become an amiable citizen. "Fat chance," Anne muttered under her breath.

She stepped back through the hedge, cringing as branches scraped her legs. Maybe her children had been right about this move to the wilds of Wisconsin. As the November air nipped at her cheeks, Anne thought of warmer, welcoming climates. She might be sunning on a beach somewhere or at least on the veranda with a glass of lemonade. But in spite of everything, Grace Arbor still held her heart.

Reluctantly, she dragged the cumbersome ladder from the shed and prepared to inspect the roof with its muddy contents. She'd have to clean it up herself or live with this insult to the order and serenity of Grace Arbor. Hostile neighbors notwith-standing, she was determined to make it her home.

She turned at the sound of a car coming up the driveway. Propping the ladder against the shed, she watched Tess climb out of her blue Toyota. After years of getting around only on the bicycle, Tess had finally realized her dream of a car. Anne's heart brightened at the sight of the girl moving lithely across the lawn, gazelle-like, copper hair swaying. Such grace and beauty were surprising, given the awkward models with whom she'd been raised until her 21st birthday.

"Hello. How are you?" the girl called, her voice loud on the morning air.

She often spoke too loudly or too softly, and why should anyone be surprised? How were the Deaf to gauge velocity? Tess, though, was incredibly good at judging vibrations and often astounded people with her sensitive perception. As a driver, her record accorded with national statistics that prove Deaf drivers have fewer accidents than hearing ones. Anne called back a good morning.

"I brought egg cartons for Aunt Vera," Tess said and shifted the ungainly stack in slender arms. "She needs them for … " Tess broke off, frowning as she stared at the trash strewn around the shed. "What happened?"

Anne sighed, wishing Tess hadn't come just at that moment. "Well, it's only a guess, but it looks like the contents of those chicken coops got over the hedge onto my place."

Tess's eyes darkened beneath amber brows. "I'm sorry," she said, looking down and shifting her weight from one foot to the other. How often had she been embarrassed by Vera's rude behavior? How often had she been the target of the woman's unreasonable temper?

"Don't worry," Anne said. "It's just chicken debris. It'll clean up. I was going to start with the roof."

"No, let me climb the ladder. I'll do it," she said, the garbled "L's" and "Rs" that were part of her charm exaggerated now from embarrassment. She scooted up the ladder with quick agility and held out her hand for the broom.

Together, they collected the sodden debris and rolled the trash barrel down the long driveway to the road. When the task was finished, they walked back to Grace Arbor, too weary or perhaps too troubled for conversation.

"Come in for some cider?" Anne asked.

"You don't have to bother," Tess said. She looked down at her shoes, then back to gauge Anne's mood.

"Please don't worry about this." Anne took a deep breath and blew it out slowly. "It's not your fault. Your aunt is—well—bitter and sad. Maybe we can find a way to help her understand. Come, you need a rest."

After washing up, they sat in Grace Arbor's spacious living room. Anne stirred the embers burning low in the fireplace and considered Tess leaning against a cushion on the ivory brocade sofa. The girl who had become her friend did not attempt conversation. It occurred to Anne that she had been withdrawn a lot lately—prone to long periods of silence.

Her son, Peter, had met Tess last summer when he'd come to visit at Grace Arbor. They'd met by accident when Tess was trying to help a fawn caught in the thick underbrush. The two had quickly become friends—perhaps more than that. He came back to visit when his work allowed for it, but it had been several weeks since he had come. Had something happened between him and Tess?

"If you're worried about that fiasco with the chicken coops and the trash … " Anne began.

Tess shook her head. "No, I—I—" She stammered, reverting to signing as she spoke, something she only did when she was nervous or unhappy. "It's nothing. I'm sorry." Her eyes roamed over her cup of cider and stopped at the photos that hung above the fireplace.

Looking out from one of the frames was Peter, tall and angular with his father's sandy good looks and sharp eyes. Peter worked as a microbiologist for a Chicago company that researched environmentally safe products. His job involved long hours of experimentation and study. He wasn't wearing his glasses in the photo, but if he had been, they would surely have slipped just below the bridge of his nose. Anne smiled. Peter hated it when she referred to his nose as "aristocratic."

"An aristocratic nose," he had mourned, "is just a euphemism for a long snout!"

Peter hadn't been able to get away from Chicago for almost a month, and Anne missed him. He'd been a rock in helping her get settled and working through the events surrounding last summer's investigation at Grace Arbor. Meeting Tess, it seemed, had a strange but welcome effect on him. He was beginning to heal after a series of emotional blows, not the least of which was his father's untimely death—an injustice aimed squarely at the Almighty.

Was death ever timely? Richard's death had been a shock unlike anything she'd ever experienced. They had made such plans, sure they would have years together, and then, in one devastating moment, he was gone. The hollow feeling in her stomach threatened to overcome her, and she turned her attention back to Tess.

Was she thinking about Peter, wondering why he hadn't visited recently? Had he been in touch with her since befriending her through the horrible episode when Alexei's death had been under investigation? "Peter's been working very hard these days," she said, hoping to ease the girl's mind.

"I know," she said, looking down at her hands, which were wrapped around a china mug of delicate blue flowers and vines. "He—he emails and we talk." She looked down into the amber liquid absently, a sign of distraction, perhaps unease.

Anne leaned toward her, inviting close attention. "Are things all right at work?" she asked brightly.

The girl nodded, returning her eyes to the mantel pictures. "Yes," she said softly.

Anne passed the plate of maple sugar brownies she'd baked that morning, but Tess gave a quick shake of her head and continued to caress the rim of her cup. Anne helped herself to a brownie from the matching china plate. Except for the crackling and hissing of the fire, silence reigned.

Presently, Tess looked up through troubled eyes. "Is Miss Morris going to be okay?"

She caught her lower lip in her teeth, and her astonishing blue eyes clouded. Was she reliving the events of last summer, the reason the old woman was ill? The harrowing night when she and Anne had been taken hostage had demanded a toll on Margaret's 80-year-old body. If it hadn't been for Tess protecting her and calling for help, the frail lady might well have died in the chilly woods.

"The doctor says she'll have to get much stronger before she can go home," Anne said. "She's been very sick." She followed Tess's gaze out the wide bay window to a house that was little more than a tiny square on the distant rise. "The pneumonia has left her very weak."

Anne shuddered and hastened to reassure her. "Margaret's a fighter. She'll come through. She'll be at Rutgers' for a while until she's well enough to come home." Anne moved to pour more cider into Tess's cup, but the girl tossed her tawny head in a decisive shake.

"No, thank you. I have to go."

Anne watched her gather her jacket and egg crates and turn toward the door. Over her short life, Tess had lost a lot—her hearing, a real home with loving parents, her dear Uncle Alexei, and even Shane Eldridge, a young man who had proved to be the worst kind of scoundrel. What if yet another thread were pulled from the fabric of the girl's life? What if Margaret, who had become as close to Tess as a grandmother, didn't get well?

Chapter 2

Margaret Morris lay on the narrow bed at Rutgers Nursing Home, where she had been transferred to recuperate from her siege of pneumonia. It was mid-afternoon. She could tell by the sun's slow decline, casting its shadow across the dresser. On the wall, a calendar with large numerals read "November." It hung slightly crooked on the beige wall and portrayed a garish wash of orange trees. Margaret closed her eyes. Oh, to be home beneath her spreading maple trees, to bask in their sheltering beauty! In spring, their leaves were a chartreuse splendor, and in autumn, a crimson riot of color. Oh, to lie at peace and look at them.

Suddenly, she became aware that someone was in the room. She opened her eyes and found Erma Tanner staring at her through eyes magnified by coke-bottle glasses.

"Erma, what are you doing spying on me like that?" Margaret asked. She raised herself on one elbow. "A woman needs her privacy, you know." Irritation crept up and settled in a spot on her left temple. She drew in her breath, relieved that at least she felt no urge to cough. Maybe she was indeed getting better.

"I'm sorry. I didn't mean to spy." Erma Tanner backed her wheelchair away from Margaret's bed. "I just wanted to see if you were awake. I—I … " Her lower lip, which bore the remnants of yesterday's lipstick, trembled in her fleshy face as her words fell away. Her heavy glasses made a deep ridge on the top of her broad nose. Her eyes, magnified and comical, misted. Dyed red hair stuck out in spikes on the left side of her chubby face; it lay flat on the other as though she'd crushed it in her sleep and never thought to comb it when she woke up. She looked, Margaret thought, like a sad clown.

"I'm sorry, Erma. I didn't mean to snap at you." Contrite, Margaret knew she'd been unkind. She had been yearning to go home—home to her own little house with its window open to the sun and stars—and she had felt embarrassed, as though Erma had read her thoughts. "It's just ... well, it gives a person a start to wake up and find someone gawking at you."

"I just wanted to talk," Erma said, looking down at feet that protruded awkwardly in their boat-like slippers. They had to be two sizes too big with foolish pompoms affixed to their tips. She blew her nose hard and wiped it with a tissue, which she then tucked into the cuff of her long-sleeved blouse.

Margaret shrugged. "What time is it?" she asked in an attempt to make amends. She knew it was afternoon, but how much after? She'd have to get someone to bring her clock with its lighted dial, but thinking about it made her feel all the more homesick and at odds with herself and the world. It troubled her that days and nights sometimes ran together without regard for order and pace.

"Just a little after three," Erma said, rocking slightly in her wheelchair. She leaned forward and looked at Margaret tentatively.

"Pull up closer," Margaret said, penitent for having been rude. "You know I'm glad to see you." She attempted to smile and raised an eyebrow in anticipation.

Erma came from a small town in northern Minnesota. More than thirty years earlier, she had lost her husband. Her family had disappeared into some vortex that made them forget the past and those they had loved. Thirty years was a long time to be alone, Margaret thought, tracing the indentation on the bridge of Erma's nose. What demon made people shut others out and turned them inward like a night flower? Wasn't she doing the same thing to Erma, who needed someone to talk to?

"So, what do you know?" Margaret ventured, smiling into the round face. Erma's eyes were as blue as irises washed by rain. She must have been a very attractive woman once, but life had not been kind. *What had happened to Erma's legs*, she wondered for the first time. Why was she stuck in that chair?

Erma glanced beyond her to an empty bed across the room where a curtain had been partially drawn. Pauline Hodges, her roommate, who had been at Rutgers for three years, had died there. Three years! To lie in this bed for three years! Margaret swallowed against the palpable gloom that settled around her. She didn't want to look at the vacant bed with its white sheet folded crisply over a waffle-weave blanket.

"One moment you're alive, and the next you're gone," Emma said wistfully, and her eyes grew even wider in her cherubic face.

"What did you think of lunch?" Margaret asked, eager to break the somber mood. Food was one of Erma's great interests, and her bulk could testify to that.

"Cardboard and sea mulch," Erma said, wrinkling her nose. "And that pie! Well, I wish you could have tasted my homemade blueberry pie." She began to rock faster in her chair, the dark mood vanishing as quickly as it had come. She was clearly in her element now. Her mood had lifted. "People used to say my pies were the best in the whole county. Betty Crocker wanted my recipe, but I wouldn't tell." She stopped and looked sheepishly at Margaret. "Well, it really was good, you know."

Margaret laughed. Judging by Erma's dramatic performances, maybe it was true that Erma had acted in summer stock theatre before the years took their toll. She spoke often enough of her exploits on the stage.

"Are you having company again today?" Erma asked.

"Maybe," Margaret said with a shrug. "Anne may drop in. You know, Mrs. Westin, who bought the old Grainger Estate. It's called Grace Arbor now."

"Oh, she's nice," Erma said eagerly.

Erma might well be thinking about the diabetic candy Anne always brought and hoping for more. Anne didn't buy bargain sweets but the kind of confection sold in fancy shops. It was one of her nicest qualities, the way she took time for people. Margaret sighed. Many visitors drew a curtain around themselves and the object of their visit, but Anne was sensitive to everyone. Few had ever visited Pauline Hodges.

Erma wheeled her chair close to the dresser and reached up to touch Margaret's photographs backlit by the sun's rays. She examined them with a faint smile, her gaze moving from one frame to the next. Cousin Noella, who died in '78, and a nephew shot down in Vietnam. She touched the gilt-framed photo of a man in a charcoal gray suit: Alexei Popov with eyes as brown as acorns beneath brows shaped like cricket legs. His dark hair rose from a high forehead in a smooth pompadour, and his lips curved in a smile as vibrant as a spring day.

Margaret felt herself smiling. She would always remember him like that, but he had looked much different when they laid him away last summer. She felt a rising in her chest, a pain threatening to launch a spasm of coughing. Grief was odd and unpredictable. She had worked through the process, at first disbelief, then anger, and finally acceptance of a sort. But without warning, the process could begin all over again.

Their friendship had spanned nearly a dozen years. It began in an unlikely way: Politeness between neighbors, a shared affinity for birds and dogs. Confirmed "spinster" through three decades of teaching Ladystone's elementary students, she hadn't expected to feel anything more than that. What might it have been like if they had married, if Vera hadn't managed to keep them apart? Then there was the accident that took him from her, took even his memory of what they had once shared. Yes, she'd lost him long before last summer.

Erma's fingers shook slightly on the frame that held Alexei's likeness. She cocked her head to one side as though trying to make up her mind whether or not she liked him. "Your husband?" she asked, looking at Margaret over the glasses that dipped even lower on her broad nose. At the shake of Margaret's head, Erma remarked with a little burst of joy, "A beau! Well, aren't you the one!"

"Erma, don't be melodramatic! He was a friend, that's all." Margaret feigned lightness, but sudden tears welled up, and the pain in her chest deepened. She could hear her own voice breaking. "I do miss him," she said softly.

Erma set the picture back almost reverently. She rolled away from the dresser and back to Margaret's bed, concentrating on the slow movement of the chair's huge wheels. She waited a few moments before looking up cautiously.

Recovering herself, Margaret reached for another framed photo on a stand next to her bed. She studied it a moment and then held it out toward Erma. "This is Tess. She's Alexei's daughter. Well, she's not really his daughter, but she lived with him and his sister until last summer." Margaret cleared her throat resolutely and reached for a tissue. "Isn't she a lovely child?"

Erma leaned in so close that her nose almost touched Tess's bright hair, the clear, young skin pink-tinged like a new petal, blue-violet eyes like bruised clouds. She traced her fingers over the girl's cheekbones, nose and mouth.

"She was only a baby when her mother died. Then her grandmother died too," Margaret said huskily, adding in a whisper, "Alexei loved her." She recalled how he had watched over her with such tenderness, even after the accident left him childlike and fragmented. She tamped down something hard that clutched at her chest. Life could be so terribly unfair.

"She's pretty," Erma said dreamily. "Who will take care of her now?"

"She's going to be fine," Margaret said firmly. Now that her inheritance was secure, Tess wouldn't need to depend on anyone, especially Vera. Margaret set the photo back on the night table. Tess would be fine, but Alexei was gone. Never again would they sit side by side on the porch swing. No longer could they watch the sun make jeweled prisms on the grass. She heard a small, strangled sound that she knew with surprise had been hers.

"Margaret? You all right?" Erma stopped the rhythmic rocking and pursed her lips anxiously. She clasped her arms over her stomach as though it hurt or needed protection.

"Of course," Margaret said sharply. She was angry at her own flight of mind as much as being called back from it. Was she turning into a taciturn old lady, tormented by memories? She looked up to see Erma's chin tremble and realized she'd been unkind once more. "I'm sorry," she stammered. "It's just that— well, I will miss him."

"I know," Erma said, brightening. "I had someone once, too. A long time ago. Sometimes, it's like he's right here with me, and then he disappears, and I can't remember what he looks like anymore. Isn't it the strangest thing?" Her eyes clouded and then brightened again. "But he was a real star more dashing than Tyrone Power or Rudolph Valentino."

Margaret laughed in spite of herself. Did Erma know that nine of ten people living didn't even know who those two swashbuckling heroes were?

The door opened, and a tall woman entered in a green business suit the color of grass at sundown. Her blonde hair was drawn back in a chignon just above rigid but handsome shoulders. Intelligent eyes as green as her suit scrutinized them behind fashionable tortoise shell glasses. Helen Rutgers, the stylish nursing home manager, looked more like a travel agent or CEO of some city conglomerate. Who would have thought the skinny, unpredictable girl in Margaret's fifth-grade class would be responsible for her well-being so many years later?

"Well, I'm glad to see you two enjoying yourselves." Helen flashed perfect teeth.

Margaret nodded, recalling that Helen had worn braces in junior high and had been an intrusive thing even then. Shouldn't even nursing home directors knock? Margaret sighed. Helen's quick smile tempered the irritation that seemed all too quick to surface in her these days. She smiled awkwardly in return.

"And how are we today?" Helen asked pleasantly, looking over her spectacles to scan the chart that hung over Margaret's bed.

Didn't the director trust her employees? How odd that she should be checking patients' charts. "Well, this part of *we* is feeling a little better, thank you," Margaret said wryly. She had always hated the condescending "we." What was it about the horizontal position that made some people treat you like a child who needed to be placated? Still, she regretted her sarcastic remark. It certainly wasn't one of her more agreeable days, and

Margaret realized that she'd had more than her share of disagreeable moods lately.

Helen raised a shapely eyebrow. She appeared mildly amused at Margaret's remark but made no comment. "Be sure to drink as much as possible, Mrs. Morris," she said amiably.

"*Miss*," Margaret corrected perversely. She bit her lower lip and softened the quick rebuke with a smile.

"Water keeps the lungs and mucus membranes lubricated," Helen added without missing a beat. If she had intended to say more, Margaret could not have told, for a young woman in a pink smock appeared in the doorway, her face a study in fearful guilt. Had she done something wrong? Neglected something? There'd be a severe accounting for any failure. Margaret had witnessed Helen with her staff. The director trusted no one and ran a very tight ship.

Helen smiled, directing her comments to Erma without looking at the nervous aide. "Miss Morris is looking much better, don't you think?" she asked breezily. She had emphasized the "Miss." Without waiting for a reply, she returned the chart to its place and smoothed the line of her tailored skirt with one shapely hand. "Well, I hope you ladies have a nice afternoon. Don't forget the craft classes this afternoon. I believe it's to be Japanese lanterns." She gave them a wink and turned to depart.

Erma pushed her wheelchair forward, obstructing her path. "Ms. Rutgers?" She looked at the director with wide, innocent eyes. "Is Pauline's name going to be in the paper?"

It was one of Erma's quirks to read the obituaries first thing, even before the front-page story. It was a morbid preoccupation, but Margaret realized it was shared by many.

"I looked this morning, and it wasn't there yet," Erma continued with the insistence of a displeased child.

Margaret hadn't read the *Ladystone Lectern* much since her illness, relying instead on Erma to fill her in on the latest news. As she studied her friend's petulant face, she wondered if Erma was about to launch one of her theatrical scenes.

Helen smiled, revealing a gold filling in a lower left tooth. Her glasses, attached to a black cord, swayed a little on her chest as she turned. "Of course," she affirmed politely with a slight narrowing of her eyes. She moved to the door, her smile waning. No doubt, she was weary of complaints by residents who were disappointed by life and hungry for attention. She put on the glasses and regarded Erma over their gaudy rims. "These things take time," she said patronizingly.

She had handled Erma's interrogation well enough, but something about Helen Rutgers had always irritated Margaret, brought out the worst in her. Years earlier, when she was the child's fifth grade teacher, she had given her extra tutoring. She had felt sorry for her because she was the only child of a vain mother and a philandering father. Helen had graduated and even risen to a managerial position as an adult, but she hadn't been above cheating on a final math exam. Ah, what a disadvantage for Helen to be remembered as a less-than-stellar student.

The director paused at the door and flashed them both a professional smile. "Don't worry now, girls. And don't forget the concert in the solarium later."

Girls? Margaret fought back a quick retort. *Who was she kidding? Girls!*

"Bye, now," Helen said merrily. Her tapered nails shone with perfect grooming as they slid slowly from the doorframe.

Margaret listened to the staccato click of high heels as Helen's steps grew fainter, but the heavy perfume she always wore lingered. Why did strong smells bother her so much these days? She reached for a tissue.

"I don't like her," Erma said petulantly.

"Ms. Rutgers is efficient. We'll have to give her that," Margaret snapped. She had been irritable and out of sorts all day, and most likely, she'd been unfair in her responses to Helen, who was, after all, the hand that fed her, so to speak. Now, Erma's childishness annoyed her. She sank back against the pillow and sighed deeply. The respiratory therapist would arrive soon, and the prospect made her even more impatient and tired.

Erma grew quiet, her fingers working absently in her lap as though they were detached things. An uncharacteristic frown caused her glasses to slide even further off the bridge of her nose. She pursed her full lips. "Harry died two years ago," she said trance-like, "and Loretta died last March on the day of the big snow…" Erma's usually effusive voice took on a flat quality. "They didn't get written up in the paper either."

"Oh, you must be mistaken," Margaret said. "Their families would make sure of that."

"Wasn't any family. No friends, either. They were alone, like us."

"Still, it's a matter of practice to publish an obit," Margaret said. If only Erma would go away so she could rest!

"Just isn't right," Erma said pensively. "Everyone should have someone to remember them." The indignant tone changed, and her voice grew weary and fragile. "Nobody cares about you when you get old."

"Of course they do, Erma," Margaret said. "You must be mistaken." Margaret was exasperated and so tired. "Why don't you go—go bake one of your pies or something!" It was a cruel thing to say, and Margaret regretted it instantly. Erma would love nothing better than to whip up some delicacy in a kitchen of her own, but her baking days were over.

Erma shrugged, apparently unfazed by the rebuff. Still in the throes of reverie, she released the lock on her chair. "At least they finally put Harry's name in last November," she said absently. "I clipped it out for my scrapbook." Erma wheeled herself out of Margaret's room, pausing to wave and smile tentatively as though she'd already forgiven Margaret her careless remarks.

Margaret listened to the slow creaking of the wheelchair until she was engulfed in silence once more. A year's delay in printing an obituary? Most likely, Erma's mind was on permanent. She didn't want to think about obituaries or dates or anything else. She was just so tired. She let her eyes drift to Alexei's face in the gilt frame, trying not to see his sad, vacant face when he left her for the last time.

Maybe it was good to grow senile or to live in an imaginary world like Erma Tanner. Perhaps it was a curse to be alive in every nerve and brain cell, vulnerable to the sorrow life could bring. She thought of Annie, who believed that God had control of the whole sweeping labyrinth of life.

Margaret felt tears pushing against her closed eyelids as she lay on her side, her body turned toward Alexei's image. She had trusted God through years of joy and pain. Why was she doubting Him now? Tears squeezed through her eyes and washed into her ears and hair, obscuring Alexei's dear face.

Chapter 3

A visit with Anne Westin usually bolstered her courage and put her at ease. She was so good to her, opening new and exciting doors that had once been closed to her. Tess went downstairs but turned to wave. Mrs. Westin was old enough to be her mother, but in a turtle neck sweater and designer jeans, Anne didn't look in the least matronly with eyes flecked with gold, chestnut hair curling softly around finely-sculpted ears. Tess always noticed people's ears; they were fascinating. What special property made them hear?

She wondered what people saw when they looked at her—a tall, thin girl with coppery hair and a too-long neck. Did they mark the awkwardness of her speech, the quick downward cast of her blue eyes? Were they fascinated by her hands and fingers, which spoke a language they could not speak? Who could tell?

Peter had told her she was pretty, that her eyes were the color of lupine. She'd had to look it up and discovered that lupine was deep blue—nearly purple—not the lovely sunlit blue she wished her eyes were. She frowned at her foolish disappointment in the comparison. A young woman should be concerned with deeper things than physical appearance, things that really matter.

You're an intelligent, gifted young woman, Tess. Look what you've accomplished despite your disability. The mention of her disability didn't offend her. She had begun to feel proud of herself and to believe she had a place in the world, too. She breathed in the sharp, cold air. Perhaps it really didn't matter if a person could hear so long as they lived each moment, knowing it mattered.

She shifted the ungainly egg crates and walked away from Grace Arbor, the house that once had belonged to the grandmother she could not remember.

"Alexei and Vera traveled with your grandmother to this country," Margaret Morris had told her, using Uncle Alexei's Russian name. "They took you in when she died."

Tess had been astonished by the story. How could she have grown up in this town and not known? But gossip spread in whispers behind cupped hands, putting the Deaf at a disadvantage—or advantage, depending on how one looked at it. It was hard to know since she'd never experienced sound, apart from a faint rushing in her head that might have been real or imaginary.

Passing Grace Arbor's south wing, she swept her gaze over the browning flower beds. She had tended them there before the house had been sold for back taxes. Before Mrs. Westin had come. Tess wondered why she had found such joy in sifting the black soil in her fingers and why the only time she felt peace was among flowers. It was as if her subconscious mind knew what she did not—that once she had belonged to that land.

Aunt Vera didn't like it. "What you do here?" she would demand, the elegant brooch she always wore flashing in the sunlight. Vera loved the sparkly bauble and never guessed it was worth thousands. "You got no business 'dis place," she would scold in her thick accent, eyebrows crawling over stormy eyes like caterpillars.

"My *lapushka* does no harm," Uncle Alexei always said, using the Russian word for a *kitten*. "She does good thing. Someone buy land one day and find happy flowers grow." Then he'd lift his battered hat and regard them both through dark, patient eyes.

In childhood, Tess hadn't questioned why Uncle Alexei and Aunt Vera were so much older than the parents of other children and why they spoke differently. But so much had been different for her. She had herself been different. In their bold prejudice, children were often cruel. Sometimes, they would stick their fingers in their ears and pretend that they were deaf, too. Other times, they jumped out from behind a bush and laughed at her.

She swallowed a lump in her throat and, with one foot, brushed away drying grass and weeds from the hardy chrysanthemums along the garden border. Mums were survivors, the last in the flower beds to retain their burnished color and form after everything else had dried up. She felt suddenly akin to them. She was a survivor, too.

Until Uncle Alexei's accident turned him vulnerable, life had been good enough. Alexei had given her the affection denied by those who believed her different and, therefore, unworthy. Even when he became oddly childlike and forgetful, Alexei had found a way to send her to the school where she learned how to live in the world of the hearing.

She stooped to pick the last yellow flower in the patch of browning chrysanthemums. Its center was as brilliant as the sun—as bright as her prospects should be. After all, she had her own apartment and a job in the hospital records department. She was developing abilities she never knew she had. And she had met gentle, sophisticated Peter, who knew so much but who never laughed at her ignorance, who had guided her through those harrowing days after Alexei's body had been found in the woods. Had it really been six months since she had received an inheritance left by her long-dead grandmother?

It was almost too much to take in, and as she moved slowly now toward the shabby little house beyond the hedge, Tess felt strangely at a loss. She didn't really belong here anymore, but where did she belong? Vera wouldn't welcome her. She had always made her feel like a burden, a disappointment. She wouldn't want her now, but someone had to take care of the aging woman. She had no one now that Uncle Alexei was gone.

Tess opened the ancient screen door and prepared to walk in. Then, pausing, she knocked. After all, it wasn't her home any-more. She had her own place in town, not far from the hospital. Vera's wooden door shook in its frame like old bones. She'd have to convince her to have some repairs done on the old house. There was no need for her to scrape a living out of those tired old hens that left their feathered detritus everywhere. How long would Vera scrunch up her bulky shoulders and refuse to take any money offered to her?

Foolish old woman, Tess thought and knocked harder. Suddenly, her inner senses told her she was not alone. Some stirring of air or an unfamiliar scent caused her to turn. A woman was coming up the uneven walk, and at the curb behind her was a boxy sedan on which the letters "City of Ladystone" were printed.

Tess felt a catch in her chest. Who was this woman striding confidently toward Vera's old shack? She was young and lean in a leather coat with a belt tied around her tiny waist. Her stylish boots came up to her knees, stopping just short of her three-quarter-length coat.

"Excuse me. I'm looking for the owner. Are you Mrs. Popov? Mrs. Vera Popov?" The name rolled off her waxy red lips with lightning speed.

Tess frowned, not sure she had interpreted the words cor-rectly. At that moment, the door opened, and Vera stood framed in the passageway. A larger-than-life portrait, she furrowed dark eyebrows in confusion.

Tess marshaled her thoughts "This lady is looking for you, Vera." How long since she'd stopped calling her "Aunt Vera"?

"What you want?" Vera frowned at the lady, and fear flashed in the lusterless eyes.

The woman from the city pulled a tablet from the pocket of her coat. She peered over her glasses after checking what was written there. "I'm here to check your property, ma'am, and to ask if you've cleared up the violations listed in the form we sent last year. Let's see ... yes, the outbuildings ... You keep chickens. Proper fencing was to be installed." She paused, pursing rose-colored lips. She gazed over her left shoulder where the chicken coops stood, bleached and disheveled in the late autumn light.

Tess squinted at the notepad. She'd warned Vera about the coops being so near the road and without adequate fencing. Alexei was going to take care of it, but in the months before his death, he had largely lost contact with the real world.

"My house," Vera said through pouting lips. "You go away." She folded her arms under her ample breasts and took a step backward as though she would shut the door in both their faces.

"Aunt Vera ... " Tess began awkwardly.

The inspector took a step forward. "Ma'am, your house is within the city limits, and there are rules for animals, both domestic and farm. Property owners must abide by the rules." The eyes behind her stylish sunglasses flashed with confident authority.

"Please," Tess said carefully, trying hard to make the "l" correctly, "This is my aunt." She broke off. How could she say her aunt wasn't really her aunt, that she didn't always understand, and that she needed help with things such as city rules and violations? *How can I say that Vera Popov didn't take kindly to strangers for any reason, that she would be voted the most stubborn person in the entire county if a contest was held?*

Tess shifted the stack of egg cartons. It was hopeless to say just what Aunt Vera was. She turned to the inspector. "Do

29

you—have a copy of the form?" she asked, willing herself to sound confident. "I will see that the matter is taken care of." In her nervousness, she'd signed the last sentence with her one free hand.

The city of Ladystone representative peered at her curiously. "I see. Well, there's a duplicate at the courthouse. You can pick it up there. But I must warn you..." She paused to remove her sunglasses, revealing severe gray eyes. It was a gesture clearly meant to intimidate. "There will be a fine added to the year-end tax bill if it's not done by January 1."

Tess nodded, willing the woman to be on her way. She stepped past Vera and closed the door. An arm's length away, she frowned at her disgruntled aunt until the dark eyes dropped away.

Vera pouted, an expression familiar to Tess. It was a hard face with deep lines in skin tanned from outdoor work. But something vulnerable lingered there, and Tess felt again that childish longing for an affectionate touch, a kind word such as a mother might give her child. If she hadn't been born different. If she'd been whole...

Tess felt a lump rise menacingly in her throat. Hadn't she worked through that? Being Deaf didn't mean... *Oh, stop,* she rebuked herself severely. Vera was what she was, who she was—foolish, unfriendly, even mean at times. Even if she hadn't willingly taken in a motherless child, she had at least cooked her meals and washed her clothes. Perhaps it was all the love she was capable of. Tess swallowed and forced herself to be calm. If only she could penetrate Vera's cold exterior, which kept even hardy souls at bay.

"Why didn't you tell me about the fences?" she asked, dropping the egg cartons on the couch by the door. A tiny living room and bath, a slightly larger kitchen, and two bedrooms upstairs comprised the house. She cleared her throat. "We have the money now to do the repairs. There's no need to... " Tess floundered, exasperated.

"Is *your* money," Vera said, emphasizing the pronoun. Adroitly, she scooped up the cartons and marched off to the kitchen, where she spent most of her time. Alexei had bought her a tiny black and white television to watch while she cleaned eggs. "Is all yours," she re-emphasized, her heavy European accent rising to the surface, as it always did when she was agitated.

"Aunt Vera, please... " She broke off, feeling sudden tears blur her vision. Would she never understand that in spite of their emotional distance from each other, Tess wanted to thank her for the years she gave to a child who was not her own?

Vera jerked her head, and the movement jarred the green brooch on her sweater. Loving all things that sparkled, Vera had accepted it and nothing more. For all Tess knew, she wore the thing to bed. She watched as Vera fled to the haven of her kitchen with its odd mixture of odors—onions, eggs, and pine cleaner.

Tess followed her, a dowdy figure in a flowered housedress and faded gray sweater. It must have seen a decade of winters. She supposed all women from the 40s and 50s dressed that way. She sat down uninvited at the old kitchen table where she and Uncle Alexei had so often eaten together, Vera serving them like a hired servant and then eating her meals alone when they were finished. She'd insist on doing the dishes alone after they had gone to sit outside and watch the twilight descend.

"Doesn't Aunt Vera like us?" she had asked Uncle Alexei in sign, the only language she'd known as a child.

Alexei's arthritic fingers could move like lightning. He never missed a nuance. But he had been slow in answering, looking beyond her to the landscape of shadowy woods. His rheumy gaze was remarkably perceptive. "My sister had hard life—hard life. She's afraid to love. Be good to her, my *lapushka*."

Tess groaned. She had tried, but nothing she did was ever right. Nothing was enough to bring a smile to the grim mouth or a tender look from the restless eyes. *I'm here! I'm here*, she'd wanted to shout. As time passed, she'd learned to expect nothing beyond the grudging meals, the clothes scrubbed in the old-fashioned way in the kitchen sink with its pipes covered by a checkered skirt.

Only with the hens and sometimes with the old collie that traipsed behind her did something like pleasure soften the hard lines in the old face. Tess breathed a long sigh and watched Vera fill a crate with clean brown eggs. Her back was turned as though she'd already forgotten anyone was there.

"I saw what you did today," Tess said slowly. There was no sign Vera had heard except for a slight stiffening of the broad back. "It was wrong to throw that stuff onto Mrs. Westin's roof. You're going to get in trouble." She stopped and watched Vera for several moments before rising from the old wooden chair. She sighed, knowing that no apology or explanation would come. "I'll get another copy of the form," she said, "and we'll see about the fences."

Tess turned away as tears threatened. She closed the rickety back door to cut back through Grace Arbor, where she had left her car at the bottom of the winding driveway. She was glad now to walk in the brisk autumn air, to feel the wind wrap itself around her like comforting arms.

She passed through the lilac bushes, now stiff and bare, and onto the path that led past Grace Arbor's shed. She slid the fingers of one hand along its siding and remembered the summer that had changed everything. In that shed with the rescued fawn, she'd felt strong stirrings of goodness—not her own but some essential virtue that existed outside her. Beyond all reason or fate, it seemed to embrace her.

She had desperately needed the injured deer to live, to respond to her touch, and grow strong. She had prayed to some distant God of whom she'd never asked anything. Peter had covered her trembling hands with his and assured her that the fawn would be all right. Perhaps it was a foolish hope, but she felt that if the deer grew strong, perhaps she too would be all right.

There in that warm shed, she had begun to think of herself as something more than the unfortunate Deaf child without a mother or father. And after the daring escape from Shane Eldridge, Peter had said she was brave for helping to rescue his mother and Margaret Morris. He had praised her for having the courage to strike out on her own, to put her unusual dexterity to good advantage. The data processing department had hired her on the spot.

But that early exhilaration was gone, and Peter was gone, too. His job in Chicago was keeping him busier than ever. Or perhaps there were other girls he found far more enchanting, easier to be with. Had the attraction been hers alone? Had she fooled herself into thinking he might really care for her, a simple Deaf girl who'd never been farther than the Minnesota border?

Leaves curled at her feet. Once fiery orange and gold, they were brown now and fell away, tear by tear from grieving tree eyes. She felt suddenly akin to them, shivered, and pulled up the hood of her green anorak. Did the leaves make any sound when they were tossed about in the careless wind? What did children hear when they leaped into great stacks of them, opening their mouths in incredulous joy and saying words that she'd never learned?

"Leaves laugh," Uncle Alexei had said when long ago she'd stopped to stare at them. "Happy noise. Your heart make happy noise too, my *lapushka*." Then he would swing her up to his bony shoulders and carry her, bending low to avoid protruding branches. He had protected her when she was left orphaned and alone. Now, he was dead. Did he know, wherever he was, that his sister did bizarre things like throwing away bills from city hall and swamping out the chicken coops onto her neighbor's lawn?

She stepped away from the shed and back onto the path, her earlier sense of significance and hope waning. She felt suddenly small and weak and began to run. She ran like a child as the north wind blew through her jacket, chilling her to the bone. She welcomed its fierce stinging against her face, causing her eyes to blur with cold and tears. She was alone, the child of parents she never knew, never would know—a young woman but still a child who didn't know who she was.

Chapter 4

Overnight, the snow fell, and Grace Arbor became a white-robed queen, her pristine train swirling below a pearl-gray sky. Dark pines formed an emerald belt, and diamond flakes glistened. Shovel in hand, Anne stood, awed by the scene and by a poignant sadness that sometimes crept up when she was touched by beauty or pathos. This was to be the perfect place for her and Richard, a haven to welcome guests, a compass point for their children and grandchildren. But at 53, she was alone on the turn-of-the-century estate, and things were far from perfect.

She gazed across the wide expanse toward the line of snow-dotted lilac bushes. Something red appeared in the lilac hedge—a bright babushka, perhaps? She frowned. She and Tess had cleared away the debris just in time, or it would have been left to rot under a blanket of snow. Was that scarlet flash Vera bent on wreaking further havoc? No, it was a cardinal—red as blood against the white backdrop.

The image of blood startled her. Perhaps such images were normal after the trauma she'd experienced in recent months. But she wanted to banish the painful memories, even as snow erased the dull brown ravages of time. She shivered in the wind that whipped with sudden savagery, stinging her cheeks. Things hadn't gone as she'd hoped, and now winter descended with its harsh beauty. She had weathered Alexei's death, Lance's secrecy, and a thief's attempt to grab jewels buried on her property. She'd even survived being kidnapped and held in a mine shack. Her entry into widowhood and her new life had been nothing, if not traumatic. After that, winter at Grace Arbor would be a breeze, wouldn't it?

There had been times when she had wanted to run back to her former life where the rigors of nature were less severe, to the safety of a predictable salary, to old friends who understood her. And she might have gone back. But something held her here— something more than the grim resolve to stick it out, to prove that she could live on her own—without Richard, without her children on this handsome estate. She could handle this without them and without Lance Crane, who, among others, had discouraged her from remaining at Grace Arbor.

"It's no place for a woman alone," he had said. And that, she realized, made her even more determined to stay.

She dug her shovel deep into the snow. She and Lance had moved beyond the turmoil of the previous summer. After all, Shane Eldridge had nearly brought them all to the brink of disaster, and he was Lance's nephew, the boy he had brought to town as a favor to his sister.

Anne hadn't blamed him for the boy's actions, and gradually, they had settled into a comfortable friendship. But she was determined to make her way without leaning on this intelligent, sensitive man who stirred her in ways she'd not expected.

She'd seen little of him since the start of Advent, and she realized now, in spite of her self-proclaimed independence, that she missed him. He had invited her to a production of "Fiddler on the Roof" at a local theatre, and though the musical ranked among her favorites, she'd turned him down. He hadn't called again, and the weeks passed in silence. She had convinced herself the hiatus was welcome, but suddenly, a wave of loneliness swept over her. She dug her shovel in deep and tossed a great mound of snow over her shoulder. Never had her porch and winding driveway seemed so massive.

An efficient county maintenance crew had cleared the main roads. Soon, they would be heading up her little stretch of county. But she would need to call a private contractor to clear her driveway or be stranded until spring.

Lance had made her promise to call on him when she needed help. Why hadn't she? Before she could dwell on the question further, she heard him turn into her driveway as though magically summoned.

With a huge shovel affixed to the grill of his jeep, he was forging up the long driveway. She answered his wave and realized that despite her determination to conquer nature's challenge alone, she was uncommonly glad to see him.

The plow made wide, practiced sweeps, and soon her driveway was clean. The jeep came to a stop in front of her garage, and Lance strode toward the redwood deck, his hiking boots making great indents in the snow. Nearly six feet tall, he was well-muscled, a tribute to his love of outdoor sports. In his red and black plaid coat, he looked more like the great icebound explorer than a real estate agent who owned several sizeable properties. Grace Arbor had been one of them. In spite of the many properties available to him, he chose to make a modest lakeside cabin his home. A black wool cap pulled low over his forehead covered thick silver hair. He pushed it up higher as he came toward her, eyes like two blue beacons in his ruddy face.

He reached for her shovel. "I'll get the rest of the deck for you. This is no work for a lady!"

She'd done most of it and was about to say she could handle the rest, but she stopped before the words got out. Protests about doing things on her own often triggered a sparring match between them, and she had no heart for argument now. "Thanks. The driveway looks great." She stepped back as he leaned into the shovel. After weeks of silence, she'd expected awkwardness, but the invitation was out of her mouth before she had time to consider it. "Have time for coffee? I made strawberry Danish this morning."

"Can't say no to that," he said with a grin and pressed his weight against the shovel as she went inside.

He made quick work of the porch and let himself in. He took off his boots and eased out of his parka. "First snow of the season's a whopper," he said, ruffling the hair that had flattened under his cap. He had a distinct northern accent that she liked to tease him about, especially when *you betcha'* came out of his mouth.

Would he apologize for not calling? Give excuses for his long silence? She fitted his coat over the back of a chair, liking the woodsy smell that came with it. "It's a beauty though, she said. So how have you been?"

He rubbed weather-roughened hands together. "Can't complain," he said and accepted the steaming cup Anne held out. He took a long swallow. "And how about you? It's been a while. Too long, in fact." He looked over the rim of the cup, a teasing glint in his eyes. "Decided I couldn't leave you defenseless in all this snow."

"You don't think I could dig myself out?" she asked, challenging him good-naturedly.

"I've no doubt you could lick your weight in wildcats if you had a mind to," he said. He helped himself to a large slice of Danish. "I thought you could use a hand this time." He drew in his breath and directed his gaze outside.

Through the wide bay window, Grace Arbor stretched in blue-white elegance. From her vantage point Anne murmured wistfully, "I've always loved winter."

"Well, you're in the right place. We get a lot of winter around here."

She sat down across from him and, hearing the amusement in his voice, joined in the game. "If I had an excuse, I'd make a snowman or stage a snowball fight or something."

"Maybe your next-door neighbor would oblige you," he said with a sardonic grin. He had listened to her laments about Vera Popov on more than one occasion. "But you better watch out. I bet she could pitch one mean snowball."

"After yesterday, I might take her on." She sighed, recalling Vera's handiwork.

Lance paused in mid-chew, a tiny crumb of Danish lingering on his mouth. "Yesterday?"

"Oh, it's nothing really," she said wearily. "Vera just decided to clean her chicken runs and threw the whole mess over my shed." She didn't want the previous day's disquiet to intrude on these pleasant moments with Lance. But his gaze was narrowed and penetrating. He was obviously waiting for more. She shrugged. "Tess came by, and we took care of it. None too soon, though. It would have been a mess if we'd had to wait until the snow melted."

He frowned and resumed chewing. "You really should report her," he said philosophically. "Let the authorities make her act like a responsible citizen."

"That would just make things worse." She set her cup down on the saucer with a sigh. I hate having her at odds with me all the time. Will she ever stop thinking of me as the enemy?

He leaned back and folded his arms across his chest. "She shouldn't get away with stunts like that," he said, shaking his head disapprovingly.

"I'd have confronted her if I could have found her," Anne said. "Poor Tess. She was really embarrassed at what Vera did."

Lance frowned. "I'm glad she's out of that house. She deserves better after all she's been through."

"Hmmm," Anne assented softly. "She's doing well, and she's such a lovely girl." She poured more coffee into Lance's cup, and they sat in companionable silence, studying the winter landscape. It was strange that she could feel so comfortable with him, as though the long weeks apart had been only a matter of hours. In the distance, the brick chimney of Margaret Morris' house rose above the snow-covered roof. "I bet Margaret's place is packed in, too, after this storm," she said.

He raised dark eyebrows that contrasted handsomely with silver hair as thick as the snow billowing beyond the window. "Well, not anymore, it isn't."

"You shoveled Margaret's place out, too?"

"Wasn't much to it," he said. "I couldn't leave Ladystone's venerable school teacher to fend for herself, not now that she's been ill. By the way, how's she getting along at Rutgers, do you know?"

Anne frowned and absently traced the rim of her cup. "Not very well, I'm afraid. She's having a rough time. I know Tess is really worried about her. I thought she was getting better, but she's just not herself. I don't know what to do to help her."

Lance rubbed his thumb over the handle of the porcelain cup without speaking.

"It's really been hard on her," she continued. "Margaret's always been so independent. She misses that old house of hers." Anne could barely make out her neighbor's roof in the distance. "I tried to cheer her up the other day when I went to Rutgers, but I have to tell you she's feeling pretty low."

"Anyone would feel low in a place like that." He paused and narrowed his eyes. "Rutgers may not be bad as nursing homes go, but they all give me the creeps."

A pair of cardinals had hopped onto the feeder and dipped their striking red crests in the snow. Anne watched them peck at the sunflower ring and recalled Margaret's pain-filled eyes. "Since Alexei died, she's lost her old sparkle. I guess she misses him more than any of us knew."

They studied the cardinals in silence and watched one of them fly away. Its mate darted left, then right as though realizing it was alone. *Like Margaret,* Anne thought sadly. Margaret and Alexei hadn't been mates in the traditional sense, but theirs had been an intimate and enduring relationship that even Alexei's dementia and Vera's antipathy hadn't broken.

Anne rose to clear away the pastry plates, aware that she was no longer thinking only of Margaret Morris. In the lonely cardinal on the porch, she was seeing herself as well. Would she ever get over that empty place in her heart?

"Habits of years can't be broken so easily," Lance said quietly.

She rinsed their cups at the sink, aware that Lance was still intent on the bird feeder. He knew what it was like to lose someone, too. Was he thinking about Rose, who had died two years earlier? She noticed the shadow that lay like a veil over his usually vibrant blue eyes. Could they ever talk about such feelings together? Didn't he know that a sorrow shared loses half its sting? Perhaps it was the way men dealt with things, but friends should be open with each other.

She brushed away imaginary crumbs on her placemat. "The lady in the next bed died the morning of my visit."

Lance looked up, startled out of his private reverie. After a moment or two, he said quietly, "That must have been hard."

Anne recalled the elderly lady whose raspy hum and jaunty movements had reminded her of an android or robot. "Her name was Pauline Hodges—a tiny bird of a woman always on the move in her pink tennis shoes. "I don't think she ever sat still. I really liked her."

"Hodges?" He searched some imaginary memory bank. "I've been around Ladystone for a long time, but I don't recognize that name."

"She was younger than Margaret but in good health except for diabetes." Anne felt suddenly relieved that at least she wasn't alone on this winter morning to contemplate death and ailing neighbors. She loved her solitude, but at this moment, she was glad Lance was there. "Do you know what she told me?"

When he searched her face but said nothing, Anne continued. "Margaret said that it might be her turn to go next. Isn't that morbid thinking for someone like her? She was always so happy and full of life."

He looked away, his fingers moving slowly over the delicate handle of his cup. "Grief does odd things to people," he said flatly.

She saw the sadness deepen in his eyes and regretted the tone their conversation had taken. He'd been through a lot, as they all had. She leaned toward him, eager to turn the subject toward something more positive. "I have an idea. Why don't you bring Grover to see Margaret? They allow pets at nursing homes, and it would cheer her up."

Grover was Margaret's great black and white sheepdog, which Lance had taken in after Margaret went to Rutgers for convalescence. Yes, Grover might be just what Margaret needed now. "What do you think?"

"Old Grover's been moping around for days," Lance said, leaning back and folding his arms across his chest. His mouth turned up in a half-smile. "It's worth a try. Let's take him to see her together," he suggested in a rush of words.

"Oh, yes! Margaret would love it." She grasped his arm in excitement, then, embarrassed, drew away. Nursing homes gave him the creeps, but he offered to go there with her. She couldn't help being touched.

Abruptly, he pushed back his chair and reached for his boots. "Then it's settled," he said. "We'll take old Grover visiting. It'll give him something to do besides getting into my garbage." He laced his boots with precision and stood up. "Yesterday, he ate a whole package of moldy cheese and a Bavarian cream donut."

Laughing, she held out his coat and helped him ease his long arms into it. She was feeling lighter than she had in weeks. "Thanks again for clearing my driveway." Her heart skipped when he leaned over to give her a quick farewell kiss on the cheek.

"Well, out into the wind and weather!" he said, good humor back in full sway. "Neither sleet nor snow can hold me back! Me and the U.S. postal service!" He pulled his wool cap low over his ears and grinned.

He looked so comical bundled up with that hat hunkered over his ears that she couldn't help laughing. She reached up to tuck his scarf more firmly around his neck, as she might have done for Peter when he was a child. "You look like an escaped convict!" she said, giving the end of his scarf a playful toss.

Instantly, his smile faded. The remark had struck too close to home. His nephew's crime and subsequent arrest were just too raw. Her words had brought back the whole embarrassing episode that had caused him such hurt. How could she have been so careless?

"Lance, I'm—I'm sorry…"

"Thanks for the coffee," he said quietly, the warm mood between them broken. He bent his head against some imaginary wind.

Why didn't she think before she spoke? Metaphors were such powerful devices. She reached for the doorknob, hoping to bring back his happier mood. "Would Saturday be a good time—to take Grover to see Margaret, I mean?"

"Can't, I'm afraid." He tapped his fingers on the doorframe as though searching for an explanation or an excuse. "I'm picking up Jimmy at the airport on Saturday." At her look of surprise, he said flatly, "My nephew."

She stared at his averted face and saw that his knuckles were white on the walnut doorframe.

"My sister's youngest son—eleven at his last birthday, as I recall. He's been in a foster home since his mother died. He got himself expelled from school until the first of the year. So, he's going to spend Christmas holidays with me."

"Oh, Lance." But she didn't know what else to say. Another troubled family member after all he'd been through with Shane.

"Funny, isn't it?" he mused bleakly. "My sister always thought her big brother could handle anything."

She touched his arm, rigid even through his thick hunter's coat. "I'm sorry. But, you mustn't think … " She wanted to say that just because he'd failed with Shane, it didn't mean he couldn't help this other nephew. It hadn't been Lance's fault, after all, that Shane was greedy and had brought such turmoil into everyone's lives.

He opened the door, ushering in a blast of frigid air. "It's all right, Anne. It's all water under the bridge, but I hope this old bridge still has some strength left in the girders."

She lay her hand over his briefly, but the awkwardness stretched between them.

He seemed not to notice the chilling wind as they stood on the threshold. Finally, he said, "We could make it later on Saturday afternoon, I guess. I'll have to bring the boy along, of course." He began moving slowly down the steps, shoulders drooping.

"Of course," she agreed. Lance was the kindest of men; he deserved so much better. She watched the jeep until it became a tiny square and then was swallowed up in a sea of white.

Job's words flashed into her mind as she stood in the doorway, the cold wind whipping her blouse. "Man is born to trouble as the sparks fly upward." She stood pondering the winter solstice, the season when they would celebrate the One who had chosen to walk the troubled paths of the world with them.

She stood at the door a long time after Lance had gone. She clasped her arms across her chest as the wind pierced her silk blouse and set her teeth chattering. She peered into the endless winter sky and whispered, "You've conquered the worst that life can bring. Dear Lord, stay with us and help us."

Chapter 5

Tess studied her fingers as they flew, independent but perfectly choreographed, over the keyboard and felt a strange sense of anonymity. Whose were these slender hands transferring black letters onto a white page? Were they like her mother's? Her father's? Perhaps her grandmother's or some great aunt whose genes were passed on to an unknown progeny? She tried to imagine her mother's hands cooking supper, making a bed, or caressing a child's fevered forehead. Had those hands tenderly caressed her?

She regarded the fingers poised in mid-air as thoughts tumbled through her mind. Disabled was the kindest of the labels people had attached to her as she was growing up. She felt the quick hurt rise to the surface and quelled it with practiced intent. She was doing something important and doing it well, wasn't she? She was a natural, people said. After all, for the Deaf, communication was closely aligned to the motion of hands. She smiled at the irony or the simple truth of it.

She was an able person, though not a hearing one, and she was making her way in the world. She was grateful—profoundly grateful. Lately, though, she had found it hard to concentrate, and it worried her that sometimes she made mistakes. Her fingers would strike of their own accord, exchanging a 6 for a 9, a

Joanne for Jeanne. People's health was far too important for such distraction. What was bothering her anyhow?

She tried to analyze her odd discontent. She should be glad for the changes in her life. Except for losing Uncle Alexei, they were good changes. After so many lonely years, she had a job, an apartment, and friends. She should be happy—or at least satisfied. She had learned so much and come so far. As Mrs. Westin often said, God had been good to her. But on this winter day, as Advent approached, she felt little joy. Despite bright displays in store windows, tantalizing aromas from cafes and bakeries, or the magical light in the eyes of children, she felt sad and troubled, and she didn't know why.

It hadn't helped that Peter broke their date to go skiing on Saturday. He had apologized profusely and promised to come at the very first opening in his heavy work schedule. She sighed. Perhaps his promise had only been a polite overture. Maybe it had never meant anything special at all.

Melissa Martin peeked around the corner of her cubicle, interrupting her dispirited reverie. She waved as she approached and asked in slow, deliberate sign language, "Want to have lunch?"

The sprightly blonde girl bent to pull her purse out of a bottom drawer and flung it over her shoulder. Tess waved back. She closed out of the database and leaned back in her chair. She was ready for a break. It would be good to eat lunch with Melissa instead of sitting alone in the hospital cafeteria—one more thing to be grateful for.

"I'm hungry," Melissa said, coming over to Tess's cubicle and leaning against the wall. She patted a flat stomach and made small repetitive circles with her hand. Rings glittered on each of her fingers. How could she type with so much weight bearing down on them?

Tess smiled at Melissa's stumbling efforts at sign language. It was awkward and sometimes wrong, but it pleased her that her new friend wanted to learn her language. "This way," Tess corrected with careful precision, striving for accuracy both with the signs and spoken words. She grabbed her sweater and purse and hooked an arm through her friend's. "Never mind," Tess said, laughing. "Let's go eat."

She had accepted Melissa's overtures of friendship guardedly at first. From long experience, she resisted, fearing that she would be viewed as a curiosity or a charity case—someone to feel sorry for. But Melissa had proved to be genuine and open-hearted.

"That's a fabulous outfit!" Melissa said, admiring Tess's turquoise skirt that clung to her hips and flared gently just above her knees. A silky white blouse ruffled softly at the neck and sleeves; a gold chain belt hung loosely from a wide clasp. "And your vest is a perfect match," Melissa gushed.

Tess blushed. She knew she was lucky to be working at the hospital and to be among friends like Melissa. Growing up Deaf had been a lonely experience. She had often been considered abnormal or lacking in intelligence. She hated being stared at when someone saw her speaking with her fingers. Deaf and dumb, the old couplet went.

As she walked with Melissa toward the cafeteria, she recalled reading those words on unsuspecting lips. They were said about Vera too, she suddenly thought. Though she could hear, she wasn't educated and had little interest in fashion or homemaking or things most women cared about. She wasn't affectionate either and had no time for coffee with a friend or going to a play. Tess sighed. Vera remained cold and rigid—especially with her. She shivered, remembering the criticism with which she had grown up. She no longer had to endure it; she was free from those harsh, forbidding eyes.

Still, she couldn't help feeling a stab of guilt. Vera had given her shelter and food. She should be grateful for that, grateful not to be left in an orphanage or on the street. She felt a familiar yearning to put her hand in one of her aunt's big ones and feel she was important to her. But the truth was that Vera had more tenderness for her brood of laying hens than for her.

Uncle Alexei had loved her, though. She was sure of that. Dear Uncle Alexei with his gnarled hands and deep-set eyes. They haunted her even after all these months. She felt a lump rise in her throat. He was gone, leaving only Vera as family.

"A penny!" said Melissa.

"What?"

"For your thoughts. A penny for your thoughts." Melissa smiled, fluttering her pale lashes.

"Oh, I'm sorry. I'm not very good company today." Tess tried to explain but found herself floundering. Even her fingers were inarticulate. She walked on, moving one foot ahead of the other, the strange discontent hovering over her like a cloud. What was wrong with her? She wasn't a child anymore. Why should it matter so much—this longing to be loved by your family?

Uncle Alexei told her that her mother had died when she was a baby. Her grandmother, too, had died shortly after bringing her to northern Wisconsin. She had come from Russia—a mysterious woman who left her grandbaby in the care of hired servants. Only Uncle Alexei had known about the inheritance. Guarding it had cost his life and changed hers in ways she was only beginning to absorb.

"You can do anything you want, Tess," Peter had told her. He wrote often, wanting to know how she was and what she was doing. He wrote about his work, his evening class at the university, and how crazy Lake Shore Drive was during rush hour. He told her he missed her, too, but perhaps he was only being kind.

No, she would not sink into that despair again. She had so many reasons to be thankful. So, what was wrong with her?

Melissa tugged at her arm, commanding her attention. "Get a tray," she said. "You need a tray."

"Oh, of course." Tess grinned apologetically. She was so deep in thought she didn't realize they had reached the cafeteria line. She pulled a tray from the rack and chose silverware from a large ceramic jar. Drops of water from the still-wet tray sprayed the front of her skirt.

"I bet I know what's wrong with you," Melissa said with a wink. "It's Peter. I don't blame you. He's a real hunk. If I had a date with somebody like him on Saturday, I wouldn't be able to concentrate either."

"He's not coming; he has to work," Tess said. She filled a glass with ice, pretending nonchalance, but memories of Peter Westin gripped her—the summer they had shared, the walks in the woods, puzzles by the fire in Grace Arbor's spacious living room. Mrs. Westin had waited on her son with such loving attention when he came to visit. And he was affectionate with her, always careful to see she had what she needed. How wonderful it would be to have someone who cared about you like that, someone you could belong to, really belong.

She didn't allow her heart to dream of belonging to Peter. He was so far above her, after all—a scientist, a man of the world. But he had been a good friend to her. At first, she thought he only felt sorry for her or, worse, that he was curious about a Deaf girl—a novelty. He had kissed her that Sunday at the waterfall when the world was hushed and green, and time had fallen away.

You've been so brave through everything. Tess hadn't felt brave when she was taken in for questioning after her locket turned up in the woods where Uncle Alexei had died. She had clung to his reassuring presence beside her. She tried to thank him as they watched the water cascade into a pool of foam beneath the high rock face.

He had chosen the name Tess for her. *It's perfect for someone brave and beautiful.* He had copied the sign, his fingers so close that they brushed hers with every stroke. She loved the idea of having a name chosen especially for her. She was determined to live up to it.

Her heart fluttered as she remembered his arms around her when they parted. Did she love him? She pressed the soft drink button and watched the slow action of the liquid as it splashed into her glass. Perhaps it wasn't wise to fall in love so quickly. Or was love ever wise? It was more than she could consider now.

She followed Melissa down the aisle to a table in the cafeteria's bustling center where nurses, accountants, interns, and visitors ate. Most of them looked industrious or purposeful; a few appeared anxious or sad. No doubt these sad ones were taking a respite from the bedside of a loved one. Bits and pieces of anonymous conversation transferred from their lips to her mind in no discernible stream, and she consciously looked away to give them their privacy.

Carefully, she balanced the tray with its plate of sliced turkey, potatoes, vegetables, and cut-up fruit. When they were seated, she automatically bowed her head to say grace. When she looked up, she found her friend's curious eyes on her.

"We used to say grace when we were kids," Melissa said, pausing to take a bite of her turkey. "Got away from it somehow, but it's nice, I guess. I mean, it never hurts to say thank you. Who likes an ingrate anyhow?" Melissa rambled on as though language might cease to exist at any second, and she'd never get a chance to use another word. What a noisy place the world must be if there were many like Melissa, Tess thought.

"Like what do you say in those prayers?" Melissa asked, scooping up a forkful of salad.

Tess took her time answering. She hadn't always prayed before meals or even thought much about God's provision until Mrs. Westin had come to Grace Arbor. "I just say thank you to God," she said, "for the blessings he gives."

Melissa munched thoughtfully. "I guess it's easy to take things for granted. To forget to say thanks."

Tess nodded. It was nice to talk to God because He understood everything; He didn't need the labored precision of syllables and consonants or even the intricate lacing of fingers. She wondered if He understood this strange sense of abandonment she'd been experiencing lately, the sense of belonging to no one.

"You're funny," Melissa said. "I mean funny as in unusual." She took a quick sip of iced tea and went on. "Not because you're Deaf or anything. I mean, because you really think about things deep down. Kind of like a poet or an artist or something." She stopped long enough to take a drink of her coke and added, "Your folks must be pretty special. I'd like to meet them sometime."

Tess felt as though she'd been slapped. It was as if everything had coalesced in Melissa's innocent remark: Family, a mother and father who played games with their children, who taught them right from wrong. A family that took you on picnics and to basketball games and who reminded you not to talk to strangers. They tucked you in at night, and in the morning, they were still there, and you were still part of them—always a family.

"I'm sorry," Melissa was saying. "Did I say something wrong?"

"No. I'm sorry," Tess said. "It's just…" She rubbed her fingers over the lip of her glass. "It's just… I don't know." She struggled against the lump in her throat and the tears that were stinging her eyes.

"What?" Melissa asked, incredulous. "You can talk to me. I'm your friend, aren't I?"

Tess put her glass down. "I didn't know my parents," she said slowly. "My mother is dead, and my father … well, I don't know who he is or where he is."

Melissa reached across the table and touched her hand. "I'm sorry, Tess. I didn't know."

Fearing that her friend might see the gathering tears, Tess kept her eyes on her lap as the awful emptiness consumed her. She would never know who her mother had been or what her hands might have felt like when she touched her. And what about her father? Did he know about her? Whoever he was, he must have been cruel to leave them. Tess pulled her hand away and scooped up her roll. She didn't care if she ever found out who her father was. She didn't need to know him, and she didn't want him to know her!

"It's nothing. It doesn't matter," Tess said.

"I didn't mean to upset you. I'm sorry," Melissa said plaintively. Then her eyes flashed left and right as she cast about for a new subject. "Why don't you and I go somewhere this Saturday? There's a new mall in town. Can you believe it? A mall, right here in Ladystone!"

Tess rummaged in her purse for a tissue. "I'm sorry," she said, wondering how many times she had said those two words that day. "I have been a real bore."

"It's okay," Melissa said with a shrug. "Do you know how many times you've said you're sorry?" She gave Tess a playful punch on the arm. "I know, let's go to that new Italian restaurant on Fourth Street for lunch. The servers sing real opera. Can you believe it? In this one-horse town!" She broke off, flushing pink. She'd forgotten that the beauty of an operatic aria would be lost on Tess.

"I'd like that very much," Tess said, stumbling over "much." It was a word she usually avoided.

"Or we could go to that seafood place," Melissa offered. "Whatever. It'll be fun!" Her lips moved perpetually as she stacked her tray with the soiled plates and silverware. That was something about Melissa. You could always count on her to make conversation, even all by herself.

Suddenly, a startled look appeared on Melissa's face. "Oh my gosh!" She leaned in toward Tess, pointing. "He's coming this way! Look!"

Tess followed the blue shining of her friend's eyes and turned back to her. "Who?"

"Dr. Brevitz. You know, the new doctor." Her hands flew to her cheeks, and she blushed like a high school cheerleader. "He's so handsome."

Tess looked up. The man coming toward them wore charcoal gray slacks and a royal blue shirt under his white doctor's coat. His eyes were compelling—gray and translucent as light breaking through a cloud or like the mist at Harper's Woods. Thick, dark hair waved back from his forehead and curled stubbornly over prominent ears. He moved with a confident air, as though he knew exactly where he was going and what he wanted, and unlike the rest of humanity, he knew everything there was to know.

She'd seen him at the hospital from time to time, usually with one of the nurses or interns. He always made her feel like a shy schoolgirl with his pompous manner. She turned away but kept him in her peripheral vision, not missing the splashy tie that lay askew on his chest or the sunglasses angled rakishly in the pocket next to a coiled stethoscope. Nor did she miss the bulge of muscle inside his shirt. She felt his eyes on her, willing her to look. Was she blushing, or did she only feel like a summer heat wave had passed through her?

When he came nearer, close enough so she could smell his cologne or aftershave, he closed one eye in a decided wink. Then, without a word, he strode importantly past her.

"David Brevitz," Melissa breathed. "He's so … so … " She broke off, overwhelmed. When she recovered her composure, she said, "He's from an important hospital back East."

"So?" Tess said. New doctors were always appearing, many from India or China or some other faraway place.

"So, he's an important doctor. So, he comes to the hospital for consultations and to see his private patients. So, he's an absolute hunk." Melissa followed him with admiring eyes until he disappeared.

Tess bent to gather her purse and sweater. She didn't care who he was. He had taunted her with his frank gaze, then quickly ignored her. She hated being treated like that.

"He's so … " Melissa stammered again.

"So old," Tess supplied emphatically.

"But men in their forties are so mysterious." Melissa sighed, and once again, superlatives failed her.

Tess hurried back to her department, not sure if Melissa followed or not. If hospital gossip could be believed, Dr. Brevitz had come from Philadelphia and quickly earned the reputation of a playboy who loved running his outboard motorboat at break-neck speeds. She didn't need that kind of attention. When Melissa grabbed her arm to slow her down, Tess said scornfully, "He flirts with all the girls."

"I think he likes you," Melissa said, staring at Tess meaningfully. "You really are quite a catch, you know."

Tess swallowed. Could a Deaf girl with skinny shoulders and unruly red hair be a catch? Was Melissa making fun of her? *How could you tell about people?* Men were the least trustworthy of all. Hadn't Shane pretended to like her when all the time what he wanted was her inheritance? She swallowed against the hurt.

And what did Peter really think of her—a girl with no family, no roots? Would an educated scientist like him ever really take her seriously? It was hard to be 21 and not know who you were or where you came from. She felt all her earlier affirmations fall away like mist. Peter, a job, an apartment, friends—none of these could fill the deep sense of abandonment that held her. She grabbed her purse from the chair. "Let's get back. We'll be late."

Chapter 6

"There he is," Lance said, squinting to get a better look.

The photo Anne had seen didn't do justice to the electric wire of a boy coming toward them with a rolling, slightly pigeon-toed gait. Unlike Shane Eldridge, who was dark-haired and well-muscled, the child descending the jet way was skinny and pale with a thatch of shockingly red hair. His face was narrow, pitiably small, with astonishingly large eyes in whose depths kinship with Lance's troubled nephew was undeniable.

Anne felt a sinking in her stomach as she recalled the harrowing summer night she'd spent as Shane Eldridge's hostage. All the snows of a Wisconsin winter wouldn't serve to bury the painful memories of her first June weeks in Ladystone. Now, she was looking at Shane's brother, having accompanied Lance to the airport. From there, they would stop at Rutgers Nursing Home to visit Margaret before going home.

Jimmy declined the hand of the slender, platinum-haired attendant but stood obediently by her side as Lance pressed forward to greet his nephew. He drew out his driver's license, identifying himself as the receiving party of a minor child traveling alone. The attendant carefully reviewed his I.D. and consulted her passenger list as travelers swerved around them, eager to get to waiting relatives.

Anne studied the boy. His ears were small, round spheres like delicate shells. He had a thin, reedy neck that seemed too fragile to sustain the weight of his head; a spray of red freckles dotted his upturned nose. His eyes were large, accentuated perhaps by slightly bluish shading beneath them, as though he might have been ill or away from sunlight too long. Yet his wiry body disavowed any hint of fragility. Beneath a fleece jacket, he wore faded blue jeans with tears in both knees and a splashy Hawaiian shirt that hung loosely on his small frame. He was hardly dressed for winter. The laces of his high-top tennis shoes hung at his ankles like flat gray spaghetti.

Jimmy shook his uncle's hand stiffly, glancing from Lance to the flight attendant as though unsure what to do next. With a nod of her head, the attendant left them.

Lance pressed Anne forward, his fingers clutching her elbow. "Jimmy, this is my friend, Mrs. Westin."

It would be hard to say which of the two was more nervous, the boy standing on shifting feet or the man with his hand tight on her arm. How strange for Lance, who'd never had a boy of his own, and how difficult for Jimmy to be placed in the hands of an uncle he barely knew.

"Nice to meet you, Jimmy," she said. "I hope you'll enjoy your stay here. Winter in Wisconsin can be a lot of fun. There's so much to do outdoors."

Under the spray of freckles, Jimmy's face flushed. He continued his nervous dance. "Hello," he said in a tight voice through chapped lips. She'd seen him run his tongue over his bottom lip several times. Was it a chronic habit, or was he only anxious?

"Well," Lance said, "let's get your bags. I hope you have some boots and gloves somewhere. You're in the frozen north now." He frowned and moved to take the boy's hand. But Jimmy squirmed and stuffed both hands inside his jacket pockets. They proceeded to the baggage area, Jimmy staying a step or two behind, and soon, they heard the shuffle and squeak of the bag claim conveyor belt.

They waited without speaking. Anne could sense Lance's anxiety. He had fretted earlier about caring for an eleven-year-old, and she knew he was thinking of his first attempt to shelter one of his sister's boys. Shane Eldridge was behind bars, and it had happened on Lance's watch.

She had tried to reassure him that he had done what he could, but a haunted look still shadowed Lance's fine features. She knew he visited Shane at the prison, though he never spoke of it. Now he had agreed to let this boy come, this child who'd been expelled from school for petty thefts and God knew what else. Even his foster parents had decided to enjoy their holidays without him and had begged Lance to take care of Jimmy while they were away. Did they even know this uncle in whose hands they had so glibly placed their charge?

The luggage carousel bumped along with its clumsy cargo as arms reached for a bag or valise. Passengers pulled carriers and duffle bags off the moving belt, each trying not to step on the other's clambering feet. Suddenly, Jimmy reached out a hand and, with quick agility, yanked a large canvas duffle bag off the line.

"That it?" Lance asked.

"Yeah," Jimmy said, shuffling his feet once more. "It holds a lot." He had a high, unchanged voice, but it was not without a pleasing resonance.

Anne felt a quick pathos that often came when she was near children. An odd sorrow overcame her whenever she heard a child cry, even an ornery one weary from shopping. Her eyes would sting, her throat would tighten, and she would hasten to distance herself from the unhappy voices.

"I'll get it," Lance said, reaching for the bag and nearly losing his footing. "You got the crown jewels in here?" he quipped, transferring the bag to his other hand.

Jimmy licked his lower lip and walked on without comment, screwing up his shoulders and jamming his hands once again into his pockets.

Anne rushed around Lance to Jimmy's side. "I hope you won't mind a stop at McDonald's on our way," she said, hoping to redeem the awkward moment. She'd felt Jimmy's quick offense. That crown jewel comment had been a thoughtless cliché, not unlike her comment when Lance pulled his cap over his ears, affecting the caricature of an escaped convict. She put a hand out to ruffle the boy's wiry red hair and was surprised at his quick recoil. She should have remembered. Boys Jimmy's age weren't into tactile expressions of affection.

Grover began to leap and bark a noisy welcome long before they reached the car and quickly bonded with Jimmy. He proved an excellent buffer on what might have been an awkward ride back to Ladystone from the distant airport. Jimmy even saved part of his Happy Meal from McDonalds to share with his new shaggy friend.

When they reached the nursing home two hours later, Lance let Jimmy take Grover's leash. When they'd deposited their outer gear in the foyer, they proceeded down the corridor, Anne and Lance exchanging looks of grateful relief.

They found Margaret sitting up in bed, wearing a dressing gown of pale blue with a dusting of pink rosebuds. Her snowy hair was brushed back from her forehead and drawn up like a frothy cloud around her face. She looked startled and then beamed at the sight of Grover, who leaped on her in one bound and began to rake his long tongue delightedly over her face.

Margaret wrapped her arms around the dog's shaggy neck, disregarding the shower of fur and tongue. "How did you smuggle him in?" she asked incredulously. She crooned softly to him and then began to cough from the exertion.

"Oh, it wasn't too difficult," Anne said, worried as Margaret's coughing intensified. She waited until Margaret lay back, exhausted but still laughing. At Lance's command, the great dog settled down and contented himself to be cradled in her lap.

Margaret noticed Jimmy in the doorway. "And who is this?" she asked in her sober teacher's voice.

"Meet my nephew, Jimmy," Lance said, motioning for the boy to come in. "He's going to spend Christmas holidays with me."

Jimmy shuffled in slowly, shaking back his thatch of red hair as he stepped hesitantly toward Margaret's bed.

"This is Miss Morris," Lance said. "She belongs to Grover. That is, Grover belongs to her."

"Hello," Jimmy said, looking down at his shoes and licking his lower lip. As though sensing the awkward moment, Grover ambled over and gave the boy a friendly nudge with his great furry head.

"Grover likes you," Margaret said warmly. "I'm very glad to meet you, Jimmy." She turned to Lance with quick reproof. "Why have you brought this boy to visit an old lady in a nursing home on a perfectly good Sunday afternoon?" she scolded. "Why isn't he out on the slopes enjoying this new snowfall?"

"Oh, we'll make the slopes," Lance said quickly. "But we wanted to see you. We've only just come from the airport."

"I see," Margaret said. "Well, you're a dear to bring Grover." At the sound of his name, Grover gave Margaret another raking of his tongue. She nuzzled her face in his collar, an action that started her coughing again. When the spasm ended, she whispered, "Thank you. I've missed the big galoot."

Meeting Anne's worried eyes, Lance grabbed Grover's collar. "We'll get out of here now so you can rest." He turned the dog over to Jimmy, clapping a hand lightly on the boy's shoulder as he steered him out of the room.

"I'll be along in a minute," Anne said, hesitant to leave Margaret. Had the excitement of bringing both Grover and a little boy been too much? She smoothed the blanket over Margaret's feet and plumped the pillows behind her head. The bed was raised into an upright position customary for pulmonary patients.

"I'll be fine, Annie. Don't worry. This nagging cough is just a nuisance. I'm sorry to be so much trouble." Margaret closed her eyes briefly. "I'm just a little tired, but I'm so glad you came."

Anne waited for her labored breathing to ease, noting the shadows under the old eyes. It was proving to be a long convalescence for her. "Just rest now," she said gently and determined to come more often—every few days if she could manage it.

Suddenly, the door to Margaret's room opened. Had Lance forgotten something? She turned to see a stranger in royal blue slacks and an open-collared shirt. He wore a gold chain around his neck, and the maze of dark hair on his head looked in need of a good combing. He paused only briefly, giving Anne a cursory glance, and rushed in, the white coat over his yellow shirt creating a breeze like a wake from a speedboat.

Anne stared at the stethoscope coiled around his neck. He had to be the physician from the hospital who made scheduled visits to the care home. But he looked more like the intrepid hero in a Victorian novel just stepping off a windy cliff in Scotland.

The dashing doctor bowed slightly and fixed his gaze on Margaret, dark eyes quick and appraising. "You have company.

That's good," he said with precise, staccato speech. He punched his fists into the pockets of his coat and surveyed his patient.

Anne found her voice. "Margaret's been waiting for you. I'll just step out."

"No need. No need." The doctor thrust a hand toward her. "David Brevitz," he said.

"Anne Westin," she replied, feeling strangely tongue-tied and, to her surprise, intimidated. The color of his eyes was hard to identify—gray or charcoal but rapidly changing—like water altered by sun or wind.

He pressed the stethoscope to Margaret's chest and narrowed his gaze. Anne waited for him to finish, anxious to ask about Margaret's treatment plan and why she wasn't getting well. But she could hardly confront him here, nor did it seem fitting to ask such questions of a man who looked more like someone who'd just stepped off a pleasure yacht than the doctor in charge.

"I am going to increase your inhalation therapy," he told Margaret, scrawling something on her chart. Then, dropping a hand loosely into the pocket of his coat, he nodded and turned to leave.

"May I speak with you, doctor?" she ventured as he made to brush past her.

"Certainly," he said. "Come to the nurses' station in … " He paused to check his watch. "I can meet you there in five minutes." He favored her with an ingratiating smile that didn't quite reach his eyes and was gone.

Anne spent a few more minutes with Margaret and promised to return very soon. When she arrived at the appointed spot, she found the doctor conferring over a chart with an attractive blond nurse. Anne waited to be noticed, embarrassed at having interrupted what seemed less like a doctor/nurse consultation than a pleasant personal aside.

She waited until Dr. Brevitz looked up with an affable expression and a raised eyebrow. The nurse tucked away the chart with a flutter of her shiny nails and busied herself at the desk as Anne approached.

Anne set her jaw, determined not to be put off by the doctor's unnerving manner. "I wonder if I could ask you about my friend, Margaret Morris," she began. "She has no family, you see, and I need to know what we might do to help her."

"Of course," he said, meeting her stern gaze, a hint of humor in his own. He bowed slightly, tucked a hand under her elbow, and led her to a waiting room a few feet from the nurses' station. "She is making some progress," he said when they had stepped inside. "However, the residual effects of pneumonia take some time to clear completely."

His speech was measured and careful, and his accent was decidedly not mid-western. She'd heard he was an Easterner—maybe a Bostonian whose accents had always seemed foreign to her.

"I've ordered an additional breathing treatment each day." He paused. "Of course, if you can do something to relieve her depression, it will speed recovery."

So, it wasn't just her perception that Margaret was depressed. Anne studied the lapel of the doctor's coat, her thoughts moving backward. It was to be expected, of course, after all that had happened. Alexei Popov had been more than Margaret's neighbor; he'd been a long-time friend and might have been more but for his accident and his sister's efforts to keep them apart. Now he was dead, and Margaret was alone.

"Margaret's been through a lot," Anne said wistfully.

Suddenly, they both looked up to see a striking woman in a jade green suit, platinum hair swept up on her head and anchored with a fashionable clip. She walked toward them, her high heels making sharp little clicks on the tile, one hand extended as though to command their attention. As she drew nearer, Anne could see that her green eyes were as vivid as her suit and wary as a crocodile's.

She stopped directly in front of Anne and exhaled an exasperated breath. "I must insist that you remove your dog." She peered over tortoiseshell glasses toward the rear door from which Lance and Jimmy had recently exited with Grover. "We do not allow animals in this facility."

"He's not mine," Anne began innocently, feeling a little shiver of apprehension. Hadn't Lance arranged the visit with the nursing home staff? And hadn't this woman ever heard of animal therapy—particularly in places like nursing homes?

"We have rules here for the good of our patients. I'll not have them breached by someone who feels she can do as she ... "

Doctor Brevitz stepped into the narrow space between them. "Now, Helen, surely a concession is in order." He put an arm around the woman's shoulder in a surprising display of camaraderie. "It is to bring cheer to one of our patients that they have come," he cajoled, his tone conciliatory but firm. He smiled and spread his hands. "And the animal has already gone. You see? There is no need for concern."

Helen's eyes smoldered with green fire, but she dropped them down to the elegant little buckles on her shoes. The color in her cheeks spread to her blond hairline.

Brevitz leveled his gaze to Helen's. "The visit was therapy, yes?" He lifted an eyebrow in an imploring gesture. "It's just what the doctor ordered, you might say." He clearly was enjoying the confrontation, and he was winning.

Helen gave an exasperated shake of her head and stepped out from under his arm. She drew in another quick breath and let it out. "Very well, but if you bring the animal in again, it must be strictly confined. He must not bother the other patients." Giving Dr. Brevitz a withering look, she turned on her heel and walked away, smoothing the hem of her jacket at her willowy hips.

An interesting bedside manner, Anne thought. The doctor appeared to have not only the nurses under his spell but the tough-minded Helen Rutger as well. She hefted her heavy coat and boot bag from a chair and nodded her thanks. Lance and Jimmy would be waiting for her. If she were lucky, they'd have the jeep warmed up. She strode down the corridor, feeling the doctor's dark eyes on her. She quickened her steps, unnerved at his ability to make her feel like a self-absorbed adolescent.

She had almost reached the door when someone called from a doorway. "Hello, do you remember me?"

Anne wheeled around. "Erma, how nice to see you." Reversing her steps, she bent to greet Erma Tanner, who was pushing herself forward in her wheelchair. Erma seldom had callers of her own, Anne knew. The poor woman was obliged to enjoy someone else's visits vicariously. She often shadowed Anne when she was there. Anne covered the pudgy hand poised on the left wheel of the chair. "How are you, Erma?" she asked gently.

"I've been sick," Erma said in a pouting voice, perhaps affected to solicit sympathy. "They won't let me have anything good." She looked down with a nervous smile and then raised her head inquisitively.

It was a familiar ploy. Her intake of sweets and carbs was monitored because of diabetes. At least, she hoped it was so at Rutgers, for Erma had a powerful craving for things like chocolate brownies and cream pies. Anne patted Erma's crocheted laprobe into place over her knees and tried to think of a way to divert her attention. In the press of things and picking up Jimmy at the airport, she hadn't thought to bring diabetic candy for Erma today. "Have you seen the snow?" she asked brightly. "It's really beautiful."

Erma shrugged and raised her eyebrows, rouge blooming like clown spots on her plump cheeks. Two buttons were missing on the bright red sweater drawn across her ample chest.

"Let's go have a look," Anne said, though it was getting late, and Lance would be waiting. He was most likely not happy to be left alone with his new charge. She shepherded Erma into the sunroom, where wide windows afforded a clear view of the winter landscape. Afternoon shadows lay across the land, and the blue hills were tinged with lavender and pink.

Erma began to wax eloquent about her childhood, her experiences as a performer, and how she'd almost married her "Valentino." How much of it was true and how much was the result of a vivid imagination Anne couldn't know. But she knew Erma needed to tell her story; she needed someone to care about it and the woman who had lived it.

"I have to go," Anne said, "but I have something for you." She leaned down close to Erma's ear, remembering that she had a little package of sugar-free gum in her purse. "Close your eyes and open your hand," she whispered. She was against "talking down" to seniors, but Erma, who was more child than woman, seemed to love it.

"Oh, my," Erma said with a giggle.

Anne dropped the fragrant strip of gum into the outstretched hand. An idea suddenly formed in her mind. "Erma, would you like to come to a Christmas party at my house?" She had been planning it for weeks. It would be wonderful to entertain family and friends for a special celebration for her first Christmas at Grace Arbor. Why not include this woman who seemed to have no one to care about her? Transportation would be difficult, but surely she could find a way. Lance's jeep was roomy enough to accommodate a wheelchair.

"Could I?" Erma asked incredulously. "Oh, my!"

"Leave it to me. I'll tell you all about it next time I come," Anne said. "But for now, it will be our secret." She took Erma back to her room, expecting the bubble of ceaseless chatter that was her normal pattern, but Erma grew strangely quiet. Was she overwhelmed at the prospect of an outing, or was something troubling her? Perhaps this time she really wasn't well; maybe this time she wasn't feigning illness for sympathy's sake.

"Annie?" Erma began when she had been safely delivered to her room, "I want to ask you ... " She broke off and squinted up through her thick glasses. "When I die, you'll see my name gets in the paper, won't you?"

Startled, Anne said, "Of course, but let's not be talking about such things now." She kissed Erma's powdery cheek and patted her hand. "Now, no more of this. Remember our secret—the Christmas party. We'll have music and holiday treats of all kinds. You think about that. Everything will be all right."

Erma nodded, pushed her heavy glasses up on her nose, and smiled shyly.

Anne left her with a heavy heart. She had told Erma everything would be all right, but would it? Everything wasn't all right. Erma was alone in a world moving too fast for her; she was possibly sicker than anyone knew. All she wanted was to be assured that she would be remembered when she passed away. What was right about that? For Margaret, too, things were far from right. She wasn't coping well with her illness and was removed from the home she loved. *Surely, by Christmas ...*

"Dear God, comfort them," she whispered, feeling the sorrow of two women who had lived long in a world that no longer seemed to need them. He who marks the sparrow's fall must weep for love of those the world forgets.

She was determined to remember.

Chapter 7

Tess zipped her fur-lined jacket and pulled the hood over her head. The snow that had been falling off and on throughout the day now poured from the heavens like flour through a baker's sieve. She'd seen on the weather channel that a storm was heading their way. It was one of many they could expect in northern Wisconsin, but it wasn't due to begin until after midnight. It was only five o'clock, but darkness had fallen, and the wind was picking up. Powdery gusts swirled across the highway as though driven by some furious broom.

She peered up at the leaden sky. It had been a long day. She wanted nothing more than some hot vegetable soup and a good night's sleep, but she would call on Vera as she had planned. She lifted a rectangular box from the trunk of her car—a gift for her aunt. It shouldn't take long to deliver the Christmas swag—blue spruce pine boughs and tiny glass balls of vivid blue. Organza streamers of the same penetrating blue were woven among the branches, creating the effect of undulating sea waves.

She approached the sagging door of the house that had once been her home and felt a vague yearning. Uncle Alexei had kept up repairs on the little house until he was injured and no longer able to work. Now drafts were held at bay with bits of cloth between the cracks. She could see that Vera had taped a sheet of plastic over the east window.

Tess gingerly climbed the first wooden step and saw that the next had split. Carefully, she stepped up to the back door. None of this had been lost on the city inspector, Tess was sure, but at least the fencing around the chicken coops and runs had been installed.

The window of her old room on the second floor was dark like the others in the house, but one small light shone from the kitchen at the rear where Vera always prepared her eggs for sale. She gave the small black and white television propped up on a shelf little attention but went about her work with lips tightly sealed as the pictures flashed on the screen. Perhaps the sounds that came brought comfort, though that was beyond understanding.

She shifted the box to her other arm and knocked, allowing herself to hope that Vera might be glad to see her. Maybe, just maybe, she would be pleased with this hand-crafted gift. Might she even be proud of the girl whose hands had fashioned it? After all, didn't everyone feel a touch of goodwill at Christmas? She knocked again, more strongly this time, as though to summon courage.

When suddenly the door opened, Vera stood with a dishtowel slung over one plump shoulder. Breathing heavily, as though she had just done an aerobic workout, she rubbed callused hands together and wiped them on the stained apron tied around her waist. The apron gave her a sectioned look, like an aging snow-man melting in a warm wind. The ever-present green brooch Vera loved was pinned to the middle of the apron. Tess smiled sadly, recalling her aunt's love of shiny baubles.

"Hello, Aunt Vera." Tess held the box out, surprised to realize her hands were shaking. "I brought you something." She formed the words carefully without signing. "I hope you like it."

Vera made no move to take the box. Her little coal eyes darted from Tess to the package, revealing nothing. Strands of hair that had escaped the knot at the back of her head wisped around her florid face.

"Can I come in?" Tess asked. She didn't wait for an answer but stepped inside and closed the door behind her. She put the box on a chair, pulled off her hat, and gave her hair a toss. Tess signed. "It's for Christmas. I made it myself."

Feet apart, arms folded, Vera cast her eyes down to her dusty canvas shoes. Her lips formed the stunted words, "Busy. Got big order tomorrow."

Undaunted, Tess raised the cover of the box to reveal the pine swag with its glistening ornaments and ribbon streamers. "It's your favorite color. Do you like it?" she asked, assuming a nonchalance she was far from feeling.

"Got no room," Vera said, pushing her lips into a childish pout. Her thick eyebrows formed a solid line of defense over stormy eyes.

"It might look nice over the mantel," Tess suggested in sign language. She led the way into the living room and held the swag up against the faded wallpaper.

From the doorway between the two little rooms, Vera fingered the green brooch on her chest absently as she watched. Then, without a word, she turned abruptly and went back to her tasks in the kitchen.

Tess laid the swag on the crude mantel and sat down on the couch with a leaden heart. She traced her fingers over the familiar brown coffee stain on the sofa's arm. Here, she had poured over *The Velveteen Rabbit, Silas Marner, Little Women,* or a book of children's poetry—books Miss Morris always brought when she came to visit. Uncle Alexei would sip coffee while Aunt Vera stood stolidly at the stove.

Tess felt fatigue settle in her bones as though she'd run a long way and still found no rest. She looked around the shabby room. There was nothing for her here anymore. She no longer belonged, if indeed she ever had. Vera had never wanted her; Her grandmother had died before Tess could know her as her mother had. Whoever her father was, he had abandoned her long ago. She stood wearily, leaving the forlorn swag on the mantel.

In the kitchen, Vera filled cardboard crates with brown eggs. She looked up briefly as Tess entered.

"I have to go," Tess said, weaving the words with dispirited fingers. She reached for the old-fashioned door knob. She should not have come. Vera didn't care two brown eggs for her and never would. What had she expected, anyway?

The old woman's eyes focused on something beyond the door. She paused, and for a moment, the old face softened; the restless eyes clouded. "Bad storm," she said without looking at Tess. "You go home quick." Then she bent to pick up a wire basket from the floor by her feet.

Tess watched her transfer the eggs from basket to carton with surprising gentleness and wondered why such tenderness had never been offered to her. Would she ever understand this strange, unhappy woman with whom she'd shared the formative years of her life?

She knew Vera resented anyone who had lived in the big house next door, especially the city woman who had purchased what she felt should have been hers and Uncle Alexei's. It made no sense, but there it was. Shane had been clever to exploit her aunt's simple-minded, jealous love of the property now named Grace Arbor. Why couldn't Vera understand and move on with her own life? Anne Westin had been a kind and sensitive neighbor and wanted to be her friend.

Thinking of the coming holiday, Tess allowed a tiny ray of hope to enter her heart. "Won't you please come to Mrs. Westin's Christmas party?" she asked.

"Got no time for fancy tea parties," she retorted. An egg suddenly cracked in her fingers, oozing yellow liquid into the carton. Quick anger flashed in Vera's eyes. "Look what you make me do!"

Tess pulled the door open, ushering in a blast of icy wind, and raced down the steps, relishing the sharp sting of the pellets against her face. She could feel the tears start and wondered if they would freeze in mid-passage.

Once inside her car, she pulled away from the curb, wheels spinning on the wet pavement. She had thought there could be no more crying; that was part of the childish past she had put behind her, but the tears were running down her face, and she could barely see. She flicked on the wipers, but the vigorous fanning was no match for the fast-flying snow and sleet that clung to the windshield. She should never have come! She should have gone directly home to her apartment.

With growing alarm, she realized she was driving in near blizzard conditions. She urged the little car on, willing herself not to panic. The panoramic mirrors she had ordered to give her greater visibility had not arrived, and she felt vulnerable driving for the first time. The hospital was closer than her apartment; she could wait out the storm there. Surely, she could make it that far. She set the odometer with shaking fingers. When it marked 2.3 miles, she'd know she was there.

Snow whipped across the windshield in a blinding sheet, and the wind rocked the Toyota like a child's sailboat on an ocean. "Dear God, please help me," she whispered.

Did God care about people caught in blizzards? She clung to the small faith that had sprung up in recent months, a seed first planted by Anne Westin. In the still moments when she reached out to God, she felt an unexplainable sense of being loved, even as she simultaneously doubted her senses. Perhaps God would tire of her ambiguity.

She had slowed to near stand-still as she desperately tried to gain visibility. Suddenly, something hit her rear bumper, pushing her forward. It wasn't a hard impact, but it was bad enough to startle her. Headlights beamed into her rear window, practically rendering her sightless. The car nudged her forward, its lights flashing until she stopped. The offending car behind her stopped, too. A huddled figure sprang out, ran to her, and pulled her door open. Was she about to be robbed or attacked?

"For God's sake, what are you doing out here?"

With giddy relief, Tess recognized Dr. David Brevitz. The collar of his overcoat was pulled high around his neck, and snow clung to his dark, unruly hair.

He slid in beside her, the blinkers from his car lighting up the interior. "Where are you going?" he demanded.

"I'm going home," she stammered. "I stopped to see my aunt. I didn't know the storm was so bad." He was very near her, wet snow clinging to his bushy brows.

He flung an arm over the steering wheel and glared at her. "Didn't you hear me honking!" he demanded, the color high on his forehead and cheeks. He raised a hand and let it fall in frustration against the steering wheel. "Of course, you didn't!" he said, answering his own impulsive question.

She shivered in misery and embarrassment but couldn't tear her eyes away from his angry face. For days, she'd seen him eyeing her at the hospital. He had to know she was Deaf. Everybody knew.

I think he's sweet on you, Melissa had said, and Tess had hushed her with an angry rebuff. She felt that same anger now and wanted to yell at him to leave her alone.

"I was almost home when you nearly ran me down!" he said. "It is crazy to be out on a night like this! Crazy!" He may have said more, but he had turned, and she couldn't read his lips anymore.

His superior air was enough to halt her panic. What right did he have to bump her car? What if he'd damaged it or, worse, sent her flying through the windshield? "Well, *you're* out on a night like this," she said imperiously. "Besides, I knew if I got to the hospital, I could wait out the storm there." She hated his scolding, she hated the blizzard, and she hated the fact that he was right. She couldn't make it by herself in this weather.

David narrowed probing eyes and ran a gloved hand through his sopping hair. "I am going to get in front of you, and I want you to stay directly behind me, close enough so I can feel your bumper hitting mine! Do you understand?"

Tess nodded meekly. She was too shaken and weary to assert herself any longer. And she was so cold!

He dashed out the door and got back into his car. She followed obediently behind his sturdy four-wheel drive until he stopped in front of one of the new Glenwood River condos. In a moment, he was propelling her toward the door, the wind pressing them forward. She felt a heady sense of relief as they rushed inside and slammed the door against the storm.

Roughly, he helped her out of her soaked parka and slung his wet topcoat on the rack by the door. He pulled up a chair behind her and motioned for her to sit. "Take off your boots," he instructed, as though she were five years old and didn't know enough to remove them on her own. "I'll get the coffee. You do drink coffee, don't you?"

She grimaced as he left the room. She looked around his cluttered but oddly cozy living room in which books and papers were scattered on a squat, marble-top table. Ashes from an old fire had spilled over onto a braided rug covering the hearth. A black leather recliner and a plaid couch were drawn close to the fire.

She huddled in a corner of the couch uncomfortably. She wasn't in the habit of visiting single men in their homes, especially men like Dr. Brevitz, who everyone said was some kind of heroic ladies' man.

She watched him covertly, wishing she could think of something witty to say, some way to prove she was not demented or too addled to take care of herself. He'd invited her to dinner shortly after the day they'd met in the cafeteria. Melissa had nearly passed out when he'd walked toward their table. *He's got his eye on you,* she'd said with surprise and envy.

He had wanted to take her to the newest, most popular restaurant in town, and she'd taken delight in turning him down. Still, she couldn't help being pleased that he'd found her attractive, perhaps as attractive as other girls. "No thanks," she had stammered.

She didn't like men with big egos. Besides, no one had really interested her since she'd met Peter Westin. Did the suave, sophisticated Dr. David Brevitz really like her in spite of her handicap, or was he only sorry for her? She was flattered by his attentions but, at the same time, annoyed by his gratuitous behavior.

He came toward her carrying coffee in two thick mugs on a tray alongside sandwiches, which were cut raggedly and spilling over with lettuce and what looked like ham and cheese. He had donned a sweater the color of old metal, which made him seem tame, domestic, like a long-married professor who spent his evenings smoking a pipe and reading the classics. Still, she knew that benign-appearing old men could sometimes prove the most dangerous.

"Eat," he said roughly, thrusting a sandwich toward her. She noticed then that there were strands of gray in his dark hair. "And take this. You're shivering." He threw an afghan at her impatiently as though she had deliberately contrived to inconvenience him by getting stranded in the snowstorm.

She took it meekly and drew it up to her chin, hating the series of sneezes that shook her. It was hard to appear capable, let alone charming or sophisticated, when your nose was red and running.

He slumped across from her in a big leather chair shoved nearer to the coffee table. "Eat, eat!" he demanded. "And drink up. It will warm you." An amber light softened his eyes and gruff manner. He chewed and swallowed with careful concentration.

She hesitated, aware of the rugged angles of his face and the swarthy, well-past-five o'clock shadow. Her hands trembled around the cup. If she could just get up and run out, leave him sitting there like some medieval ogre too dull to chase her.

"What troubles you? Do you think I put something in the coffee?" He made a clucking sound with his tongue. "You should not listen to everything you hear."

She picked up a sandwich, frowned at its asymmetrical shape, and realized she was hungry. She took a generous bite, determined not to be intimidated by his high-handed manner and the rumors that circulated about his philandering ways. *Never let them think you're afraid.*

"Thank you," she said politely. She nibbled and looked at him over the sandwich. The rumors about his love life might be merely trumped-up nonsense from small-town gossips intrigued by a sophisticated doctor from Boston. On the other hand, maybe he was waiting for just the right moment to lunge at her. She gave her head a little toss and turned her gaze to the window.

Through the Venetian blinds, she could see the snow thickening on branches and roofs. The wind keened and whistled around the windowpanes. Oddly, she had a sense of being sheltered and began to feel almost comfortable.

"And who was it that you simply had to visit on the worst night of the winter?" he asked, breaking the silence between them and leaning back in the big chair.

It was a question rudely asked, and it was none of his business, really, but she found herself answering. "My aunt." She paused. "She is not really my aunt, but she raised me after my mother died—she and Uncle Alexei."

It seemed to take him a long time to speak again. She watched his eyelids open; the irises darken like charcoal and fall away to the floor. He put the mug to his mouth, swallowed, and coughed as though something had gone down the wrong way. He pulled a handkerchief from his pocket and wiped his mouth.

He said nothing for several seconds and drank more coffee. Then, in an off-hand manner, he asked, "He was good to you, this Uncle Alexei?"

She cradled her coffee cup and looked away from him deliberately. She gazed out the window over his head, studying the winter landscape. Uncle Alexei had liked snow. *Is not so much snow. Not like we had in old country*, he would say, and a faraway glaze would wash the light from his eyes. She thought of his gnarled hands and her small, quick ones working together to build a snowman. Those had been the best times when she was small and certain that this dear old man loved her.

She swallowed, surprised that grief could still be raw. "He was good to me," she said and realized that she had crossed her arms across her chest—the sign for love.

"And your aunt ... Vera, is it?"

She took a deep breath. "She's mad at me," she said with a shrug. "She is always mad at me for something. Who knows why? Now it is because I moved out." She studied her hands on the blue mug. It was a sudden moment of knowing. Yes, that was true. For all her complaints about being "saddled with a Deaf child," Vera hadn't wanted her to go away, had resented her packing up her few belongings and putting them inside her blue Toyota and driving away.

"Tell me about your parents," David said as though he was a psychologist and she a timid patient.

"My mother died when I was young," she said, looking away to watch the swirl of snowflakes beyond David's shoulder. It was embarrassing to have to stare at his lips to know what he was saying. "My grandmother brought me here to the house where Mrs. Westin lives. I don't remember living there. I was a baby when she died."

"I know her," David said and passed a hand over his jaw where dark stubble was forming. "I met her during my rounds at the nursing home." A hint of a smile touched his eyes. "She and a very big dog were visiting one of the patients."

"Margaret Morris," Tess supplied.

"Ah, yes, he said with an impassive expression. "Recovering from pneumonia. Too bad."

"Miss Morris was my teacher and my friend," she said, tracing the cuticle around her index finger. "I owe a lot to her; I just wish she'd get better so she can go home."

She waited, but he offered no further comment. He leaned back in the leather chair, legs stretched out, arms folded across his chest. He seemed to be thinking about something. His eyelids fluttered as though he were fighting sleep, but she could see that he was watching her.

After what seemed a long time, he asked, "And what about your father?"

She played with a loose strand of yarn from the afghan. "I don't know." She didn't want to talk about her father, that shadowy figure she had never seen and who was never spoken of. As a child, she had read the mocking whispers that she had no father, that she was a foundling or illegitimate. That was no big deal. It happened to lots of kids. Still, the idea made her cringe, and she felt a resurgence of fear or anger or some unspeakable emotion. "I hate him. I hope he's dead."

Where had those terrible words come from? She had never said anything like that before in her life—nor had she thought it. She must sound like an impetuous child denied some indulgent treat. She looked at David's lips. He didn't move or speak, just sat still, eyes closed, as though she'd said nothing surprising or important.

After a few silent moments, she said, "So there you have it, the story of my life," nearly adding *I'm not only Deaf; I'm a bastard!* She wanted to shock him, to hurt him.

His eyes remained closed, his arms folded across his chest like some bored barkeeper after all the guests had gone. She put the plate and mug down on the coffee table and swept the afghan aside. "I've got to go home."

He was instantly alert. "Do not be a fool." His dark brows furrowed over suddenly flashing eyes. "We are in the middle of a blizzard. You would not get two meters down the road. You must stay here."

Spend the night in his house? The possibility had occurred to her. Now, it sprang full-blown to life, and she grew nervous, tongue-tied.

"Don't worry," he said. "There is a lock on the bedroom door. I will sleep on the couch." The matter was decided, and he had no plan to discuss it with her! He rose and pointed to the stairway. "Top of the stairs, turn right."

She stared at his back as he poked the dying embers in the fireplace and shoved the tray aside before flicking off a lamp.

"Tomorrow is a long day, and I must be at the hospital at six for rounds. If you need anything, help yourself. Good night."

Tess stared at him, stunned at this dismissal. All right! So, she was going to spend the night with Dr. David Brevitz. So what? He was proving to be about as romantic as an old shoe! She made her way up the stairs, marveling at the mix of relief and disappointment she felt.

Chapter 8

Anne drew the last card from the box of Christmas cards. She had chosen a simple design incorporating the nativity scene in soft blues and lavender. She added a personal note to each card. With the cost of postage at record-high rates, she couldn't bear to simply sign her name and seal the card in an envelope. The last name on the list was Vera Popov.

She drew in her breath. The celebration of the Lord's birth was a perfect time to express friendship and neighborly camaraderie. She traced her finger over the name, sensing the irony of a goodwill wish for someone who continued to wage a private cold war against her. Vera had not answered the RSVP request on the first invitation to Anne's Christmas party to be held in a scant two weeks. She wasn't likely to acknowledge a second, but Anne tucked another invitation inside the envelope.

The guest list included Tess and Lance. And Jimmy, of course, who, according to all reports, had been settling in quite nicely with his uncle since coming to Ladystone nearly three weeks before. He'd been slow to accept the hand of friendship from anyone except perhaps Grover and Tess. Lance had done everything he could to make the boy feel welcome, and no complaint of trouble had arisen as the Advent season marched on in a hectic wave.

She tucked Vera's card on the stack next to her Bible and regarded it silently, thinking of the paradox of the angel's greeting, "Peace on earth, goodwill to men." Peace in this world's charged atmosphere could come only if people chose God's goodwill. As it was, most people stumbled from one Yule-packed day to the next, decorating with frenzied fervor, eating too much, and buying like there was no tomorrow.

How she longed for a clean Christmas with no gift but God. And for the peace that reigned when neighbors lived together in harmony. Perhaps it was an old-fashioned ideal that one should no longer expect in the 21st century. But she was determined to do her best to make it happen.

If God were willing, Margaret would be well enough to join them for the celebration along with Erma Tanner whose life seemed so colorless and friendless. Anne shivered inside her bulky-knit sweater, recalling Erma's odd behavior and talk of obituaries. She wanted to forget the sights and sounds that were part of Rutgers Care Home, including the stark image of the empty bed next to Margaret's. Who was the woman who had once occupied it? Did anyone care that she was dead or that her passing hadn't merited a notice in the obituary section of the Ladystone Lectern?

"Will you see that my name gets in the paper?" Erma's fretful query when she'd wheeled her back to her room unsettled Anne. *Such dark thoughts,* she chided herself. It was a brilliant Saturday afternoon, and she could have been enjoying the slopes with Lance. He had taken Tess along with Jimmy to ski for the first time in their lives.

The troubled youngster and the lovely Deaf girl seemed to have bonded quickly. Did Jimmy see in Tess the big sister he'd never had? Perhaps the mother who might have loved him? Backward and afraid to trust anyone, he was much like Tess had once been. Peter had suggested "Tess" as a fitting name for Beatrice Popov. Like the well-known protagonist in British literature, she had overcome so much.

"Is Tess okay?" Peter had asked when he'd phoned the day before. The autumn months had been his busiest at Rotak Industries, and he had been required to work weekends in addition to his weekday schedule. Then, the Christmas season with staffing problems had descended, and his visits to Grace Arbor became even fewer.

He'd been deeply affected by meeting Tess and helping her through the loss of her dear Uncle Alexei. It had been quite a summer for both of them. She wondered now if Peter had heard the hospital gossip that Tess was seeing Dr. David Brevitz.

Anne caught the inside of her cheek as she evened up the stack of cards and bound them with a rubber band. It wasn't surprising that the new doctor, with his penchant for pretty young women, would be attracted to Tess. But it seemed an odd choice, given his level of sophistication and his age. And what did Tess see in him? It wasn't her place to question the girl's choice in dinner dates, Anne realized, but it worried her that Tess might become one more addition to Dr. Brevitz's burgeoning collection of ladies.

It started the night Tess was caught in the season's first blizzard, and the good doctor came to her rescue. "He seems nice," Tess had told her shyly when they'd shared a cup of tea at Grace Arbor a few days later. "He wants me to go to the Royale for the Christmas show. It's a Dickens' play." A pink flush had spread over her face; her blue eyes shone. "They are doing my favorite, *A Christmas Carol*."

Anne sighed. Tess was 21 and had the right to make her own choices. She and Peter had no claims on each other, so far as she knew. Surely, Tess needed to make friends and discover life for herself, but was she opening herself up to being hurt? For today, at least, Tess could be a girl enjoying winter fun, thanks to Lance.

"I'll probably break my leg," he protested when he volunteered to take the young people skiing. For all his grumbling, Lance had come alive with Tess and Jimmy vying for his attention like two spoiled children. It was sad that Lance had never had children of his own. He'd lost his life's companion as she had, but he was alone while she had Dawn and Peter, who were testament to a life of shared love.

She put away the unused cards and tucked pens and stamps into the drawer of her antique drop-leaf secretary. It was nearly four o'clock, and she'd promised to have pizza ready in half an hour. Hurrying upstairs, she exchanged her comfortable sweats for attire more suitable for entertaining. Black wool slacks and her red knit top might fit the occasion. She decided to add a pendant to accent the outfit. Yes, that would be just the right touch. She opened her jewelry box and drew in her breath with sudden alarm.

The grooves that held her wedding band and diamond engagement ring were empty. She swept aside necklaces, brooches, and assorted pieces twined together in the deeper section of the box. Maybe the rings had become entangled there. She lifted the upper tier to search beneath it and felt a wave of panic. Her rings were gone.

How long since she'd opened the jewelry box? A week? Two? She hadn't worn the rings in months but often fondled them, remembering the years of love they represented. Could she have moved the rings and forgotten? Taken them for cleaning? She searched for an answer but instinctively knew that she hadn't done any of those things.

Had someone entered her house and taken them? She searched her memory. Was anything else disturbed? Nothing had been taken except the many-faceted diamond ring and the matching gold band, worn thin from the passing years. Why would someone take these personal treasures?

Suddenly, a stomping of feet on the porch and accompanying chatter announced approaching guests. She heard Lance's deep-throated laughter, Tess's slow, affected speech, and Jimmy's little boy chatter. Jimmy! She dropped down on the bed, stunned by her thought.

Jimmy had been in her house frequently since he had come to stay with Lance. There was the night they all played Monopoly after a church-sponsored basketball game and the time Jimmy played video games on her computer. The boy could easily have entered her room and taken her rings.

Lance had advised her of Jimmy's reported misconduct and the fact that his foster parents were threatening to return him to the court for replacement. The details were sketchy, and she felt sorry for this child who had been dealt many a hard blow in his short years. Could he be acting out for attention? Was Jimmy really a thief? Would he do this?

"Anybody home?" Lance's resonant voice pierced her consciousness.

She'd left the door open, knowing they would arrive soon. She usually kept it locked, especially since the trauma of Alexei Popov's death. Now, the feelings of vulnerability and violation deepened as she closed the jewelry box lid.

She nearly stumbled over the shoes she had kicked off earlier. "I'm coming!" she called and hurriedly put the box back in the cabinet, her mind whirling. Why would a thief take only those two pieces and leave other items more valuable behind? Was it a child's clumsy effort— grabbing the first things he saw? Items he could quickly slip into his pocket? *You're jumping to conclusions. Don't be paranoid.*

There was no more time to think or to look. Later, she would turn the house upside down, but even as she planned a search, she knew that someone had stolen her cherished rings.

Having left their wet outerwear in the hall, her guests were gathered in the living room. Tess and Jimmy warmed their hands over the fire, laughing and chattering about the day's adventure. Tess signed words as she spoke, her fingers flying furiously. Her eyes and complexion glowed, and Anne thought she had never looked happier.

From the top of the stairs, she caught sight of Jimmy dancing up and down, his red cowlick sticking up like straw on fire. He was wearing a blue and white striped tee shirt and jeans that hung loose on his nebulous hips. His dingy white socks had holes in both heels.

If he turned around, would she be able to read his expression and know if he were guilty? She couldn't tear her eyes from the child she had befriended, trusted, and let into her home on numerous occasions. She wanted to spin him around and demand the truth. How dare he hurt Lance like this? *Wait until you're sure, she* cautioned herself.

Lance stood at the bottom of the stairs, silver hair tousled, his face red from wind and pleasure. "There you are!" he said warmly. "We're a little early, but it was beginning to get dark on the slopes. It's hard enough to keep from breaking my neck in the light, let alone in the dark." His eyes narrowed. "We did say four, didn't we? Is everything all right?"

She hurried down the remaining stairs. "Yes, yes," she stammered. "Of course." Was the shock visible on her face? With a brave pretense at nonchalance, she took his arm and walked with him into the kitchen. She had often chided him for working too hard, not getting out more. He was investing himself in others now, and it agreed with him. Tess and Jimmy had been good for him. He desperately wanted to succeed with Jimmy after the disastrous experience with Shane. She couldn't tell him about the rings and her suspicion now when he seemed so happy.

"You're looking lovely tonight," he said, regarding her closely. Then, a puzzled look flashed across his face. Was she that transparent, or were they beginning to be able to read each other's moods?

She looked away and hurried to get napkins, plates, and forks. She longed to tell him what was wrong, to let him console her and tell her it would be all right. But it would spoil the whole day. She couldn't hurt him now when he seemed happier than he'd been in months. "The pizzas won't take long," she said. "Help me get them out of the fridge, will you?"

"Sure." He headed to the refrigerator obediently, glancing at her over his shoulder with the same quizzical expression. "You should have come with us, Anne. It was great fun, even on the beginner slopes, which is where I stayed, believe me. I know my place."

She mumbled something to show she'd heard, but all she could think about were the empty grooves in her jewelry box and the gnawing in the pit of her stomach.

"How did it go?" Lance asked, handing her a pepperoni and green pepper pizza from the bottom shelf.

Pepperoni and green pepper would go down hard. She deflected a slight wave of nausea and tried to remember what Lance had just said.

"The work you had to do," he repeated. "All that work that kept you from joining us today."

"Oh, yes," she said lamely, feeling a flush creep up her neck. "It's all finished. Ready to post tomorrow." She began to fill glasses with ice, aware of Lance's covert glances in her direction. "Sorry," she said. "I'm a bit distracted. Never mind." She busied herself, shooing Lance out of the way. "Go sit by the fire and warm up! I'll take care of this."

Tess came into the kitchen, tendrils of copper hair slipping from her ponytail. "Can I help?" Her eyes glistened. No trace of the sadness that sometimes gave them a wounded look. Their blue clarity could take one's breath away—something the charming new doctor had no doubt noticed.

"Thanks," Anne said, careful to face her so Tess could read her lips. "But you go on and enjoy the fire. You're shivering! When the pizza's ready, you can help me serve."

Suddenly, Jimmy peeked around Tess, bumping her arm playfully. "Is it pepperoni?" His cap had flattened his orange hair, and his freckles stood out in bold relief. "Pepperoni's my favorite."

Anne stared into the pale eyes with their sharp black centers. Above them, one brow arched higher than the other as though in perpetual angst. Was there a hint of embarrassment or guilt? The shy, brooding little boy she'd first met at the airport had changed.

She remembered the night soon after his arrival when Lance had brought him to Grace Arbor for sundaes after a basketball game. He had disappeared, and she found him in the living room beside the piano, holding Richard's photo. He didn't look up when she came in and spoke to him but simply stared at the picture. In a small voice, he had asked, "What's it like to be dead?"

It had brought her up short. Children sometimes asked difficult questions, and one was never quite ready for them. "No one really knows," she said, groping for a way to explain a subject that was so complicated. "Maybe it's a little like going to sleep and then waking up in another room."

He hadn't said anything; he just stood there, staring at the picture, at Richard's patient eyes, the sandy hair gone gray at the temples, and the teasing lines around his mouth. "He was my husband," she said softly. "I still miss him very much, but I know he's with God, and someday we'll be together again."

Jimmy blinked and swallowed. "My mom's dead," he said flatly. "She's dead, but I don't care." And he had let the picture fall hard on the shiny surface of her Kwai grand and ran out of the room. She'd been stunned and hurt, as though he'd deliberately made a mockery of her memories, her tender hope. Later, when she returned to the kitchen, she found him gulping ice cream from a huge bowl, chocolate syrup dripping from his chin. The outburst over his mother's death had been forgotten, but she'd felt her own hurt like a searing wound reopened.

Had Jimmy seen something pretty and been overcome? Or was he more calculating? Would he try to sell the rings for whatever took his fancy? He couldn't have known his brother well since ten years separated them, and they had not lived together. It was a good thing they hadn't been close. Shane Eldridge was not the kind of brother a boy like Jimmy could look up to. But was there some intrinsic likeness, some in-born bent toward evil that the brothers shared?

She picked up two pizzas and felt the heat surge through the potholder as she balanced them in her hands. She wanted to forget about the theft, to burn away the image of her rings clutched in small, freckled hands. Jimmy surreptitiously nicked a potato chip from the bowl on the table and popped it into his mouth. The benign act of which anyone might be guilty seemed a telling detail.

"Let me help you," Tess said in her careful diction, interrupting Anne's thoughts. She took one of the trays and placed it on a quilted mat in the center of the table. "There's room for the other one here," she said before casting Anne a puzzled glance. Tess had uncanny powers of observation and could easily perceive that something was bothering her.

Anne squared her shoulders and gave the girl a wide, deliberate smile. "Come on. Let's eat!" she said with a brightness she didn't feel.

Once seated around the table, tales of maneuvers on the ski slopes dominated the conversation. There was considerable discussion about Christmas plans as well. Resolved not to spoil their evening, Anne tried to mimic their enthusiasm.

When there was a lull in the conversation, Tess turned to Anne. "Aunt Vera says she won't come to your party." She caught her lower lip and released it. "I asked her twice, but she said no."

Anne knew how much Tess wanted Vera to be part of her life, how much she longed for a real family. "I know. I'm sorry, Tess. I sent her a second invitation. Maybe she'll reconsider."

Doubt lingered on the delicate face. "But Miss Morris will be coming home soon," Tess said, eyes brightening. "Right?"

"And we should get her something special for Christmas," Anne suggested as she poured Coke into tall glasses. Margaret had been as close to Tess's Uncle Alexei as anyone could be, and she'd become a surrogate grandmother for Tess. The girl clung to the slightest hint of love or approbation. It made her vulnerable to the charms of people. *Like David Brevitz*, Anne worried.

"I painted Miss Morris a picture of Grover," Jimmy said, looking profoundly proud of himself and reaching for the biggest slice of pepperoni pizza.

"Great idea," Lance agreed. "And I'll get that new back door installed for her. The old one is ready for the chopping block."

"We can all thank God that she's finally getting well," Anne said. "It's been a long recuperation. And just in time for Christmas."

The phone rang at that moment. As though summoned by the conversation, Margaret said, "Something terrible has happened. It's Erma…"

"Oh, Margaret, no," Anne breathed. *Erma?* Only the other day, she had wheeled her into the sunroom at the nursing home. She'd been so excited to be invited to a party.

"She collapsed; they found her in the bathroom. She was such a dear person, and now she's ... "

Anne caught her breath, aghast. "Do you mean—?"

"Annie, she's dead."

Anne clutched the receiver. "I'm so sorry," she whispered. "I'm so sorry about your friend."

Margaret's voice trembled. "I wasn't a good friend, Annie. I should have been. I should have paid more attention to her ... but sometimes she got on my nerves, and I brushed her off like a bothersome gnat." Margaret began to cough, the harsh, rasping sounds amplified over the receiver.

"Please calm down, Margaret," Anne urged. "It's not your fault." More coughing, a click, and then the line went dead.

Looking up, she met three pairs of anxious eyes. No one spoke, just stared at her, their faces blank, unmoving. Why was this happening now? Just when Margaret was getting well and when Erma was so excited about coming to the Christmas party?

The missing rings were completely forgotten. Anne stared into the eyes fastened on her. Her heart beat a silent prayer. Margaret would need the Almighty's help and the support of her friends. She'd need them all now more than ever.

Chapter 9

"She always came to visit and to talk." In the raised bed at Rutgers, Margaret spoke almost reverently, leaning her snowy head against plump white pillows. She wore a blue sweater with tiny pearl buttons over a white silk blouse. A patchwork quilt no doubt covered the long skirt it was her habit to wear.

A book lay sprawled across her lap with its marker at midpoint. Anne Tyler's *A Patchwork Planet*. Anne smiled to herself. She admired Margaret's penetrating mind and forays into eclectic literature. It was wonderful to find Margaret in Ladystone. She was a flower sprouting from cement, a refreshing and literate surprise.

Anne sat by the bedside without speaking. She wanted to comfort her friend but sensed her touch would not be welcome right now. Margaret looked so lost, so forlorn. Though she wasn't given to hysterics, she was taking Erma's death hard. She prayed that her friend wouldn't sink into depression, which she knew could be a problem with the elderly sick.

"She liked to recall the old days, her lovers, her dreams," Margaret continued in a melancholy tone that matched her expression. "She'd lean over me with those big owl eyes and with such sweet angst. Oh, Annie, this shouldn't have happened to her."

"No," Anne said softly. She bowed her head as though in apology for Nature's lapse, but she knew there was no explanation for some things. In happier times, they had enjoyed many theological and philosophical conversations, but lately, Margaret had little to say except to ask questions. But surely she knew that God would not turn away the hard questions.

The ancient Hebrews who penned the Psalms had included God in every aspect of their lives—their emotional ups and downs. They not only praised Him "with timbrel and dance" for His mighty works; they railed against His seeming failure to involve Himself in terrors that afflicted them. With humanity's narrowed focus, it was hard to remember the Scripture from Isaiah: *For my thoughts are not your thoughts, neither are your ways my ways,"* declares the LORD. *"As the heavens are higher than the earth, so are my ways."* (55:8-9).

In the midst of Margaret's deep sadness, what could she say that would really help? "Erma enjoyed your friendship, Margaret," Anne said gently. "She told me how nice you were to her."

"Nice," Margaret sputtered. "What a completely bland and useless quality that is."

Anne drew in a deep breath. "You're determined to flog yourself, Margaret Morris. And even if you do it in your finest pedagogical manner, you're quite wrong." She heard the sharpness in her own voice and hastened to soften her rebuke, but raised voices in the hallway caused them both to turn their heads toward the door.

Helen Rutger's authoritative voice, each syllable clearly enunciated, carried from the nurses' station half-way down the corridor. Another voice, deeper and softer, came through equally firm. Anne detected a vaguely familiar accent. She stepped to the door and peeked out just in time to see David Brevitz stride to the exit and disappear through the double doors.

At the circular counter in a pin-striped suit, Helen stared after the departing doctor, her face dark and brooding. Anne stepped into the hall. Apparently, the two were not always as congenial as they had seemed on the day Grover had caused such a ruckus. She held up a hand, indicating that she'd like a word with the administrator.

Helen quickly covered her anger or embarrassment with a smile that didn't quite reach the intractable green eyes. She closed a manila folder and walked toward Anne, shoulders rigid. "Mrs. Westin," she acknowledged.

Anne moved back into Margaret's room, signaling for Helen to follow.

"What can I do for you?" Helen asked, her gaze sliding briefly toward Margret propped up in bed.

"Margaret is—that is—*was* Erma's friend," Anne said. "She's very upset about her passing. Can you please tell us both what happened?"

"She seemed just fine this morning," Margaret broke in, chin set. She had removed her glasses, and two bright spots appeared on her cheeks as her eyes bored into Helen's. Margaret had reserved some ire for Ms. Rutger, Anne realized.

"Blood clot," came the blunt, even response. "Erma's circulation has been poor for years and getting worse." Helen waved fuchsia fingernails in a dismissive gesture. "It's often that way with diabetics." She cleared her throat and continued. "Erma's disease was acute. "And she didn't eat right; she was always sneaking sweets into her room."

Had the woman no tact, no heart? Couldn't she see how aggrieved Margaret was? "But are you certain?" Anne asked. "Has there been an autopsy?"

Helen shrugged her elegant shoulders once more. "The doctor has completed his findings and signed the certificate. The cause of death was multiple pulmonary emboli—blood clots in the lungs. There's no need for an autopsy."

"Has her family been notified?" Anne asked.

Helen pursed sharply sculpted lips and drew her penciled brows together in a frown. "Ms. Thaddeus had no family, unfortunately. There was no next of kin to notify. I'm sorry."

"Thaddeus?" Anne and Margaret repeated simultaneously.

"Yes. That is her name."

"But her last name was 'Tanner,'" Margaret quipped, sitting up straighter and pushing back the wisps of hair that strayed around her face.

"She liked to call herself that," Helen said. "Tanner was her stage name." She gave a light, offhand laugh. "You know how Erma liked her little dramas." She gazed down at Margaret indulgently. "I am truly sorry about your friend, but I must get to a meeting now. Perhaps we can chat later, or maybe you'd like to speak to the social worker." She left the room, her heels making sharp clicks on the tiled floor.

Anne folded her arms across her chest to keep them still. *Chat later? Chat about the pain of a friend's death?* Even her language was inappropriate. "Margaret, I'm so sorry," Anne said quietly.

Margaret lay back against the pillows, the spots of color still prominent, and closed her eyes. She folded her hands over her stomach, and Anne could see that they were trembling.

Anne went to her side and covered the thin, veined hands with her own. They were white and cool, like marble. *No*, Anne corrected herself. *Like fine bone china. Helen's hands would feel like marble.* "I know Erma was a good friend to you," she whispered.

Margaret's eyelids flickered. "I was not a good friend to her," she said adamantly. "I was impatient. I scolded her about eating sweets. I told her she was silly when she made up those dramatic stories of hers. And when I grew weary of her prattle, I all but asked her to leave." She turned her face to the window, and Anne knew she was hiding tears. Her breathing grew more rapid and uneven.

"Margaret, try to calm down."

She whipped her head back to Anne. "You know what she used to tell me?"

"No."

"That people who died here didn't get written up in the papers, that as long as the government didn't know when someone died, the checks kept coming in."

Anne stared. "But that's impossible. The attending physician always makes a report, and it's filed with the proper authorities."

"I told Erma she was being foolish and dramatic. You know how she was with those stories of hers. She was once invited to Buckingham Palace for tea with Queen Elizabeth, you know."

Anne's mind flashed back to a conversation the day Erma had wistfully extracted a promise that the news of her death be printed in the newspaper. She often said shocking things like how she danced in a Broadway play with Maurice Chevalier, the famous actor of a bygone era. *Charming little fibber*, Anne thought, remembering the powdery feel of Erma's chubby cheeks, the frizzy, henna-rinsed hair, the scent of lavender. A lump rose in her throat. *Oh, Erma, dear Erma.*

Anne smoothed Margaret's hand gently and watched the rise and fall of her chest grow more even. Margaret pressed her lips into a firm line and said nothing. The watery eyes glittered, but Anne saw no resignation in them. Margaret was angry.

She prayed a short prayer, thanking God for Erma's life as well as asking for comfort for Margaret. When she finished, she pressed her friend's thin fingers lightly, but there was no response. Margaret's eyes were closed, but she clearly was not sleeping.

Anne drove home through the darkening afternoon. It was nearly four o'clock. She loved winter, but for all its stark, white beauty, she begrudged the early loss of light. Now, the extended hours of darkness seemed appropriate, a fitting requiem for the dead. She would miss Erma Tanner or Thaddeus or whoever that charming woman was. Still, there was nothing to be gained by regret. Margaret was the one who must be considered now. She had been doing so well and had made plans to come home. Why must this happen now?

Hating to leave Margaret at Rutgers for even one more day, she had urged her to come to Grace Arbor. "I would love to have you, and we could arrange for your breathing treatments at home."

"Oh, I wouldn't think of imposing like that."

"It's not imposing. We're friends, Margaret. And friends should take care of each other." But all her cajoling and rationalizing had not convinced her. When Margaret Morris made up her mind, there was no point trying to change it.

As she drove, she mulled over their conversation. Could something really be wrong at Rutgers Nursing Home? Were Erma's comments just the raving of a high-strung woman who lamented her advancing age? The obituary page carried the name, Erma Thaddeus, proving that Erma had been mistaken in her claim about obits in the newspaper and proper death notices. She would surely have been disappointed, though, that the name hadn't read "Erma Tanner."

She climbed the stone steps of Grace Arbor and reached into her purse for the key. The sun had been in hiding most of the day, and now the gloom deepened. It would be fully dark soon, and she was tired, very tired. She turned the key in the lock, sensing an uncommon foreboding. Death, that unnatural interloper, always put one on edge, even the death of a woman she hadn't known well.

She usually experienced a sense of haven when she came home to Grace Arbor. The sheltering oaks, broad-armed porch, and the welcoming light in the window made her feel secure. But as she stepped into the foyer, she felt vulnerable and alone. Her missing rings rose ominously to mind. She had nearly forgotten them in the face of Erma's death. Now, the fact of their absence struck her full force as though she'd been accosted and robbed at gunpoint.

She switched on the kitchen light and, without removing her shoes, inspected the living room, the dining room, and the kitchen. Everything was as she had left it—cookie sheets laid out on the counter, the box of Christmas paper and assorted ribbons on the credenza, and her best crystal bowl, which she would later fill with fresh pine and holly.

She moved from room to room, vaguely disturbed. People who had been burglarized talked about the residual effects of such a trauma. She gave herself a mental slap, which did little to lessen her sense of anxiety. It had been a long, unnerving day. She leaned wearily against the dresser in her bedroom. She hadn't said anything about the missing rings, hadn't told Lance or reported the theft to the sheriff. But something would have to be done. She had looked everywhere and concluded what could not be avoided. Someone had stolen her wedding rings, and the most likely culprit was Jimmy.

She would have to talk to Lance and the boy soon. With a heavy heart, she changed into sweats and went downstairs. Work was good therapy. There were cookies to be made, gifts to wrap, and a sacred holiday to be honored. She would put these gloomy thoughts behind her, at least for now. As she bent to open the refrigerator for butter and eggs, she wrinkled her nose at the faint odor of onions.

The ring of the telephone startled her. Her heart thumped as she picked up the receiver.

"Mom? How are things in the frozen north?"

"Snowy," she countered with a flood of relief, surprising herself. "Peter, it's so good to hear your voice. Is everything still okay for next week? I can't believe how quickly Christmas is coming!"

"I plan to be there with bells on. Jingle bells, that is," he said. "How's Tess?"

The inevitable question. "Oh, she's fine, Peter." She probably should say something like *Tess misses you. She'll be glad to see you. She asked about you.* But she said none of those things. Nor did she mention that Tess had apparently found a friend in Dr. David Brevitz. "She's been busy at the hospital because of the holidays. People taking time off for shopping and parties, I guess."

The empty places in her jewelry box burned in Anne's mind. She wanted to tell him about it, but what could he do except worry and ask her why she hadn't confronted Lance about it or the sheriff?

"And Miss Morris?" Peter queried.

"She's still not able to come home." Anne paused. "A friend of hers in the home passed away. Margaret took it really hard." Anne felt her voice tremble. She swallowed. "I wish I could convince her to come to Grace Arbor to stay with me for a while, but she won't hear of it."

"You sound tired, Mom. Are you all right?"

That was Peter, perceptive, even over 300 miles of telephone cable. She hastened to reassure him but was suddenly gripped by a sense of loss, as though Richard's death were a fresh reality. Did one ever really get over the loss of someone as close as your own heart? "Things have been ... busy around here," she said lamely. "And I've been playing catch up." She struggled to overcome the tears gathering in her throat. "Nothing to worry about, dear. I'm fine."

In the pause that followed, she could almost hear the wheels of Peter's mind going around. She didn't want to deal with further questions. She straightened her shoulders. "I'm about to stir up a batch of your favorite cookies," she said. "I'd better get off the line, or the cupboard will be bare when you get here."

"Okay, Mom. I'll see you soon."

She hung up and switched on the radio. With firm resolve, she began pulling butter, eggs, and pecans from the refrigerator. The music of Bach's "Jesu, Joy of Man's Desiring" washed over her, and she felt the gloom in her heart begin to lift. Snow was falling again. Thick flakes fell against the oaks outside the kitchen window and gathered on the porch rail. *If only God were truly the object of all our desires.*

As she cracked eggs into the bowl she prayed for them all, for Peter, Tess, and Lance, for grieving Margaret and Jimmy.

"Jesu, joy of man's desiring, holy wisdom, love most bright." Martin Janus's words to Bach's timeless melody bore her up sweetly. "Drawn by Thee, our souls aspiring soar to uncreated light."

Whatever else was going on in her world, or anyone's world, she could cling to the knowledge of Immanuel, the God who is present, though He sometimes seemed unreachable. But that was what faith was for. To know God was with you even when there was no obvious evidence of Him. Faith might seem blind, but the very blindness of it had eyes that pierced the darkness. She reached out to Him, clinging to the wonder of His presence.

When Bach's beautiful hymn ended, Anne picked up the telephone and dialed Lance's number. Lance must be told, and something must be done. When there was no answer at home, she tried him at the realty office.

"Lance. I'm sorry to bother you at work."

"That's all right, Anne. I had a few things to tie up. I was about to leave the office. I told Jimmy to throw a frozen pizza in the oven for us."

She didn't say she had phoned his house and that there had been no answer. Was the boy outside playing? Running with Grover? In her mind's eye, she saw the unruly red hair, the jaunty gait, the small, busy fingers.

"Is everything all right?"

"Oh, yes," she responded hastily. "I just wanted to—well— to ask you ... " She must speak about the rings, but how could she talk about this on the phone? She had to see Lance. She paused in an effort to collect her thoughts. "That is ... " She stumbled awkwardly. "It's just that I'm worried about Margaret," she said, delaying the inevitable.

"I know," he said quietly. "Miss Morris was doing so well, and now this."

"Lance, could you come by?" *There's something I need to dis-cuss with you. Your nephew has stolen my rings; I want them back. I'm as sorry as I can be. Your nephew is a thief!* Out loud, she stammered, "I—that is, it would be very helpful to me if you picked up a bag of canned goods I've been collecting to take to the radio station. Tomorrow's the last day of the drive, and I thought maybe you might take them in for me. I've so much to do to get ready for next week." She knew she was rambling.

"Sure," he answered briskly. A curious pause followed as though he were trying to read between the lines. "Try not to worry about Margaret too much, Anne," he said gently. "She'll be all right."

The tenderness of his voice nearly unhinged her, and she felt tears stinging her throat. If only she didn't have to tell him about Jimmy, to hurt him yet again. Shane was in prison on a robbery charge; now another nephew—only a child—was following in the footsteps of his brother.

"Thanks," she said softly, swallowing against the lump in her throat. She didn't want to think how Lance would take this news, how those clear blue eyes would cloud with fresh pain. "See you tomorrow." And she hung up quickly, the phrase of a song hammering in her head with a mocking lilt: "The sun will come out tomorrow."

Chapter 10

*L*ance rubbed the small electric sander over the Rosie-O's hull. Little nicks and abrasions disappeared in a whir of warm sawdust. When the boat's surface was petal smooth, he would touch up the paint to a gleaming white, and by the time spring came, there would be no signs of summer's excursions into the briny deep with the inevitable toll on wood and chrome.

He had risen early and carried his coffee to the garage, where his boat was dry-docked for winter. Real estate moved slowly during the cold months, giving time for catching up on paper work and repairs around the house, but he preferred to work on the Rosie-O—readying her for the next season's rendezvous with sun and wind.

This was where he was happiest, if not sailing the Rosie-O, then working on her. He touched the raised letters, which he had painted in deep burgundy with silver highlights. They'd have to be touched up, too. His wife, for whom the boat was named, had loved speeding down the Flanges River in a blast of summer wind. Together, they would drift lazily, fishing rods perched over the side and the sun pouring over them like love.

She'd been gone seven years. Seven was supposed to be the perfect number. What was perfect about watching a beautiful, energetic woman become a mere shadow of herself until she vanished? What was perfect about all the things you might have done for her and could no longer do? What was perfect about the ache that never quite went away? What was perfect about loneliness? His fingers trembled as he gripped the sander.

Not that there hadn't been diversion and friendships to fill the years that passed with amazing speed. He'd lived for more than five decades, but he could hardly be considered an old man, could he? Lance shifted his position to relieve the pressure on his left knee, the one that sometimes reminded him he wasn't exactly young either.

Yes, there had been friends to go bowling or fishing with and business acquaintances to buy him lunch or coffee. He had no intentions of becoming a hermit, but neither was he willing to invest himself in someone again. Relationships were fragile things. When they broke, they sapped the life right out of you.

He chipped away at a stubborn barnacle until the surface was smooth, unlike his troubled thoughts as the snow drifted by the garage window. He let out a long breath. There had been women, too, but none had interested him seriously—not until Anne, that is. Her face appeared in his mind as he dipped the flannel into the chrome polish.

There was much to be admired in her—her cultured elegance, her easy grace. And she had a figure women half her age would envy. He liked the way her chestnut hair waved back from delicate temples, the mixture of sagacity and mischief that danced in her hazel eyes. Richard had been a lucky man. He felt a heady rising. It would be easy to fall in love with her. He wasn't sure he wasn't already halfway there.

He paused, stunned by his thoughts, and scrutinized a strip of chrome on the boat's hull. What was he thinking? One should learn caution, if nothing else, with age. Commitment was costly, and love without it was an oxymoron. He was certain she would think so. Besides, he'd failed her. He'd been so wrapped up in his miseries that he hadn't seen what was going on with Shane before it was almost too late.

Could he have stopped Shane from burglary and kidnapping last summer? For a while, Anne had even suspected he was involved in a conspiracy to defraud Tess and prevent the sale of Grace Arbor. The truth had come out in the end, and she'd understood and forgiven him, but would she ever completely trust his judgment again?

He paused, suddenly conscious of a warm draft of air. He looked up to find Jimmy standing in the doorway, hands in his pockets, small face pinched in the early morning light. Blanched freckles and close-set eyes rendered him something of a caricature in faded blue jeans and a tee shirt that read 007. He'd run from the house to the garage without his coat, and his tennis shoes were thick with snow.

"Morning," Lance said, touched by a sense of the boy's vulnerability. He'd been moved from pillar to post from the time he was four with no family to provide a stable, loving environment. Little wonder that Jimmy was far too serious for a boy soon to be twelve years old.

Jimmy stamped the snow from his shoes and gazed at the Rosie-O with wide, curious eyes. "Your boat go fast?" he asked timidly.

"Like a streak of lightning," Lance said. "Next summer, I'll show you." He closed the jar of chrome polish and realized he'd just hinted at a promise he was not likely to fulfill. Jimmy would be back with his foster parents after the holidays. Their threats to return him to the court were probably just that, threats to goad the boy into better behavior.

"You mean it?" Jimmy asked with sudden enthusiasm.

"We'll see." Lance set the chrome polish on a wooden crate. "Maybe you can come for a few days in the summer." He put out a hand to ruffle the boy's hair and was surprised by the quickness with which the boy stepped back.

Boys his age weren't much for displays of affection, he knew, but it seemed to Lance that Jimmy was almost afraid of him. Hadn't he done everything he could think of to make the boy comfortable and happy? Hadn't he put his work aside to be with him? Taken him skiing, skating, or ice fishing? He'd worked at home rather than at the office since Jimmy had come. And when he had to show the occasional property, he'd taken Jimmy along. Only rarely had he left him at home alone, and then only for an hour or two in midday. Taking care of a boy sure changed things. Today, he'd promised him a Christmas shopping trip. He'd been surprised when the boy said he wanted to buy a gift for Tess.

Lance felt suddenly tired and discouraged. He hadn't expected wild enthusiasm, but he'd hoped Jimmy would see he was trying to be his friend.

"They won't let me come next summer. I know it," Jimmy said sullenly.

Lance turned. "Now, how do you know that?" he demanded more gruffly than he'd intended.

The boy shrugged and darted his light blue eyes back and forth. He slumped down on a large tool box that doubled as a chair and kicked at a pile of sawdust. "They don't like me, that's why," he said quietly.

"Then they'll be all the more glad to get rid of you for a few days," Lance said with a touch of humor. He was in no mood to dispute the parenting style of foster parents and the usual small-boy resistance to discipline. Further, he was eager to end any discussion of the future. Summer was a long way off, and the

Christmas holidays were upon them; they had to get through that first.

It was sad to think of simply getting through the holidays rather than celebrating the Savior's birth. But holidays could be so hard and solitary, especially Christmas. Well, it had been a solitary business for those involved in the first Advent, too, he realized. Mary waited alone with the poignant knowledge that her Child was destined to die. The wise men trudged alone across the desert against the edict of the ruling monarch. Old Simeon had languished alone in the Temple with his yearning to see the Lord's Christ before his life ended.

Lance tightened the lid on the polish and turned off the sander to give the boy his full attention. "You eat the cereal I put out for you?" he asked.

"Yeah. The Lucky Charms are history," Jimmy said, rubbing his flat little stomach. "Are we still going Christmas shopping today?" he queried.

"That's the plan. But first, you've got to corral that dog."

"Yeah, I know." Jimmy sprang up and headed for the door.

"But get your coat first. In case you haven't noticed, it's winter! And boots. Don't forget boots. This isn't Florida, you know." Lance watched him go, surprised at a rush of affection for the boy. He closed up the garage and headed to the house to change his shirt.

From the bedroom window, he watched Jimmy out in the yard. He was surprised by a feeling of pride in the boy's quick, eager movements. His high cheekbones and round little chin were so like Jane's. What did Jimmy remember of his gentle mother whom cancer had taken in the prime of her womanhood? He stared gloomily out the window. *So much for getting rid of depressing thoughts.*

Aware he was about to be penned up, Grover was engaging in his usual annoying antics, lunging away every time Jimmy bent to grab his collar. He'd scoot sideways, spring forward a few paces, then stop to look back with his tongue hanging out, waiting for the pursuit to begin again. Jimmy's red hair stuck out under his ski cap as he lurched after Grover, hollering for him to stop. Lance smiled as he watched the game.

Suddenly, there was a flutter of arms and legs as Jimmy tried to head off the dog. The chain slipped from his hand and splayed out in a long stream behind him, catching on a stack of firewood. In seconds, Jimmy went down in a graceless heap. He rocked back and forth in pain, grasping his leg. A few feet away, Grover stood panting and waiting for the game to continue.

Lance yanked on his boots and ran outside. He lifted Jimmy under the arms to help him up. "You all right?"

"I—I think I cut my leg."

"Can you stand on it?"

Jimmy took a faltering step. "Yeah, it's okay, but I think it's bleeding."

"Go on in and take off your boots and jeans," Lance said, holding Grover back as Jimmy limped into the house.

At the kitchen sink, Jimmy dabbed a towel against his calf, where the cut on his leg bled profusely. He flung the towel over his bare legs when Lance came in and gave his uncle a pale look of embarrassment.

"Let's have a look," Lance said. The scratch was about five inches long and quite deep at the point of contact. He soaked a face cloth in cold water and held it firmly over the cut. "Lesson is," he began quietly, concentrating on holding the pack firmly in place, "don't run with a chain in your hand."

Jimmy grimaced but made no sound as Lance worked. When the towel fell away, Lance could see a series of scars in varying sizes on the boy's leg. Most were old scrape wounds, but one abrasion on the back of his left leg near the current wound was scabbed over.

"Been running with a lot of chains, I see," Lance said evenly, though bells were going off in his head. He searched his nephew's face.

Jimmy shrugged, staring fixedly away. "It's nothing. I fall sometimes," he said in a small voice.

Looking up, Lance was surprised by the stubborn set of mouth and something veiled in the small, averted eyes. He squeezed some antiseptic from a tube and applied it gently to Jimmy's leg. "This one doesn't look too bad," he said, examining the new cut. "Should heal up nicely, but you better take it easy. We wouldn't want to start it bleeding again."

Lance turned to hang the wet linen on the towel rack and realized his hands were shaking. Jimmy's scars had looked a lot like lashes from a whip or belt, and something clicked in Lance's mind. Jimmy had avoided being touched from the first day they'd met in the airport. Could someone be abusing him?

Unthinkable. Lance had met the boy's foster parents briefly; they seemed all right, but what did he really know of them? And who had been his former caretakers? Maybe it happened while he was at some institution. He'd had no contact with Jimmy for more than two years. He'd never really been close to Jane's boys, both of whom had been born on the East Coast, and dealing with Rose's illness had made travel impossible.

He dried his hands as his mind tripped over the terrible possibility. What he'd seen hadn't been caused by small boy roughhousing. He hung the towel back on the rack with studied precision until he could trust himself to speak.

"I'm sorry about falling and everything," Jimmy muttered. "Can we go now?" He zipped up his pants and began to pull on his boots. "Can we go to town now? I feel fine."

Apparently, Jimmy was not about to tell how he had sustained his injuries. At Lance's nod, he was out the door and inside the Jeep in seconds.

The stores were full and bustling, and Lance, never fond of shopping, found his legs beginning to ache. Jimmy, on the other hand, gave no sign that his injured leg bothered him at all except when a lady's bulging handbag bumped against him.

"You all right?" Lance asked.

"Yeah," he said, limping ahead a little. He paused at a rack of colorful silk scarves and lifted out a blue-green square with tiny mauve flowers scattered over the shiny fabric. "You think Tess would like one of these?

"Bet she would, but she wouldn't expect you to buy such an expensive present," Lance said.

But Jimmy had already produced his wallet and was pulling out a five-dollar bill. Lance noted with surprise that there were still a number of bills left inside. "Last of the big spenders, aye?" he remarked dryly.

Jimmy shrugged and handed his purchase to the clerk. "I've been saving, mostly from taking care of Grover. Miss Morris paid me ten dollars—in advance. And Tess let me vacuum out her car."

Lance gave him a sidelong look. Perhaps this kid had more gumption than any of them knew. He felt a resurgence of the pride he'd felt when he was watching him in the yard with Grover. Maybe what he'd been told wasn't really true. Jimmy had been no trouble at all and did the chores assigned to him without complaining. Lance had never had a child, but he'd been around long enough to know that a parent should count himself lucky if a boy did as he was told.

Jimmy bought a rawhide bone and some dried beef for Grover and a flowery ballpoint pen for Anne. Lance realized that everything the boy had purchased was intended for his new friends in Ladystone.

"I suppose you celebrated Christmas with your foster family before coming here," Lance remarked, feigning interest in a display of greeting cards.

Jimmy shrugged and mumbled that he'd made them something in school.

"Would you like to send them a card?" Lance asked. He had suggested more than once that Jimmy should write to let them know how he was. Surely, they must be concerned. But he'd noted with surprise that no letter had come from them either. Odd, but then maybe things were different now. In his day, everyone wrote letters. Email changed all that. But they weren't staying in touch by phone or through cyberspace either. "Bet they'd like to hear from you," he finished.

"Okay," he said in a resigned voice. He grabbed a card off the rack, giving it little more than a passing glance. He paid for it quickly and tucked it inside one of his bags.

Lance blew his breath out slowly. "You sure you're okay?" he asked before Jimmy could turn away. It was odd that he never had anything to say about his foster parents, but then he didn't have much to say about anything. Of course, one had to earn a child's trust.

Moments later, Lance found his nephew two aisles over in the sporting goods section, eyeing a shiny, ten-speed with almost reverent admiration. Some things about kids never changed.

"Nice bike," Lance said, standing back and watching him inspect the thin tires and the frame with its low-slung seat.

"Yeah," Jimmy muttered, eyes shining. And Lance wondered if the boy had ever owned a bike, let alone one as fancy as this. And sadder still, he thought, why had he never taken the time to get to know his own nephew? Life's urgencies could certainly get in the way of the important things.

They had hamburgers for lunch and bought a box of ornaments. Lance hadn't put up a Christmas tree since Rose died, but a boy should have one. He let Jimmy pick out the ornaments—blue spheres with silver stripes and an ultra-modern topper that looked like a prop from a Star Wars movie.

With arms loaded, they headed for the car. "We need to stop by Mrs. Westin's place on the way home," Lance said, recalling her telephone call the evening before. "It shouldn't take long."

When Anne had asked him to pick up some canned goods to take to the radio station, he'd agreed happily. He had missed her more than he wanted to admit, even to himself. But she had seemed strange, preoccupied on the phone.

He'd bought a gift for her, a tapestry throw with a library motif in shades of burgundy and forest green. He'd shown it to Jimmy, who gave his usual shrug and added, "Nice. She's a nice lady."

She was more than nice. Lance wished he could tell her what he felt without the words catching in his throat. Instead, they kibitzed and teased, sometimes nagged each other like comfortable old friends whose idiosyncrasies could be endured only through great resolve.

"Can I walk down to the creek?" Jimmy asked when they arrived at Grace Arbor. "There's a real beaver dam. I hope the snow hasn't covered it all up."

"Sure. Don't be too long, though," Lance warned. But Jimmy was already trudging over the drifts toward the little creek that bounded Anne's property on the north. He watched him go, strangely moved at the way the harsh wind whipped at his pants, and the huge snow banks seemed to swallow up his small body. Nature, like life, didn't temper its cruelties for a fragile boy. It would not wait until he was strong enough to fight. What had he endured already in his short eleven years? And something inside him twisted, leaving him aching.

Jimmy began to run, flinging his arms out at his sides like an airplane and lifting his head into the wind. Lance stared after him. It was as though he was watching himself, looking back to an age long past and finding it suddenly, perfectly encapsulated. He could feel the sting of snowdrops on his tongue and the blood tingling through his veins. He felt like he could run forever and never stop. But life, he knew, had a way of stopping you in your tracks.

He turned away and climbed the stairs to Anne's door where a wreath with a red bow and holly berries hung. He was eager to see her, yet oddly reticent. He glanced over his shoulder with a strange sense of foreboding. When the holidays were over, he'd get to the bottom of things with Jimmy who had now all but disappeared below the little hill in search of the beaver dam.

Chapter 11

The back door opened before he'd had a chance to knock. Anne stood waiting in white slacks and an emerald-green blouse. Her chestnut hair glistened in a perfectly projected ray of light, and he felt somehow transfixed. She was like a sun-dappled evergreen trimmed in new snow; Lance could almost smell the pungency of pine. Or was he still wrapped in that childhood reverie that Jimmy had sparked a moment ago, that nostalgia that made everything in the world beautiful?

"I saw you from the window," she said, her voice lilting and warm. "Thanks for coming. I hope it wasn't too much trouble."

He gave her a quick hug and stepped back lest she hear the accelerated beat of his heart. He had missed her more than he'd realized. He collected himself and pulled a pine needle from her hair. "Nice touch."

She reached up an exploring hand and laughed. "It's the tree. I just had it delivered. Come and look." She grabbed his hand and pulled him excitedly into the living room. "It's one of those blue spruces I've always wanted—so full and fluffy."

"Sounds like a French poodle," he teased, stepping quickly out of his shoes and following her into the living room.

The tree stood in front of the bay window near her burgundy couch, on which were scattered small pillows with colorfully embroidered designs. Boxes of Christmas ornaments, tinsel, and lights that were ready for decorating covered the coffee table. He studied the tree, arms folded across his chest. "Well, it's a tree, all right," he said, narrowing his eyes. "But it's got to be the crookedest one I've ever seen! Did you pay real money for this thing?"

She sighed and threw up her hands. "I know. I've worked for an hour trying to get it to stand up straight, but it's hopeless. I never was any good at this."

He loved her innate ability to enjoy even the most mundane task. When he was with her, he forgot the troubles of life. He suddenly realized that Anne had never mentioned such things. Surely, she had troubles like the rest of the human race. He looked from the tree to her face and back again in mock concentration. "Have you tried tying it with a string from the window?" he teased.

"That's next unless you can help me," she countered. She cocked her head to one side and considered him through hazel eyes with mock pleading. Uncharacteristically, some vague apprehension seemed to linger there as well.

Her face was beginning to flush the way it did when she got excited, and he was aware again that she was a lovely woman and that his world had become decidedly brighter since he had met her. *Steady*, he cautioned himself. He pulled off his cable knit sweater, rolled up his sleeves, and shook his head at the stocky pine with its knobby trunk. "Might have to cut off a few of those lower branches if we ever hope to get it into the stand," he said. "I have some tools in my car."

"Never mind; I've got a perfectly good saw in the mud room. Come to think of it, I have some plastic drop cloths too. They'll keep the needles off my carpet, though maybe not out of our hair." She removed the stray needle from her hair with a helpless grin. "But I haven't even offered you a cup of coffee," she said. She moved toward the kitchen but glanced back over her shoulder in a questioning way. She seemed almost nervous. Something *was* bothering her.

"The coffee can wait," he said. "Let's save the tree first. By all means, let's save the tree!"

She reappeared a moment later with a saw clasped efficiently in her hand. She had a stock of handyman tools, saved no doubt from Richard's workshop. Sometimes, she made a great show of being able to wield them. She had been very proud of the electrical switch that she'd installed in the kitchen. A stubborn, independent woman. No wilting female, she, but it did make it difficult to impress her with his macho abilities. He prostrated himself beneath the leafy expanse and began loosening the loop screws.

He lifted the tree from its base and laid it on its side. It fanned out immediately, filling up the space by the window. He peered at her through the prickly branches, making a great show of the tree's enormous girth.

"It didn't look this big on the lot!"

"They never do." Lance grinned. He began lopping off a branch here and there near the base of the tree. "I remember the year Rose and I picked out the perfect specimen just right for our apartment. That thing magically grew six inches during the ride home."

He hadn't meant to talk about the past, but suddenly, he was besieged with memory—the year they turned their tree upside down to accommodate it in their small Georgetown apartment, the year hail had cut off the electricity on Christmas day. They had eaten cold beans by candlelight.

You're a fool, Lance Crane, he said to himself. *Old men grow dotty digging up memories of years gone by, nursing them like aching joints that need lineament.* He whittled away at the knobby trunk while Anne watched from a nearby ottoman, elbows on her knees. She was quiet, giving him space for private memories.

Twice the fool, he rebuked himself. He was engaging in an old man's reverie in the company of a sensitive woman he clearly wanted to impress. He was shooting himself in the foot, but then his aim had never been good, especially when the target was out of his reach. Besides, the prize, should he win it, could be snatched away in a flash.

"So, canned goods were a ploy to get my expert assistance with ye old Yule log," he quipped, anxious to derail his emotion-laden thoughts and move on to more even ground.

"You've found me out!" she said. She looked away as though to deflect a stray thought. "But I really do need you to take that box of cans to the radio station for me. The last day of the drive is tomorrow, and ... "

She left her sentence unfinished and seemed content to watch him work. But there was definitely something on her mind— something more than trees and canned goods. He cast a furtive glance through the branches as he worked and saw that she was twisting an errant thread on her sweater.

"Lance," she began slowly. "Where's Jimmy?"

"Down by the creek looking for that old beaver dam. He'll be along in a few minutes."

A silence ensued. Lance could hear the steady ticking of a mantle clock and small crackling noises—the sun melting ice on the roof. He looked up. "Can you hold the trunk right here, in the middle?"

She knelt to steady it. Her cologne mixed with the scent of the pine was sweet, unnerving him. When she brushed his hand, the quick warmth of her fingers traveled through him like a lightning rod. He moved quickly to the base and attached the stand once more, fumbling awkwardly with the screws. "There. Now, let's stand her up." As they lifted the tree together, loosened needles shook down on them. "Careful. Don't let go yet," he warned. "We may have to yell 'timber' if I didn't get those things tight enough. Why can't they make those screws big enough?"

Gingerly, they both let go a little at a time. They half lay, half sat under the fragrant branches. A little spot of pinesap had fallen on her blouse near the second button. "Hope that will come off," he said. She didn't look at the spot but rather into his eyes, and he was aware that he was holding his breath. But the moment ended.

"It's nothing." She scrambled to her feet.

He stood, too, still grasping the trunk in the center. The tree quivered like a dog after a swim, but when the beautiful blue-green branches stopped trembling, it stood ramrod straight.

"Perfect," she said, her eyes sparkling. She clasped her hands in delight. "Lance, you're a genius."

"And don't you forget it," he said wryly, amused, as always, at her childlike delight in small things.

"As if you'd let me." The electric moment as they'd lain prone under the tree seemed quite forgotten if she'd marked it. She nudged his arm playfully, then quickly began gathering up the discarded branches.

But as she began rolling up a drop cloth, Lance saw the small frown reappear on her forehead. He bent to help her pick up the needles that had escaped and gathered the bits of wood and tools to be put away.

When the lopped-off branches had been carried to the recycling box on the back porch, Anne placed a few of the medium-sized boughs in a ceramic pitcher by the fireplace. She fanned them out and studied their symmetry. "Thanks for taking the time to do this. I really appreciate it." She arched her back and stood with hands on her hips. She turned toward the tree again. "I've bought all new lights this year. I found those little white ones with crystal frames that glow like Bethlehem stars. I can't wait to see them."

Two pink spots appeared on her cheeks, and Lance thought she had never looked more beautiful. Instinctively, he moved toward her, but she quickly dropped the light string she had been admiring and whisked off toward the kitchen. "Let's have that coffee now."

He watched her go. His world had changed since she had come into it. He wondered what to do with this new rising inside himself.

She returned with a tray carrying two red and green mugs and a cut glass plate of coffee cake. "This is a new Danish recipe I tried yesterday," she said as he took the tray from her hand. "Careful, the coffee's really hot." She poured the steaming liquid into the mugs and held one out to him without looking up.

They were skirting around something, and he was eager to put things on a more even keel. "Hmm," he said, sniffing the warm pastry. "I think it might just be edible."

"If you don't like it, I have some dried-up old cornbread I was saving for the birds." She gave him a look of mock disdain and joined him on the sofa where late rays of sunshine fell through the bay window. And silence descended again.

He liked sitting there with her, even without speaking. Maybe especially without speaking. *The world is so full of a number of things; I'm sure we should all be as happy as kings.* The couplet by Robert Louis Stevenson played in his mind. He had forgotten it until today when he'd watched Jimmy walk away to explore the beaver dam.

Actually, he'd forgotten a lot of the good, simple things that Anne Westin inspired. He studied her face. What did she want from him? The frown he had noticed earlier remained perched on her forehead like an uncertain bird.

Her hazel eyes seemed to darken as she twined her fingers in her lap. He found himself longing to take away whatever it was that troubled her, to protect her from hurt. "Did I do all right?" he asked.

"What?"

"With the tree. That's why you're plying me with coffee and cake, right? Penance for dragging me here to save the Christmas tree?"

The twinkle he had hoped to see flashed briefly but disappeared. "Lance..." She paused and set her cup down on the table quietly. She traced its thin gold rim thoughtfully, causing a tiny high-pitched ping. A tiny vein appeared on her temple as she leaned forward. "Something's happened," she began. Then her words fell away.

He studied her folded hands, her thin, white wrists. Only the band of her watch interrupted their bare translucence. "What is it, Anne?" he asked gently.

"My wedding rings. They were stolen."

He looked down. The ring finger of her left hand revealed a small white band of even paler skin. He couldn't phrase his confusion.

"I keep them upstairs in my jewelry box," she whispered. "I never move them. Last week, I—I discovered they were gone."

"Do you mean someone broke in? Someone broke into the house and stole them?" He felt a knot rise in his throat. *Last week? Why had she waited so long to say something?* Had she been in danger? "Have you called the police?"

"No." She paused before stammering. "My wedding rings...they're precious to me..." Her eyes grew misty, and her voice caught. A lone tear dropped from her cheek onto her blouse near the little sap stain.

He caressed her hand gently as one might comfort a child in distress and searched her face. He had seldom seen her like this. She was usually so buoyant, so steady.

"I'm sorry, Lance. Really, I don't know what's come over me." She sniffed and wiped at the dampness on her cheek. "They're just *things*, just jewelry. I guess I didn't realize how important they were until they disappeared."

Of course, losing her rings would be important to her, but the level of anxiety he was reading seemed excessive. It wasn't like her. There had to be more. "Was anything else taken? Has someone hurt you?" He tried to read her expression, remembering those months when she had been tormented by Shane, knowing someone was watching her house. But that was all over, wasn't it? Surely, the danger was gone; she was safe.

"No. Nothing else," she said in a small voice.

"When did this happen exactly?"

"I discovered them missing last Saturday. It was the night Erma died—you know, Margaret's friend." She looked past him to the winter scene beyond the window, where frost had painted pictures in the glass.

Shadows had formed beneath her eyes, and Lance could see tiny blue veins at her temples. He thought back to the day he had taken Tess and Jimmy skiing. They had all gone to Grace Arbor for pizza. They had been having a great time until the phone call came from a tearful Miss Morris.

"There was another time when I thought someone might have been here," she said. "Yesterday, when I returned from visiting Margaret." Her voice took on a trance-like quality. "I felt it the moment I turned the key in the lock." She shook her head. "It was probably just nerves. There was no one here at all."

"Anne, you should call the sheriff."

"I didn't want to report the theft until I talked to you—and Jimmy."

Something clicked in his mind. He studied her, trying to discern what lay behind those brooding eyes. And suddenly, he knew, and the knowing hit him like a blow to the solar plexus. "You think ... you think Jimmy took them?"

She blinked, her dark lashes fluttering, but she said nothing. She had found the stray thread on her sleeve again.

"But he wouldn't do that. He—likes you. He hasn't caused any trouble at all." He could feel the pitch of his voice rising. "He's not like Shane. He's Shane's brother, but ... " His throat felt parched; his head throbbed. He dropped her hands and looked vacantly at the carpet where a few stray pine needles lay in almost geometrical precision. "You're sure you didn't misplace them or something?"

She shook her head, not looking at him.

He felt a hard knot in the pit of his stomach. "And you're blaming Jimmy ... " The coldness of his voice startled him.

She looked up, eyes wide. "Lance, I'm sorry. I—I just felt I had to talk to you about it. Jimmy has been here a lot. He's had the run of the place when we've been in the library or working on the computer. And yesterday ... "

He waited, not trusting himself to speak.

"I phoned you yesterday when I felt someone had been in my house. You weren't there, and Jimmy wasn't home. He could have been here. I mean, well, he could have ... " She put a hand to her temple. "He could have been here at Grace Arbor."

He looked at her numbly, seeing in his mind's eye Jimmy—frail and small—with belt scars on his legs. At that moment, he felt as though he was that child himself, that he was the one accused. Accused. Misunderstood.

"I see," he said. But he didn't see at all, and his head was buzzing. He got up and stumbled toward the door. "I'll—I'll have a word with the boy and get back to you."

"Lance, please…" She followed him to the kitchen, where he was already putting on his coat. Maybe it wasn't Jimmy," she exclaimed. "I don't want it to be, but I had to tell you." Her voice trailed after him as he opened the back door.

"Like I said, I'll get back to you," Lance said more harshly than he intended.

A slight dark figure encircled by harsh light came toward him—Jimmy returning from the pond. He walked toward him with a little sideways gait like an impatient skater waiting for the music to begin.

Lance stumbled down the steps woodenly, watching with dread as a father might look on a wayward son. The poem rang in his mind again, this time with irony. *The world is so full of a number of things. I'm sure we should all be as happy as kings.*

Chapter 12

Helen Rutgers entered the 40-bed care home she'd oper-
ated for three years and went directly to the front desk.
She had a headache, a pulsating pain that promised to increase in
intensity as the day wore on. She had been getting these headaches
far too often in the last few months, she realized. What she needed
was some good vanilla espresso and an aspirin. She straightened
her shoulders and stopped at the front desk. She looked at the
receptionist cautiously, for the sun was beaming in painfully
behind Catherine Kellman's head.

The receptionist's glasses fell from a long silver chain onto
her chest. Catherine was new, a deferential young woman from
Jamaica whom Helen had recently hired. She was the sort who
minded her own business and did what she was told. An asset to
good business. Helen applauded her good judgment in securing
Ms. Kellman. "All quiet on the home front?" she asked.

Catherine Kellman nodded, sitting up straighter in the chair
and giving Helen a quick, nervous smile. Dark eyes gleamed in
her bronze face, and her coiled braids formed a perfect corona at
the top of her head. "Your secretary left these for you," she said,
handing Helen a small bundle that comprised the mail.

Helen took the stack of mail she hadn't gotten to the day
before and turned away without further comment. Days were

often hectic, and recently, they had been especially so, what with that nosey Anne Westin demanding to know all the gritty details of the Thaddeus woman's passing. It was enough to give anyone a headache.

"Quit sniveling!" She could hear her father's voice in her brain even as her head began to pound in earnest. *You get what you go after in this life with grit and gall, not tears.* She wasn't sure what she hated worse, the father who hadn't cared enough to stick around or the tired epithets he left behind. She squared her shoulders, took a deep, stabilizing breath, and proceeded to her office at the far end of the south wing.

As she walked, she thumbed absently through the small sheaf of letters. There were several invoices, a communiqué from the Association of Residential Care, three "while you were out" slips, and a "request to transfer" notice from the hospital. She scanned the relevant information on the transfer notice. "Broken hip…maximum stay three months…Medicare…" Personal information listed the patient as a widow with no relatives and no name to notify in an emergency. She tucked it along with the rest of the mail into the side flap of her attaché case and felt some of the fog in her brain lift. She approached the south wing. It might not be such a bad day after all.

She turned to enter her private office, which she left open most of the time as a gesture of good will and availability. As long as the keys to her desk and private files were safeguarded in her Armani purse, she could retain her open-door policy. Only occasionally did she have to put up with the annoyance of a meandering patient. Like the one spinning around now to face her, fingers curled around the handle of a file drawer. Stunned, she grasped the door frame. "Ms. Morris?"

The petite woman's face blanched as white as her hair, high-lighting two bright spots of rouge. "Good morning," she said huskily, her eyes clouding beneath furrowed brows. Margaret dropped her hands and weaved as though she'd been startled awake. She was wearing a blue linen skirt that ended just short of thin legs traversed by faint purple veins. She sported a white blouse with a tailored bow at the neck and a pale blue cardigan. She looked every bit the venerable school teacher about to launch into the day's lesson. But school was not in session.

"What are you doing here?" Helen asked evenly, disguising her irritation and even managing a small, stern smile. The elderly were like children, after all. You had to show them who was in charge.

Margaret Morris stepped away from the filing cabinet and placed both hands on the back of the desk chair as though to steady herself. "I've been waiting to see you," she said calmly, but her face, drained of color, revealed her obvious dismay at being discovered.

"You're up very early this morning," Helen said, careful to keep the rising anger out of her voice. She hadn't thought Margaret Morris well enough to be walking the halls. She'd been confined to her room, complaining of fatigue and shortness of breath, and had asked for her meals to be delivered. What was so important that she had come to the director's office at this hour? What was the woman up to? Helen peered at her closely, waiting for an answer.

"It's 9:30. I'm used to rising at 6:00," Margaret responded crisply, her voice taking on a note of authority. A flush crept up from her neck, mitigating the ghostly pallor.

Helen's mind flashed back in time; she was looking into the implacable face of her long-ago fifth-grade teacher. The translucent hair combs that secured the thinning natural waves might be the very same ones she had worn so many years earlier. Margaret Morris was resuming her superior air in spite of the fact that their roles were oddly reversed now.

"I'm sorry to bother you so early in the day, but I really must have a word with you on an important matter."

The watchful eyes and determined lift of her chin unnerved Helen as they had in the fifth grade. She set her jaw to match Margaret's. "I wonder if you'd mind coming back later," she said in her best "take charge" voice. "I'm very busy right now. I can give you some time later on in the afternoon."

Margaret came toward Helen, clasping her hands in front of her as though about to begin the day's lesson. *Open your geography books to page 28.* "It's about Erma," she said abruptly. Obviously, she was not about to be dismissed.

Helen walked calmly to her desk and sat down, neatly arranging herself in the chair. She folded her hands over the smooth mahogany surface and made a tent of her fingers. "I see," she said, regarding her elderly intruder with a patience she was far from feeling. She'd have to handle this carefully. Margaret Morris was no fool, and she had equally formidable friends. "I know how upset you must be," she said quietly. "Erma was your friend. I'm very sorry. You must be lonely without her."

"This isn't about me," Margaret said sharply, toying with the bow on her blouse while fixing her eyes on Helen's face. The watery blue eyes flashed momentarily, and Helen could read anger in them, anger and something very like a threat. "Has anyone called about her—any of her family or friends, I mean?"

The pain in Helen's temples intensified with every beat of her pulse. She had been over all this with Anne Westin, though why it was any of that woman's business, she didn't know. Margaret Morris was demanding to know things Helen had no wish to discuss. She drew in her breath and let it out slowly. "No one has inquired," she said with studied sincerity. "I'm sorry. Erma seems to have been quite alone in the world."

"Perhaps if the name she always went by had been printed in the paper, those who knew her might have had an opportunity to pay their respects," Margaret said, narrowing her eyes but keeping her gaze intent on Helen's face.

Helen's patience was wearing thin. Children and the elderly could be such burdens. A small sigh escaped her pursed lips. "Miss Morris, I explained that to you. We're mandated to print the full given name. Tanner was a stage moniker, not her real name." Her headache was making her edgy, and she hoped her questioner hadn't taken the trouble to confirm that statement.

Helen opened her middle desk draw and made a show of beginning her day's work, but her fingers trembled slightly. Erma Tanner had been snooping into things. Helpfully, the diabetes put an end to her snooping. *Still, if anyone knew she had deliberately delayed reporting Erma's worsening symptoms.* Helen shook herself mentally. Perhaps it was a kindness after all. The woman no longer had to suffer.

Why should a person hang on for years and years to no purpose? When there was nothing they could contribute to the world? She held her lips in a firm line, aware that these thoughts no longer shocked her. Perhaps they never had. They had just evolved little by little, without conscious formation. A dim picture of her father emerged in her mind. A compulsive gambler, Hiram Rutger always had some scheme going. When he was winning, he was generous, kind, and even doting. But he wasn't always winning. And the only thing he had ever whipped her for was crying.

Don't snivel! If you want something, go for it, but don't turn on the waterworks. I hate snivelers.

She had tried to please him, a task she had never accomplished. When she was in junior high, her father left for Las

Vegas, claiming half ownership of a new casino that promised to bring in millions.

But when will you be back, daddy?

I'll see you when I see you. And if I don't make a million, I'll save the whole world the sight of me.

She'd never heard from him again, and shortly afterward, his wife divorced him, as she'd threatened so often in the heat of argument. Sometimes, she said it in a teasing way that made Helen shudder and clutch the worn teddy bear, who was her only friend.

Margaret's voice broke into her reverie. "But isn't it customary to print other names as well? Names familiar to family and friends so they'll know when a death occurs among their acquaintances?"

Helen blinked and stood up. First, that meddlesome Erma Tanner, and now Margaret Morris was picking up where Erma left off. "Miss Morris, I must ask you to excuse me. I have an appointment. I'll be glad to discuss this later." She turned and marched out of her own office with as much dignity as she could muster.

Her head was pounding more fiercely than ever. She fled into her secretary's office and closed the door, aware of Margaret staring after her, surprise and criticism in her calculating gaze. Helen strode on. The key to her files was tucked safely away. Let Miss Morris tinker all she liked; she'd never find anything!

Helen sat down at her secretary's desk, feeling more tired than she had in years. She sighed deeply and traced the smooth finish of the desk with one red-tipped nail. She scrutinized her hands as though they held some secret to what she should do next. Her mother would have coped.

Fannie Rutger owned a beauty shop where she cut and styled hair and gave manicures. She had taught her daughter how to do nails. *One could tell a lot about a woman by the look of her hands. If they're bitten down to the quick, you can be sure she's a poor, nervous type who'll never amount to anything. If they're plain and unpolished, she's a girl without ambition; she's boring. Whatever you become, don't be boring.*

Mother had been anything but boring, Helen mused. She could bend over backward to be nice and, at other times, vent a torrent of hate. Sometimes, she'd dress her little girl in ruffled dresses and coax her honey-colored hair into outrageous styles. She'd take her to town and buy her the most expensive doll in the store. Other times, she'd be gone for hours and return to find Helen hungry and crying, and there would be no comfort. Only a slammed door and silence. Helen trembled, remembering how she hid when Mother was in one of her moods.

She seldom thought of her mother at all now. She hadn't seen her since she showed up slightly tipsy at her wedding—the first and only. Helen gripped the edge of the desk with her nails. She should have known there'd be no riding off into the sunset with Roger, who'd dropped her flat after twenty-two months as her mother had predicted he would. Mother had stopped predicting. She had stopped interacting with her daughter at all and retired to a pink condo in Florida. The last Helen had heard, Fannie Rutger was traveling the craft circuit with a sculptor who created avant-garde lawn decorations from spears of twisted copper.

Helen rubbed her aching temples and felt dangerously close to tears. She couldn't be missing her mother after all those years, could she? Her father's stern rebuke echoed in her ears. *Stop sniveling. If you want something, go for it.*

Well, she had done just that. She'd worked hard and earned a degree and the admiration of the town's movers and shakers. She stood up decisively. She made a lucrative business out of Rutgers Nursing Home, and no one was going to spoil things for her.

She went back to her own office, half expecting that Margaret might still be lurking there, but the room was empty. Helen shut the door and brewed herself a cup of coffee. Before she could take the first sip, her phone rang. The display panel revealed an inter-office call.

"Doctor Brevitz is here," Catherine from reception said matter-of-factly. "He's waiting in the east wing."

Helen put a hand to her head and smoothed a strand of platinum hair that had escaped the faux diamond barrette. Few women her age wore them, but for her, they were more than utilitarian devices to hold her upswept style in place. They were status symbols, especially the more expensive variety, like the one she wore today.

She smiled a little to herself. It had been easy to work her way into the confidence of attractive, cosmopolitan David Brevitz. She'd found out just what she needed to put him in her debt, but he was becoming far too interested in her business affairs of late. She frowned, remembering the argument they'd had the day before. It was definitely time to press her advantage.

She found him bent over an elderly patient, probing for a heartbeat. She waited in the doorway, watching his hands as they moved steadily, surely. It was his hands that first attracted her. She liked the way they moved—deftly, gracefully, like perfectly matched dancers. She had longed for those hands to touch her. He was suave, engaging, and frustratingly impersonal.

His manner contrasted maddeningly with his cavalier demeanor and his reputation for flirting with pretty young women. She frowned. He'd taken her to dinner once and even for a sail in his boat, but it had been a long time since he'd invited her out. Was he just preoccupied, or did it have something to do with that young records assistant? Was she jealous of an uncultured Deaf girl, and was it possible that David was romancing her?

She stepped away from the door and walked toward him, leveling her gaze to those turbulent eyes that had captured her heart from the first moment she'd seen him. She watched him slip a pen into the pocket of his white coat. "Good morning, Doctor," she said coolly. "You're in early."

"That must be why they call them 'morning' rounds," he quipped without meeting her studied gaze. He moved past her, heading for the south wing of patients. "Any problems?"

She felt the quick hurt induced by his sarcasm. "We're very business-like this morning," she teased, pretending nonchalance.

He lifted one eyebrow and gave her a wilting look. "Well, now, it is business that brings me here after all, is it not?"

"Unfortunately," she responded, matching his stride. She was nearly as tall as he, and she was poignantly aware of the smooth angle of his jaw, the darkly curling hair, and the broad, square shoulders. She moved closer so that her arm brushed against his. A lump rose in her throat. He had definitely been neglecting her. She could feel her irritation growing. "Apart from business, I don't suppose I'd see you at all. Really, you're quite ignoring your old friends."

"As they say, a doctor's work is never done."

"Have a cup of vanilla espresso with me before rounds," she said, pressing his arm.

"I have a consultation at ten," he said without hesitation.

"But the coffee's all ready," she coaxed, giving him the benefit of her most ingratiating smile.

"Sorry," he said and lifted a chart from the rack near a closed door.

Helen drew in a long, slow breath, disappointment quickly turning to anger. "I see." She peered at him closely. His eyes were never at rest, she thought, always watching something she couldn't see. It was infuriating. In the beginning, he was attentive and even gallant. Now, he seemed bent on distancing himself from her. Well, not before she got what she needed from him. She glared into his averted eyes with their dark, furrowed brows. When he finally met her gaze, she said, "Morris in 212B has improved a lot. I think she should be released."

His face registered quick surprise. "I just saw her last night. Her oxygen levels are quite unstable."

"She's stable enough to be running around the halls, getting into people's private offices," she said indignantly. "I want her released."

"Has Miss Morris been giving you trouble?" he asked in an apparent effort to be casual.

She sniffed. "Nothing I can't handle, but that's not the point. We need the room, and I say she's well enough to go."

He turned toward her, scrutinizing her to the point of discomfort. "Miss Morris was asking me some rather interesting questions this morning, Helen. She wanted to know about the diabetes case—Ms. Tanner."

Helen felt a quickening in her stomach. "Thaddeus," she corrected quickly. "Thaddeus is her given name."

"I see," he said, and his frown deepened. "You did take care of the reports, didn't you?"

She stiffened. How she hated his superior manner. "Of course," she spat. Had someone been questioning him, too? Perhaps that Westin woman or Margaret Morris? "For heaven's sake, I look after these people day and night, and they still find something to complain about. Really, David, you should know better than to believe everything you hear." She prepared to leave, but David blocked her passage.

"You are not letting too much time elapse before the official reports?" he queried in a warning voice.

"Do I tell you how to do *your* job?" she countered, her anger only barely under control. "Curious, isn't it? You lecturing me on legalities."

His face paled. The threat had clearly hit its mark. "I want Morris cleared for dismissal by the end of the week," she said tersely and edged away from him. Turning back, she smiled over her shoulder and saw the muscles in his temples working. She realized that her headache had all but vanished.

Chapter 13

Tess glanced up with a start, sensing someone inside her cubicle. "Oh!" she breathed, wondering how long her friend Melissa had been standing there.

"Hey, you skipped coffee break," Melissa said, forming the words with over-zealous care and extending a Hallmark Maxine ® mug in one heavily-ringed hand. "It's almost time for lunch already. What's with you?"

"I'm sorry," Tess said wearily, though she welcomed Melissa's interruption. She'd been distracted much of that morning and hadn't had the heart for conversation in the department break room. Besides, it was Friday. She had the afternoon off, and she'd wanted to be sure she'd finished everything. She pushed back from the keyboard and regarded her friend with quick amusement.

"You missed Jennifer's birthday cake," Melissa said carefully, arching one penciled eyebrow beneath curls restrained by a crimson band. One blonde wave dipped over her right eye as she made a face of mock horror. "We got the leftovers no one ate at her party, and now we know why!"

"That bad," Tess sympathized, wrinkling her nose. She put her hands in her lap, realizing that she had been signing.

Her friend dropped down in the chair next to Tess's computer and put a hand over her stomach in exaggerated pain. "That bad," she agreed. "So, tell me, what have you been up to?"

"Up to?" Tess queried.

"Yes. Tell me," she urged. "I heard on the hospital hot-line that you've been seeing Dr. Gorgeous."

Tess dropped her eyes as Melissa rambled on about David Brevitz's "gorgeous" qualities. She rubbed her temple. The mild pain that had been threatening all morning had become a full-blown headache. David had likely been the cause of her inattention. Since the night of the storm, he'd begun showing up. Sometimes, at lunch, he'd appear in the cafeteria line or in the parking lot at quitting time.

He'd taken her to dinner at an Italian restaurant the week before, where candles flickered in old wine bottles. He'd been solicitous, eager to hear about her life but oddly remote when it came to sharing anything about himself. There was something terribly unreachable and sad about David Brevitz, something that drew the caring instinct in her to the fore. She wanted to help, but she could not reach him.

Maybe he didn't think she was capable of understanding a man of the world like himself or care enough to share his thoughts. She might have gotten him to open up if there had been more time, but he'd been paged just as their dessert arrived. They'd consumed it with haste, and he'd taken her home with apologies, but he hadn't suggested getting together again. Just as well.

Melissa tapped her shoulder. "Come on. This is me— Melissa. You can tell me!"

Tess looked up, startled. She'd been immersed in her thoughts. "It was just dinner," she said. What would Melissa think if she'd told him she'd stayed all night in the doctor's house? But what was there to tell? He'd treated her like a patient, insisting she drink her coffee and get warm by the fire. Nor had he pressed the slightest advantage. But there had been something about the way he looked at her, something that couldn't deny his interest.

Suddenly, Melissa got up, her skirt provoking a rush of wind against Tess's cheek. She turned to see the cause of her friend's sudden movement. David Brevitz stood in the doorway, white coat flagging over a lime green shirt and striped tie. He paused in the doorway, one hand on the wall, the other hanging loosely in his pocket.

His glance took in both girls and then focused on Tess. "Are you working through lunch?"

She held his gaze, refusing to register surprise at his sudden appearance. "No," she said flatly. "I was just finishing, and Melissa…"

"Was just on the way out." Melissa winked at Tess and wiggled her jeweled hand in farewell with an adoring glance at "Dr. Gorgeous."

"I had to deliver some records," he said. "Since I was here, I thought I might walk you to the cafeteria if you are going." He touched a hand to his mouth as though to cover a cough. Then his hands found his pockets again as he stood waiting.

Tess logged off her computer and straightened a few items on her desk. Her pulse raced, a condition confusing and irritating. This enigmatic doctor's behavior bordered on rudeness. Did he think he could just show up, and she'd be ready to drop everything? She looked up, wondering if her thoughts showed on her face.

"Come. I will walk with you," he said, but something soft in his expression mitigated the abrupt words.

"All right," she said, wishing she hadn't chosen words with such difficult consonants.

They walked without speaking. Conversation would be impossible anyway. She'd have to turn to read his lips, and then she would likely stumble over her own feet or those of the many visitors and employees leaving offices and patient rooms. They filled their plates from the busy food line, making choices with nods and gestures. Tess ran her name plate under the code reader at the register and followed David to a nearby table.

"Are you all right?" he asked after he'd removed each item from his tray and arranged them at precise angles.

Tess unfolded a napkin and found her fingers speaking in spite of herself. "Busy. I lost a whole file and had to retype it."

A hint of a smile lit David's eyes, but his mouth remained rigid. For several minutes, they ate without further conversation. A smile traveled to his lips and softened his austere features. "I dislike computers myself, but thanks to people like you, our work is much simpler and far more accurate because of them."

It was as close to a compliment as he had ever come. She could think of nothing to say in answer and felt the heat rise to her cheeks.

He broke off a piece of garlic toast. "And how is your aunt? Miss Popov, isn't it?" They had talked about her the night of the storm—and about Alexei too. She blushed, remembering how she had wanted to keep talking as the snow fell and flames danced in the fireplace. He had listened to her every word, a strange look in his eyes, a frown deepening across his forehead.

Tess studied her diced peaches—the perfect little chunks in the white glass bowl. That was the night she had gone to see Aunt Vera, the night of the blizzard. The quick hurt of Vera's indifference stung.

"She is the same." *I am nothing to her. I have no family.* But she wouldn't have him feel sorry for her or think she was full of adolescent angst. She shrugged and tried a smile. "I tried to get her to accept Mrs. Westin's invitation to the Christmas party, but she said no."

"She doesn't like parties?" He lifted a mug of coffee to his mouth.

"She doesn't like to go anywhere." *Not even to my grade school graduation when I was 12.* Alexei had come looking older than she'd ever remembered him and fallen asleep before her name had been called. She'd felt the stares of the other children whose parents shouted their enthusiasm and clasped them in strong, young arms.

"And how did you cope with such a life?" David's eyes lit with concern.

She glanced up from the dish of peaches. What an odd question. She must have told him that she lived with Vera until the summer of last year when everything had changed. She shrugged. "It doesn't matter," she said and laid the spoon down gently.

Suddenly, David pressed back from the table. "I have a meeting. I am sorry." He rose abruptly, not bothering to clear his dishes, and strode away.

His departure had all the nuances of a door shutting in her face, and she felt herself blush as though they'd been arguing and everyone in the room had taken notice. But no one was looking her way. In the brightly lit cafeteria, lips moved in animated conversation. Forks were held in mid-air or pulled toward smiling mouths in quick flashes of silver.

A sense of abandonment filled her. She had wanted to tell David about the ski trip with Lance Crane and Jimmy, how she'd felt she was flying as she swept down the white hills, the wind on her face. She'd wanted to tell him about how she'd found a way to recapture the file lost in cyberspace, how pleased she had been about the commendation of her supervisor. But he had gone without finishing his lunch or even saying good-bye.

She had no appetite to finish her lunch. She'd go home to her apartment and forget about it all. She must get used to being alone, to having no one with whom she could really be herself. She felt the lump in her throat thicken as she stared vacantly into the crowded room. After a few moments, she became aware of someone leaning against one of the cafeteria's square pillars. He seemed to be waiting for something or watching like a department store detective. His legs in khaki slacks were crossed at the ankles, and his hands hung in pockets of a camel-colored jacket. She squinted for a closer look.

The man's nutmeg-brown hair glistened beneath the fluorescent light. He was looking toward the conveyor belt that spirited David's tray into the kitchen or just beyond it to where the doctor strode away from the cafeteria. When suddenly the man turned, she drew in her breath.

Peter! Peter was here in the hospital cafeteria. She stared. Was he an apparition conjured up in her lonely imagination?

He started toward her. "Tess!" He fixed dark eyes on her face and took both her hands in his, brushing her cheek with a kiss. "I'm sorry for just dropping in." He stopped and turned again in the direction Dr. Brevitz had gone. "But if you have other plans..." He reached up to right his dislodged glasses.

"No, I was—just having lunch..." She let the unfinished sentence drop, helpless to explain. But what need was there to explain? Why did she feel guilty, as though she had somehow betrayed him? It made no sense. They had no claim on each other, and yet...

"I'm sorry to surprise you like this," Peter said, searching her eyes. "It was a last-minute decision. We've been swamped at work, but I was able to get away for a few hours. I just really wanted to see you, Tess."

"Oh, Peter." She found herself floundering, resisting the urge to smooth her hair, which she hadn't combed since morning.

"I thought we might take a ride...if you want to." The wrinkles in his forehead deepened, and he glanced once more in the direction of David's departure. "I can bring you back later for your car if you can get away." He paused, looking her up and down tenderly. "It's really great to see you."

Tess nodded, feeling again that wonderful sense of being admired and cared for that she had experienced last summer. Had it only been six months? Yet now, she felt as though it were yesterday. She bent to pick up her tray, but Peter quickly lifted it from the table, brushing his hand against hers.

"I'll get that. Come on." The smile that had been tenuous broadened to fill his whole face with light.

They drove south out of town along Highway 10, a familiar road that led to Glennis Falls, where they had met that bright summer day. She had been running along the upper ridge when she'd seen the deer thrashing below at the edge of the rushing water. She had been frantic about helping the desperate animal, and when Peter, driving by, saw her, he came to help. The memory settled deep and warmly.

Tanner's Wood stretched, a black and white etching against the gray sky. The gaunt trees were even more beautiful without their cover of leaves. Snow lay thickly on the ground between the slender trunks, hidden from the sun's melting rays. Branches appealed to the sky as though seeking comfort in the cold.

Peter stopped the Buick at the lookout point, not far from the site of their picnic those long months ago. They'd come there in late September, too, when he'd had a free Saturday. It had become their special place, and as she drank in the beauty of the icy water rushing down from jagged peaks, Tess felt a wave of anticipation or warning.

"I hope you don't mind that I didn't warn you I was coming." He turned to face her squarely and held her hands lightly. Sometimes, he used sign language, and he was very good at it, but now he simply spoke, watching her closely. "Are you all right, Tess?" he asked. "I mean, is there anything…" He broke off and looked down at their twined hands a moment before lifting his eyes to hers again.

She waited, puzzled. He was still trying to take care of her like last summer when Uncle Alexei's death was being investigated. He'd gone with her to the sheriff's office when her locket was found near the body. He'd been firm in his defense of her, and she'd clung to him in her confusion and naiveté. Perhaps she would always be someone who needed him, a disabled child for whom he felt sympathy.

"You've become very important to me, Tess. I—I hoped that you … " Once again, he seemed incapable of completing his thought.

In her emails, she'd stopped short of telling him how much he had come to mean to her. She would not say that she had lain awake wondering, hoping, praying that he might come to love her.

"I'm worried about you," he declared in a sudden rush of words. "That doctor… has he been bothering you?"

She stared at him. "Bothering me?" she repeated.

"Oh, Tess," he said, leaning forward, frustration written on his face. "It's just that he's not the kind of guy… that is, he's, well, he has a reputation of being something of a Don Juan. And you … " His hands flew up in a gesture of agitation.

"He's not like that," she stammered, trying to understand just what he was saying. "He's been kind to me and… " She broke off as Peter had done, and they sat looking at each other in embarrassment.

Could Peter actually be jealous? She was aware of the gossip about David and had been wary of him in the beginning, but he wasn't what they said. He was gentle and seemed to need her somehow, though she couldn't think why. Her feelings had fluctuated so much, and now Peter was questioning her like she was a child who needed protecting.

She felt sudden anger and pulled her hands away. "He's a friend, that's all. And I don't need to be protected, Peter. I can take care of myself." She knew it sounded ungrateful, peevish, but she couldn't help it. "We should go back; it will be dark soon." She studied her clasped hands and, in a moment, felt his hand soft on her arm. She fought against rising tears as he gently tilted her face up to meet his gaze.

"I'm sorry, Tess. I didn't mean to question you. I just don't want you to get hurt. I only want you to be happy." His eyes were soft disks behind his glasses; his lips curved into a smile that lit them from within like sunlight through amber glass.

She said nothing, but her anger had flown. She knew she would count the days until Christmas when Peter would be back. Maybe she could work through the tangled maze of her feelings by then and know just what it was she wanted from David Brevitz and what he wanted from her.

Chapter 14

"The property is about 25 miles outside of town on route 81. Go south to Emerson and make a right on Euclid Crossing. Yes, 747. Just like the airplane."

Lance hung up the phone and ran a hand through his hair. It had grown too long and was doubtless approaching his collar. He hadn't expected to show houses today, especially the somewhat isolated old Tudor he'd had on the books for three years. Buyers were rare in winter months, especially in northern Wisconsin, and he didn't want to miss a chance for a sale. The caller, with a Southern accent, was in the area for the holidays to visit relatives and had heard about the Emerson listing.

He peered through the living room window where snow was lightly falling and regretted his procrastination. He'd put off getting a haircut and planned to remedy that situation today. He'd even toyed with the idea of getting a new suit for the holidays, but clients didn't grow on trees. Besides, he wouldn't need a new suit and a haircut since he had worked a wedge between himself and the hostess of the only event on his immediate agenda—Anne's Christmas dinner party.

A haircut wasn't the only thing he needed to do. He sighed wearily and gazed at the half-decorated little fir by the window. Jimmy would want a tree. He had dragged it out of the shed, but that was as far as he'd gotten before his nebulous Christmas spirit vanished.

It had happened the afternoon he and Anne had laughed over the spectacle of the crooked blue spruce she'd purchased. He'd been struck during those pleasant hours by a rare sense of happiness and hope. It was like discovering some part of yourself you'd never known was there and feeling almost reborn.

He caught the inside of his cheek, remembering the sour note of their parting. She'd accused Jimmy of stealing! Could it be true? Could he have entered Anne's bedroom and lifted her wedding rings from her jewelry box?

Jimmy had kept his distance since he'd confronted him about the matter. "They turned up missing after you were in the house playing computer games," he'd said quietly, trying to still the anxiety he was feeling. "You know anything about it?"

The freckles on Jimmy's face had blanched, and his eyes suddenly sparked like pulsars about to explode in the atmosphere. "I didn't take nothing. I wouldn't!"

Lance's anger had flared. If there was something he hated, it was dishonesty. Hadn't he taken Jimmy into his home for the holidays and set aside his office schedule to spend time with him? And this was his reward?

And what about Anne, who had befriended Jimmy and opened her home to him, giving him free rein of her computer with its parental controls in place so that he could play his cherished video games?

He knew a bond had begun to form between them. Lance remembered the tears in her eyes when she'd told him about the rings. He'd been too angry at the time to care, too ashamed even to consider how she must have felt about such a loss.

He leaned back in his chair and stared at the telephone. He recalled only too well the wrenching moment in Anne's kitchen, the hard, bright landscape behind the ruffled curtains, and the sense of betrayal like a rock in his gut. He had felt... What was it? Offended? Ashamed? He shook his head, at a loss to understand himself.

"I didn't take nothing of hers!" Jimmy had repeated and turned his back, small shoulders rigid, arms locked. Was he hiding tears?

Lance had spun him around. "If you needed money, you could have asked! You didn't have to steal like a common thief."

He'd wanted to be calm and accommodating and remain open-minded, but he had lost control. History was repeating itself. Jimmy was Shane Eldridge all over again. His gentle, phlegmatic sister would be devastated if she knew what was happening to her children.

"If your mother were here!" he had shouted, feeling all constraint fall away.

"Well, she ain't here. She's dead!" He had said it like a curse and glowered at him through eyes drawn together like beads on a string. Then he'd jerked away and run up the stairs to his room, slamming the door after him.

Why couldn't he give the rings back? Anne would understand; she'd forgive him. "Look, son," he'd tried later when his anger cooled and Jimmy deigned to come out of his room. "Everybody makes mistakes."

"I ain't your son," he had responded under his breath, then in a high-pitched voice added, "And I didn't take nothing!" He vanished again, the small feet drumming with amazing speed on the uncarpeted stairs.

That night, they had both sought the comfort of separate rooms and gone to bed early without supper.

Lance overslept the next morning, no doubt due to a considerable amount of tossing and turning in the night. He'd roused himself at 9:30 and gone out to the garage to work on the Rosie-O. There was nothing like hard manual labor to clear the head and put things in perspective. It was almost noon when he came back into the house, expecting Jimmy to be zoned out on the couch, watching Cartoon Network, having devoured several bowls of his favorite cereal. Well, Jimmy would have to go with him to the Emerson place whether he wanted to come or not.

But the house was quiet. No TV, no cupboards slamming. Maybe Jimmy was still upstairs, sulking in his room. Lance's legs felt leaden, his heart heavy as stone. He'd been harder on the boy than he planned, but he had to get him to confess. A lot of the blame could be laid on the lousy start he'd had in life.

The poor kid had been dealt one rotten card after another. First, his father had left for parts unknown and, in spite of the government's crusade against deadbeat dads, had managed to stay hidden. Then Jane was diagnosed with cancer. Her health had declined quickly, though she had kept the truth about her illness from family members. That was no surprise. They were never close as a family, nor was there anyone in a position to take on a small boy, even if they had been so inclined. The courts had taken over before Lance was aware of what had transpired.

He thought of Jimmy covering himself with a towel to hide bruises on his spindly legs. "I fall sometimes," he had said that happier morning as they prepared to go Christmas shopping. Lance had reported what he saw to the caseworker and was promised an investigation would take place immediately, but the matter had not yet been resolved.

Lance felt old and weary as he climbed the steps to the spare bedroom. He had failed once more. Was it possible the boy was telling the truth? Lance bit his lip. Shane had declared his innocence, too, and had lied through his teeth.

God, what can I do? Things couldn't go on this way. They couldn't live in the same house and carry on this cold war.

He knocked on Jimmy's door. They would talk it out on the way to meet the potential buyers of the Emerson house. They'd ease into the topic after a stop at Jimmy's favorite fast-food restaurant. One way or another, they'd come to an understanding. He rapped louder, his knuckles making a harsh, hollow sound on the wood.

No answer. Lance turned the knob.

He stared at the twin bed with its Spiderman sheets, at clothes scattered on the floor, and the latest Harry Potter book upside down on the rug. A half-empty bottle of Dr. Pepper sat uncapped beside it.

Advancing fully into Jimmy's room, Lance pulled aside the blue checkered curtain and peered through the window into the winter bleakness. It wasn't unusual for Jimmy to go walking in the woods with Grover in tow. The two were inseparable. It would be a sad day when Jimmy had to leave the big shaggy dog behind. Grover was growing lazy with age and preferred his bed by the fireplace, especially on cold winter days. Still, when there was hope for a walk, he'd perk up, every muscle alert. Lance breathed a heavy sigh. Surely, that was where Jimmy was, but it was odd that he'd heard nothing while working in the garage.

Lance glanced at his watch. He had to get on his way, or his clients would be waiting, shivering in the snow. He'd have his talk with the boy when he got back. Maybe Jimmy needed to clear his head, too, and he'd be through sulking when he got back from his walk.

He left a note, telling Jimmy there were subs in the fridge and that he wouldn't be long. He drove down Highway 81, watching for a small boy and a dog, but the landscape was barren. Jimmy wasn't likely to take the highway in any case. He preferred walking in the woods, where he could check out beaver dams and collect fossils. Lance thought it a point in the boy's favor that he sought out Nature.

He shrugged. They'd have their talk when he got back from his showing, and then maybe they'd have a pizza in town. Pepperoni with double cheese, the way Jimmy liked it.

Lance led Charles Andover through the house, pointing out various features of the Tudor. The potential buyer was a graphic artist who wanted a get-away for weekends and summers. He followed, perceptive brown eyes scrutinizing every detail. His wife, wrapped in something that looked suspiciously like mink, raved over the "country ambiance that was to die for."

Showing them through the house turned out to be a long-drawn-out affair. They had a thousand questions and wanted to know every detail of the Tudor's history and construction. He let them wander off into a corner where they bent their heads together in conspiratorial discussion before returning to request another look at this room or that. Lance took advantage of their private corner consultations to duck into a room and call home on his cell phone. As had been the case in several calls he'd already made, Jimmy did not answer.

Lance jammed the phone back into his pocket. How do you deal with someone who sulks and won't respond, won't even answer the phone? Kids! How did one get through to them? The trip back would take nearly forty-five minutes. It would be dark soon. He had to get back.

He promised to take his clients through the Emerson property again on Monday and waved them off. He sped away toward home with a growing sense of alarm. It was snowing again, fat flakes picking up speed with every second. He took the curving road that ran along Harper's Woods, where Jimmy often went to explore, but all the way home he saw no one.

He parked the jeep in the driveway and went inside, his muscles tense with anxiety. The note he had scrawled lay as he had left it on the kitchen table. Silence loomed. He called Jimmy's name several times, but his voice echoed through the empty house like so much wind in the trees. He made his way upstairs but knew, even before entering Jimmy's room, that it would be as empty as before.

Where could the child be? Surely he wouldn't run away! But why *not* run away? Isn't that what a thief would do when he was trapped?

Lance had once run away as a boy. He'd been banished to his room for going fishing instead of doing his chores, and no one believed that he'd simply lost track of time. He'd been cut to the heart by the unfairness of it all and wanted to make his parents sorry. He'd gotten as far as the neighbor's barn before turning back, cold and frightened.

Had Jimmy run away rather than face up to what he'd done? Lance riffled through dresser drawers and flung the closet door open. Shirts and pants hung at precarious angles; some had fallen from their hangers onto the floor or were balled up in the corner. He rummaged through the messy closet. Both pairs of shoes were gone—his high-top tennis shoes and his hiking boots. Lance searched the top shelf for the big duffel bag he had brought when he first came, but only a dusty space remained where the bag had been stored since his arrival in Ladystone.

He could feel his pulse racing, his mind clicking off one possibility after another. What should he do? Call the police? But they would only tell him there was nothing they could do until the boy had been missing for 24 hours.

He ran back downstairs and onto a deck slippery with fast-falling snow, nearly losing his balance. The post and chain where Grover was restrained when no one was at home was covered in snow, and the dog's dish was missing from the porch. He ran back inside and flung open the cupboard. The 25-pound bag of kibble he had bought just last week was nearly empty.

He dropped down on the stairs, stung by the awful truth. Jimmy had run away. What would he do? Where would he go? He had no friends except for Tess and Anne Westin. He had played once or twice with the Patterson boy across the ridge. What was his name? Tom or Tim? Ted. That was it. He thumbed through the phone book and found a listing for Patterson.

"This is Lance Crane, Jimmy's uncle. I wonder if the boy might be with Ted." He barely recognized his own voice, husky with concern.

"I haven't seen Jimmy for several days." The woman's soft voice faltered. "Is—is everything all right?"

Lance stammered something and replaced the receiver. He was sweating inside his parka, and his jaw ached with tension. Tess? Would Jimmy have gone to her? They'd become fast friends. Tess often "babysat" (Jimmy hated that word!) when Lance had business to tend to, but she always came to the house. They had never gone to Tess's apartment. Did Jimmy even know where she lived?

Who else did Jimmy know? Anne? He might have sought her out once, but he'd hardly go there now after being accused of stealing her wedding rings. Lance exchanged his topcoat for a cold-weather parka and grabbed a woolen scarf from the hook by the door. He'd have to find him. But where?

He scrawled a note in case he should return: "Jimmy. Stay here. I'm out looking for you. Please, don't leave." He signed it "Uncle Lance" and, after a pause, added, "I'm not mad at you. Wait for me," he finished and dropped the pen from his trembling fingers. He turned to the door but left the kitchen light burning a bright welcome for Jimmy's return. *Dear God, he must come back.*

It was fully dark as he trudged down the back steps. The temperature had dropped. Lance shivered inside his fleece-lined parka and felt the wind whip around his legs. Did Jimmy plan to spend the night in the woods? Surely, he'd turn around and come back once he realized how cold it was, wouldn't he? He circled the area, straining to bring shapes out of the darkness, but his anxiety grew with every dead-end turn.

Then he scrambled into the Jeep and almost instinctively drove toward Grace Arbor. Anne would know what to do. He frowned as he pressed the accelerator. He shouldn't have left things as they were with her, but his pride had been hurt. He'd frozen her with his cold rebuke and blown his stack at Jimmy. Dumb, stupid pride. It had been more important to him than listening to Anne's full story or working things through with the boy. He'd simply exploded at them both. No wonder Jimmy refused to talk to him. No wonder he'd run off.

It was nearly six o'clock when he pulled up the long winding drive that led to Grace Arbor. Maybe she wouldn't even answer his knock after the way he'd treated her.

Before he could raise a hand to the door, she opened it, concern and surprise in her eyes. A smudge of flour or sugar dotted her softly rounded cheek. She was wearing a blue turtle neck sweater and jeans with a ruffled white apron tied at her waist.

He stood in the doorway, unable to speak.

"Lance?" Her usually serene features clouded. She dried her hands on the towel and stepped back to usher him in.

Feeling like a lost child coming home, he stepped into the foyer. "It's Jimmy," he stammered. "He's gone."

"Oh, Lance, no." She drew him quickly into the circle of her arms and held him for a moment, then stepped back, hazel eyes wide. "What happened? What can I do?"

Something of his helplessness shifted. "I—I didn't know where else to go," he said simply.

How would they find one small, hurting child alone in the night, a child who likely had no wish to be found?

Chapter 15

$\mathcal{E}$benezer Scrooge crouched over a counting table where a meager fire sparked by two scant lumps of coal flickered. It was the scene for the live presentation of "A Christmas Carol." Tess watched the action with rapt enthusiasm in the 200-year-old theatre in upscale Gladstone. A renowned actor portrayed the acrimonious Scrooge, surrounded by a cast of local minions who were surprisingly adept and professional.

Tess had seen David outside the hospital only once since the night of the snowstorm. The Italian dinner she shared with him had ended when he was called away to attend a patient. She was more than surprised when he invited her to the semi-professional play in Gladstone. There was nothing she loved better than a good play, and Charles Dickens was a favorite. She had read every one of his novels, some for the third or fourth time.

She was surprised by David's attention after the disastrous evening of the blizzard when he rescued her and brought her to his condo. Throughout the evening, she'd been childish, remote, and even antagonistic, put off by his superior air and the way he ordered her around like a schoolgirl.

He had been courteous when their paths crossed again at the hospital, even kind. A time or two, she'd caught him looking at her, an inscrutable expression in his swarthy gaze. In a way, it made her uncomfortable, yet she felt flattered. What was wrong with her anyway that she needed approval from him of all people!

If the date tonight surprised her, she was even more surprised by the necklace that nestled now in the little hollow space on her throat. She felt it warm against her skin and repressed an urge to reach up and touch it.

"I have something for you," he had said just before they left her apartment for the play. "It isn't new. Actually, it's quite old, but I think it will look very nice on you."

He had handed it to her in a small white box. As soon as she opened it and saw the lovely oval pendant on its fragile chain, he'd snatched it back. "Let me put it on for you," he said. "Yes, it is just right with your dress. May I?"

She lifted her hair and shivered when his fingers brushed her neck as he secured the clasp. When she turned around to face him, he was staring at the necklace, a strange brooding expression in his eyes. She had waited, puzzled. She was no connoisseur of fine jewelry, but the pendant looked expensive. Should she accept it? Perhaps he meant for her to wear it just for the evening to show her off. And she'd felt a tinge of irritation. Had she been foolish to accept this date and this man's odd attentions—even for one night?

It should not be hidden in a box like a violet in the woods. Raising his eyebrows, he smiled in the teasing way he often did. *Yes, it's perfect for you. Do you like it?*

"Yes," she had stammered, "but you shouldn't ... "

He had laughed then and adjusted her coat around her shoulders. *Come. We don't want to be late. Ebenezer is waiting!*

She folded her hands in her lap as Scrooge lingered over his accounts in the makeshift office window. A group of carolers appeared in Victorian hats and jaunty scarves vibrant under the lights. They began their song, which, of course, she could not hear, but she knew it and traced the strains of "God Rest Ye, Merry Gentlemen" on their lips.

Even as she concentrated on the action on stage, she felt the heat of the pendant against her throat, puzzled over it, and wondered about the man who had given it to her. A lot about him was hard to understand, but she had little experience in co-ed relationships. What did a girl who'd never gone out on a date until she was nearly 20 know about such things? And David was nothing like Shane Eldridge or Peter.

The night of the blizzard, she had stayed awake for a long time in the room he had assigned her—his bedroom. Eventually, she drifted into a surprisingly sound sleep, and when she woke, he was gone. Her car had been cleared of snow, and a scrawled note lay on the kitchen counter.

Good morning, Lady Beatrice. I hope you slept well. Next time, check the weather news. Stay home when a blizzard is coming.

She'd been angry without really knowing why. Maybe it was his gallant old-world manner or the fact that he treated her like a child. And why call her "Beatrice"? No one called her that anymore. And how did he know her given name?

Now, in the darkened theater, their shoulders touched lightly. Glancing up, she saw that his rugged features were curiously softened. He was dressed for a night on the town but not overdressed. He'd even skipped the tie, choosing instead a burgundy jersey shirt that contrasted handsomely with a tweed jacket and charcoal trousers. He wore an unusual watch that looked finely made with a mix of yellow gold and white gold with tiny stones around its face. It might have been almost effeminate except for its large size and the way dark hairs curled around the expansion band.

Now and then, he turned to her. Sometimes, his eyes fell on the necklace. Sitting next to him made her feel worldly-wise and important. He was a doctor with cultured tastes and sophisticated friends. And she? She had been treated for so long like an invalid or worse. *Invalid—not valid, without worth.* She despised the word. But she was Alexei Popov's Deaf niece. His charge, really—the poor child no one wanted.

But her mother *had* wanted her, hadn't she? She couldn't help her sickness, and when she'd died, her grandmother had cared for her as long as she could. This was the woman everyone had been so curious about last summer, whose life in the famed House of Romanov had stirred debate and controversy. She had been only a child, the daughter of a servant, but had escaped the Bolshevik Revolution and made her way across an ocean to a strange country. Or so the legend went.

Were the jewels buried on Grace Arbor really part of that cache of treasure? She was glad they had been sold so that history buffs and treasure seekers were no longer snooping around. Grandmother, whoever she was, had left her enough money for comfort and security, not using even a portion of it to pay the mortgage on her estate. Sold for back taxes, it was now Grace Arbor, Anne Westin's home.

Tess had no memory of her mother, but Uncle Alexei had shown her pictures. Gentle blue eyes with an odd mix of impertinence and humor. Delicate skin, auburn hair, and softly chiseled lips that looked very sad.

Ever since Miss Morris had given her the photo, she had kept it carefully pressed in the pages of the Bible Anne Westin had given her. Sometimes, she took it out with trembling fingers to study it; other times, she avoided it as though it would burn if she touched it. She folded her arms across her stomach, feeling bereft and alone in the crowded theatre.

She felt a hand on her arm. "Are you enjoying the play so far?" David asked.

"Oh, yes," she said quickly. What had touched off her reverie into the past? Perhaps it was the scene where the spirit takes Scrooge back to his youth when he gives up his sweetheart because his heart is bent on making money. She wanted to call out, "No, Ebenezer, no. Don't let her go." She swallowed and pushed back her sudden tears.

The play moved quickly, too quickly. Tess wanted to live in it, to be one with it, to break into the ring of exuberant dancers and whirl across the stage. At last, Scrooge was hoisting Tiny Tim on his shoulders, his bleak old face transformed, and his bony hands clasping the boy's small legs. The Cratchitts pirouetted behind him with unrestrained joy, looking on old Ebenezer with love. What would it be like to be part of that familial effervescence? To be loved and cherished because you belonged?

Even when the curtain closed, and people began filing out of their seats, she was mesmerized, and tears threatened to spill over. She was aware of David watching her with a puzzled, half-amused expression. When she turned to him in embarrassment, he closed his eyes slowly and opened them again as if to say he understood how the pathos of the melodramatic scenes could move a young girl. He gave her his handkerchief and waited while she dabbed at her eyes. He must think her a romantic schoolgirl. How could he be expected to understand her longing to belong to someone, to be part of a real family?

She sniffed, gathered her coat, and moved out of the aisle, not looking back to see if he was following her. Her heart ached, and she was filled with yearning.

Matching her mood, David drove back quietly, almost taciturn. Occasionally, he glanced at her through peripheral vision but said nothing. When they stopped in front of her apartment, he set the gear and waited, his fingers lingering on the ignition key. It seemed like a long time before he spoke. "Thank you for coming, Tess."

She folded and refolded the strap of her handbag. He could have taken any one of a hundred girls, but he had chosen to spend the evening with her. And she had been wrapped up in her foolish thoughts. What must he think of her? "I had a wonderful time," she stammered. "And thank you for this." She put a nervous hand to her throat and began to unclasp the necklace.

He patted her hand down into her lap. "You think I want it back?" He laughed, and then his mood suddenly altered. "Come, I will see you to your door. I have early rounds tomorrow." He scrambled out and came around to her door, the smile lingering on his lips as he helped her out of the car.

A few struggling snowflakes filtered through the hard crust of sky as they walked to her apartment, his hand tucked lightly under her elbow. She had thought she might invite him in, be gracious and sophisticated in the elegant black dress she had so carefully chosen. She'd spent a small fortune on it. She had even bought a bottle of carbonated grape juice with a real cork and a gold foil label so they could toast the evening.

But now they stood in a little circle of light like two awkward strangers. He looked down at her with something like sadness or worry and then squared his shoulders as though reaching a decision. "You are tired," he said. "The doctor recommends a good night's sleep." He touched her cheek lightly with his lips. "I will see you at the hospital tomorrow. Good night, Lady Beatrice."

She backed into the foyer of her apartment building, tracing his retreating figure to the curb where he did not bother to turn or wave. He hadn't asked to come in or even vaguely pressed his attention. This wasn't the David she heard about in hospital gossip. Where was the easy-going, flamboyant playboy who'd dated most of the young women on the staff? Or was he simply not interested in a girl like her? She put her hand to her cheek and felt the pressure of his soft, undemanding kiss.

"He's not like that," she had protested to Peter. But was he? Was she fooling herself to accept his attention, and what was this strange attraction she felt? There was no more time to think about it because when she turned the corner to enter her apartment, she nearly stumbled over someone.

"Oh!" Jimmy was sitting on the floor, elbows on his knees, chin propped up on his hands. With his Badgers' cap pulled down over his ears, he seemed to be sleeping. Unruly hair stuck out under the cap like prickly red straw, and she saw that his hands were dirty. His boots lay in an untidy heap beside him. One sock was blue, the other green.

Grover leaped up and bounded toward her. Jimmy sat up sleepily and rubbed his eyes as Tess approached. A hint of a grin appeared on the pallid face. "Hi," he said, as though it was the most logical thing in the world for him to be waiting at her door at 11:00 o'clock at night.

"What are you doing here?"

He jumped up and pulled the grimy hat off his head, releasing the shock of red hair. He hesitated, then added, "Uncle Lance told me to come and stay with you. He had to show some clients a house." He looked away as though searching for something. The truth, perhaps.

"How long have you been here?" Tess asked, her hands weaving words madly in surprise.

"I was supposed to come by the hospital earlier and ask if I could stay, but I forgot." He chewed the inside of his left cheek. "It's okay, isn't it?"

She scrutinized the pale face, the enormous eyes that didn't quite look into hers. "But your uncle never said anything to me."

In the few weeks since his arrival, she and Jimmy had become friends. They'd shared frequent outings with Jimmy's Uncle Lance and with Mrs. Westin. They'd gone skiing, played Monopoly or Uno in Grace Arbor's cozy den, and sometimes made homemade pizza or chocolate chip cookies together. It would be hard to say goodbye to him when the holidays were over.

She spied the duffel bag, which looked much too big to contain a small boy's pajamas and toothbrush. She frowned and waited for him to explain himself.

Jimmy shrugged. "I brought some books and stuff," he said simply.

Tess looked from boy to dog and felt instantly protective. She folded her arms across her chest, knowing there had to be more to this story. She fixed him with an authoritative stare.

"It's okay, isn't it? I mean, if we stay with you? Just for tonight?" Jimmy peered up at her appealingly and gave her a sheepish grin. "We don't snore much."

She threw up her hands in mock surrender. "Come in before you wake the neighbors. I'm the only one Deaf around here, you know." She grinned at her witticism.

She fixed him a bologna sandwich and poured a bowl of Cheerios and milk for Grover. "You guys can sleep over there," she said, pointing to the striped couch in the sleeping area of her apartment. "You can make it into a bed, but Grover stays off!"

Jimmy stared at her strangely, and Grover cocked his furry head to one side. Tess realized that she had been speaking only with her hands. "I'm sorry," she said. I forgot you don't understand sign language!"

"Gee, I wish I could do that!" Jimmy breathed.

She laughed, suddenly glad for his sweet simplicity. Is this what it would be like to have a little brother, a boy to shepherd through the rigors of childhood with sisterly affection? She watched him pick up the last crumb of his sandwich and was filled up with affection for him. There was nothing hidden or false about him. At least, she'd never thought so before. But why was he at her door late at night with his bag packed?

"So you want to learn sign language. It's easy," Tess said. She formed the signs for "bed" and "sleep" and guided his unpracticed fingers. "There, that's right!" She pointed him to the couch and stood with arms folded until he made his way to the couch. "It's time you were sleeping, young man," she said with mock severity. "Do you know what time it is?"

He gave a little grimace and shrugged. Then, a roughish twinkle appeared in his eye. "I saw you with that doctor. You guys have a date?"

"Now, what makes you think so, young man?" she asked, pretending annoyance. She reached up to touch the necklace David had placed around her neck. The evening had ended before she could find out why he had presented her with it. She couldn't wait to examine it more closely.

"You sure look nice in that black dress and all."

"Well, thank you, Jimmy," she said and fixed him with a penetrating stare. "I'll tell you all about it if you'll tell me why you're here so late at night with your suitcase."

"It's not a suitcase," Jimmy said sharply. Then his pale bravado gave way, and he dropped his gaze to his feet. When he looked up again, his eyes were shiny with tears.

She put her arm around his small shoulders. "Why did you run away?"

He squirmed a little as though her touch would break his resolve. "They think I'm a thief," he blurted and crossed his thin arms over his nebulous stomach. "And now Uncle Lance's going to send me back. I know he will!" He covered his face with his hands. One of his fingernails had been chewed to the quick, and dark blood was dried around the cuticle.

An overwhelming tenderness gripped her. She pulled him around to face her, watching his lips intently. "Tell me!" she demanded.

"Mrs. Westin can't find her wedding rings," he said slowly. "She told my uncle I took them." He bit his lower lip. "I didn't take anything, I swear."

She put her arms around him, feeling his hard little boy body. She knew Jimmy had been in trouble. He'd been in several foster homes, but that was before—before she'd gotten to know him. Surely, he wouldn't take something that belonged to Mrs. Westin, whom he liked a lot.

She studied the red-rimmed eyes. Could he be lying? Shane had lied to her, and he had completely fooled her. Now, this little replica with the same compelling charisma was appealing to her.

"Did you tell your uncle you didn't do it?" she asked gently.

"He doesn't believe me. Told me to go up to my room and think about how I had treated him and his friends." Jimmy bit his lip again and dropped his head.

"So you just took off without telling anyone!" She lifted his chin to look at her. "Your uncle will be worried sick."

"No he won't. He's probably glad I've gone." A sob caught in his throat. "Please … I didn't know where else to go."

She studied him, feeling fiercely protective of the little boy she'd come to love. Should she just put him in the car and take him home now? But it was late and snowing heavily again. Jimmy was already exhausted, his face smudged from crying. She cradled him against her. "It's all right, Jimmy. Everything will be all right."

But things were not all right, and the world could be a cruel, unforgiving place. She breathed a long sigh and knew she'd decided on a course of action that might be a mistake. She removed the sofa cushions and began to make up his bed.

When he was ready, she tucked him in and smoothed his hair back, smiling at the way it made a red halo against the white pillow. When Grover jumped up on the bed, she didn't have the heart to make him get down. Let Grover give him comfort.

Was Mr. Crane out looking for Jimmy right now? She should let him know he was safe, but maybe he deserved to worry. He shouldn't have called Jimmy a liar and forced him to run away. People could be so cruel. Well, maybe in a little while, she'd text him, tell him Jimmy was with her. She switched off the small, beaded lamp and left Jimmy and Grover to their slumber.

In her room, she removed her black dress and carefully unclasped the necklace. There had been no time to study it before. Now, she could relive the beauty of the play's costumes and sets, the thrilling words of the classic story. She could think about David and the sweetness of sitting beside him in the darkened theatre.

She caressed the smooth oval surface of the necklace and turned it over in her hands to study the intricate scrollwork. She touched the smooth edges of the beautiful piece and felt a tiny bulge at one side. A hinge. She tucked her fingernail in the aperture, and the locket separated.

She gasped. Looking back at her was the face of her mother!

Chapter 16

*A*nne stared restlessly into the darkness beyond Grace Arbor's bay window. The storm had slowed, and a ragged moon shimmered through the dusty pall.

It had been hours since Lance stood dejected in her doorway, the marks of strain etched in his handsome face as he recounted Jimmy's disappearance. She'd heard nothing since. Why had the boy run away in the dead of winter? Her rings weren't worth such drastic measures. If he had just returned them, she'd have forgiven him. *Dear Lord,* she whispered, trying not to think how deadly Wisconsin winters could be. *Watch over him.*

She looked down at her hands, at the fingers bare of rings. Her suspicions had sent him away. He was out alone in the snow because of her! What if Jimmy wasn't guilty? What if something happened to him?

She made a tent of her fingertips. She hadn't actually accused him, not straight out. She had only said to Lance that Jimmy *might* have taken her rings. It was a logical assumption, wasn't it? Jimmy had been expelled from school and gotten into trouble for stealing before.

She thought about the afternoon she and Lance had coaxed her Christmas tree into submission. They had laughed as they looked for its best side. She gazed at the tree, its imperfections cleverly disguised by strategically placed ornaments.

She glanced down at her silk blouse—the same one she'd worn that afternoon but without the sap. The stain had been eradicated, but not the memory of his touch. Her heart had begun a journey toward Lance, but what would happen now? Would they be left with only the burnt-out ends of a wary friendship?

Lance had reacted badly when she'd talked to him about the theft. In retrospect, it was only natural that he would be sensitive after the disastrous events his other nephew had set in motion. Now, the twelve-year-old brother entrusted to Lance was in similar trouble. She stared gloomily at the white landscape beyond the window. Things had certainly not gone well with her new neighbors. She wanted them to accept her and trust her, but so far, she was batting zero.

Well, perhaps not exactly zero. At least Tess no longer considered her an enemy. They could talk now and share thoughts as trust began to develop between them. Tess was learning to trust the God who loved her, too. It would hurt Tess to know Jimmy was following in the dishonest steps of his brother. She had grown fond of the boy, though her attention may have been diverted in recent days. Anne longed for the games and the lively cheer that had filled the house when the two visited Grace Arbor. It was sad to think that those days might be gone forever.

No, things were not going well at all. Jimmy had run away; Margaret wasn't getting well and refused to leave the nursing home where her friends were dying; Vera continued her brooding avoidance, and Tess was involved somehow with the mysterious, much-rumored Dr. David Brevitz.

"I'm sure it's just a passing fancy," she had told Peter over the phone. The uncomfortable silence that followed underscored her suspicion. Tess had become much more than a friend to her son.

Snow began to fall again. She watched the flakes flock against the panes like small white birds. She traced their busy path for a while and then looked beyond to the spindly hedge of winter bushes that separated Grace Arbor from Vera Popov's little house. Vera's back porch, usually lit all day long and through the night, now lay shrouded in darkness. Vera was afraid of the dark and always left a light burning in the house—even when she slept. How strange that Vera hadn't replaced the burned-out bulb on her porch, leaving her little house in utter darkness.

She sighed wearily and let the curtain fall from her fingers. She and Vera never shared so much as a greeting over the back hedge. She'd learned more about her neighbor's background since the story of buried treasure had hit the local papers earlier that year. Vera had been raised in an orphanage in Moscow. Alexei, also orphaned, had been sent far away from his sister. Many years later, when both were adults, Alexei brought his sister to live with him in a small Russian village near Yekaterinburg, where he was employed as a household servant to Tess's grandmother.

Local gossip suggested that Tess's grandmother might have been a child of a servant in the house of the Romanov dynasty that ended in 1918 when Bolsheviks ordered the assassination of the entire family, along with their servants. In 1991, when the bodies were exhumed in Yekaterinburg, it was discovered that two children were missing. Some believed that they had escaped their captors, possibly taking some of the family jewels with them. It was the stuff of legends, giving rise to such films as Twentieth Century Fox's "Anastasia."

The fate of the servants and the children of the servants had been largely overlooked in the search for the Romanov children and for family jewels allegedly sewn inside the women's clothing. Had the little girl who became Tess's grandmother carried jewels with her when she fled Russia?

A local Wisconsin reporter speculated that it might be so. No one knew why the woman had settled in the small Wisconsin town with her baby granddaughter or why she had put a down payment on the property that years later became Grace Arbor. When she was dying, she had entrusted the baby to the care of Alexei and Vera, who had traveled with her from Russia and for whom she had built the small house behind Grace Arbor. But if the elderly dowager had buried valuable jewels, why had she failed to make her mortgage payments and foreclosed on her property?

Vera hadn't shared Alexei's love for the little girl, but Alexei had been adamant. So it was that Tess had come to live with them, and Grace Arbor had been sold to recover back taxes. Vera's resentment was palpable. Perhaps she thought Grace Arbor should have been hers in exchange for her loyalty and for taking in the little Deaf baby with no mother or father.

Anne felt a renewed twinge of anger as she studied the dark porch beyond the hedge. Well, Vera might resent her neighbor for buying Grace Arbor, but she had no legal claim to it. And simple-minded or not, she had no business trashing Grace Arbor's land with the refuse from her hen house.

In spite of everything, she couldn't help feeling sorry for Vera. The woman's self-image had likely been deeply damaged. Who knew what she had suffered in a Russian orphanage, what terrors made her sullen, aloof, and sharp-tongued? A few historians had made the trek to Ladystone after the discovery was made public. Now, the furor had died down, but the small town would likely always lay claim to its notoriety.

Anne turned back into the kitchen. Vera must be lonely and hungry for a kind word, though she gave so few away to others. Perhaps she would welcome a bit of holiday cheer. Anne began to fill a tin with frosted angels, red-sugared bells, and green trees with white icing. She felt her depression lift. It was better to do something constructive than sit at home and wait to hear from Lance.

She put on her boots and traipsed across the snowy expanse that separated Grace Arbor from the small Popov house. She passed the wooded area where Alexei had been found dead last summer and jumped when an owl hooted. It was so dark. Why hadn't she thought to bring a flashlight?

She quickened her steps to the rickety porch where a skinny cat with luminous eyes huddled against the back door. "Out in the cold too, are you?" she crooned softly, comforted by the sound of her own voice.

The cat gave a raspy meow and threaded in and out of her legs. Anne waited on the dark porch, listening, but no sound issued from inside. She peered through the little square of glass at the top of the door but saw only reflected night. She walked around the house, snow from the high drifts sliding inside her boots.

All was dark and quiet in the front of the house as well. Perhaps Vera had gone away, though she seldom left the house. Anne began to turn back with her gift of cookies when she heard a moaning sound, low and chilling. Wind in the pines, perhaps? Her pulse quickened, and a shiver raced up her spine.

"Was that you?" she asked the cat, but it was no catlike mewling; it sounded human. She stiffened. "Vera? You there, Vera?" She rapped louder. "Are you all right?" She turned the knob and pushed the door open.

She was greeted by silence and a fetid, yeasty smell like warm eggs. The cat bounded past her, and she nearly tripped over it. "Vera?" She groped for a light switch. A dim light revealed an old Formica table on which egg cartons, rumpled towels, and dirty dishes were scattered. Anne dropped the tins on the table's scarred surface and hurried deeper into the house.

And suddenly, she found Vera on the floor, propped on one elbow, her face contorted in pain. Her right arm stuck out at a strange angle. She struggled to pull herself up, and Anne could see that there was blood on the shoulder of her dress. A lamp lay in broken shards on the floor next to her.

She rushed in and knelt beside her. "Vera, what happened?"

Vera was sweating profusely, her black hair straggling about her flushed face. "My leg," she muttered through clenched teeth. "I trip on lamp."

Anne covered her with a blanket and dialed 911 on an ancient black telephone. She found a cloth in the lean-to bathroom and gently swabbed the gash on Vera's arm. She eased the heavy woman's head onto a dingy bath towel she'd grabbed from a rack. "You'll be all right," she said soothingly. "How long have you been lying here?"

The little coal-like eyes closed, and her head wagged from side to side, but when the whine of the emergency vehicle sounded, her eyes flew open. A mask of fright replaced the contempt Anne usually saw in the harsh features.

"It's all right," she whispered. "They'll help you." Thank God they didn't live that far from town. The scream of the ambulance, the flashing lights, and the sound of strange voices seemed to terrify Vera. "Help is here. They'll know what to do," Anne whispered. She patted Vera's plump hands. "They'll take care of you. Try not to worry."

Vera was placed gently into the ambulance, but as the attendant began to close the rear gate of the vehicle, she reached out her good left arm, waving her fingers in alarm. "My chickens! My chickens!"

Anne leaned inside the ambulance. "I'll see to them," she said gently. "And I'll get word to Tess. Everything will be all right, you'll see."

When the siren's drone ended, she secured her neighbor's door and headed toward the low coops. She had promised to take care of the birds, and now was as good a time as any to make sure they were fed and secured in the storm.

The hens clucked and fretted as she entered. Feathers and debris curled and spun in the chilly air. Several of the birds rose defensively, shook themselves in warning, and then settled down again over their shelled embryos.

"There, there," she crooned softly, removing a wicker basket from an enormous bent nail. The basket was broken in several places, and sharp pieces of straw cut her hand. She grimaced, wishing for a pair of gardening gloves. "Hush. It's all right," she cajoled. "No one's going to hurt you."

Suddenly a large biddy flew straight up from its nest and fluttered high above the rafters, shrieking as it went. It perched on a top beam and peered down through glassy eyes. Anne's breath caught in her throat.

She had done this once long ago when she was a girl spending summers with her cousin. As a city girl, she'd been nervous. *Won't they bite me when I try to take their eggs?*

"Stare me down if you want," she said now to the hovering bird. "You can lay some more children later." She moved from cubicle to cubicle, reaching beneath each warm hen, extracting three or four eggs, and grinning at the silly prattle with which she comforted herself.

She liked the way the eggs felt in her hand—little smooth spheres of budding life. Really, they were little miracles.

Nearly finished, she thrust her hand under a great hen with glassy eyes and ghostly pale markings. The hen made no sound as Anne gently probed beneath it. It cocked its head nervously. Suddenly, her fingers touched something hard, something that was definitely not an egg. "Out you go," she said, prodding the protesting hen. "Let's see what you've got in there." She pushed a little more forcefully, and it fluttered off to a nearby perch to regard her fussily. Through a small, smudged window, moonlight cast a beam directly over the nest to reveal the objects she had felt—two rings with gleaming stones shimmered in concert with her racing heart.

Her wedding rings!

What were they doing under a hen in a smelly nest? Anne cradled the rings like lost children come home, wiping them on the tails of her shirt. She slipped them on her finger, her heart thumping wildly as she examined them for scratches or blemishes. She turned her hand over and over, exulting in the loved objects.

So it had been Vera all along. Vera, who always thought Grace Arbor should have been hers. She had tried to discover where her poor, demented brother had buried jewels that were to be Tess's inheritance. Why hadn't it occurred to her before?

Vera was like a child with a shiny toy. Anne recalled the intriguing brooch the woman wore so proudly in the middle of her broad chest. It might have been sold for a lot of money and gone a long way toward repairing the decrepit old shack and adding onto the chicken runs. Instead, Vera clung to the jewel, wore it continually like a badge of honor.

Anne dropped down on an old chair covered with paint spills and willed her pulse to slow down as she sniffed at the stale air. It was the same odor—a mix of yeast and onions—which she had detected at Grace Arbor. But it was, in fact, the undeniable odor of a chicken coop.

Vera had been in her house. Anne could feel the hammering of her heart. The sense of violation, of outrage, threatened to overwhelm her. She scooped up the basket of eggs and raced away from the fetid henhouse.

Snow that had been falling haphazardly now descended with a vengeance. Trees and overhead wires swayed in the rushing wind. Surprised by the quick turn of the weather, she hurried back to Grace Arbor. With sickening dread, she realized the implications. Jimmy had been falsely accused and was out alone in the night.

"Oh, my Lord! Don't let my stupidity bring him harm!" she whispered through chattering teeth. "Please watch over him."

She heaved a sigh. Power failures were nothing new. They happened in summer or winter with sometimes the slightest provocation. Sometimes, the blackout lasted only a few minutes, but at other times, it continued for hours.

She lit the oil lamps that usually served as decorations and built up the fire in the living room. She'd have to spend the night there, stay close to the fire, and wait for electricity to be restored. Thank God the power hadn't gone off before she could make the 911 call from Vera's house phone.

The phone! She grabbed the receiver and punched in Lance's number, but the line had gone dead. She sat down on the couch, pulled the afghan up, and wrapped herself in it. The house would grow chilly quickly in these temperatures. That settled it; as soon as this was over, she'd buy a cell phone. She never should have put it off this long. Peter had tried to convince her she needed one ever since she'd come north.

Wrapped in the afghan, she locked the front door and lingered at the stairwell with her hand on the mahogany rail. She was too tired to go upstairs for a gown or robe. Besides, it was too dark to see, and she was too cold to think of undressing. She sank onto the couch, glad for its nearness to the fireplace, and huddled under the afghan. She'd have to wait until power was restored to learn the extent of Vera's injury and Jimmy's fate as well.

Chapter 17

Anne woke in a daze on her living room couch. The afghan had fallen to the floor, and both table lamps shone uselessly in the morning light that crept through the blinds. The fire had smoldered into ashes, but the house was warm. Power must have been restored sometime during the night. How long had she been asleep?

She sat up, aware of a crimp in her neck, and pulled back the drapes. A snow-spent sky brooded against the pale landscape, and somewhere in the distance, plows were at work on the roads. The ever-efficient road crew, bless them! She rubbed her eyes and willed herself fully awake.

The telephone was ringing. Was there news of Jimmy? She hurried to the kitchen where lights left on the night before blazed indifferently. Stretching against the ache in her back, she picked up the phone.

"Mom?" Peter's voice broke through the mild static on the line. "Are you all right? I've been calling since early last night." She could hear the agitation in his voice and felt instantly penitent.

"I'm fine, Peter. We had something of a blizzard last night, and the power went out. I'm so sorry to worry you." She cleared her throat, still scratchy from the smoke of the fireplace.

"You have a cold?"

"No. It's just my scratchy morning throat." She warmed to his quick concern. She could almost see the little furrow that hovered between his eyes when he was worried. "I slept on the couch by the fire, but I'm fine, Peter."

"Well, that's a relief. Now, if you hadn't refused to join the 21st century, you could have kept me from going crazy with worry. You're getting a cell phone for Christmas whether you want it or not."

She laughed. She'd had the same thought. As her head cleared, the events of the previous evening replayed. She had found Vera on the floor, and after Vera was taken to Ladystone General, she had found her rings in the henhouse. But what about Jimmy? Perhaps he was home safe and sound with Lance by this time. "I found my rings," she told Peter.

"That's great news." He waited, but she felt too tired to talk about it. There were too many gaps to fill. She didn't want to discuss her suspicions and the disagreement with Lance, nor did she want to broach the subject of Tess and Dr. Brevitz. "I'll tell you about it when you get here, and don't worry about the roads. They've got snowplowing down to a science. I heard them going at it already."

"Okay, Mom. I'm hoping to quit early. See you soon."

"Can't wait. Love you," she said, replacing the receiver before he could ask about plans for the party. Besides, if she didn't get moving, there'd be no party. Then again, what kind of party would it be, given the state of things at the present moment? It wouldn't be much of a festive occasion without Lance, and she felt a vague emptiness in the pit of her stomach.

Hardly had she moved from the telephone when it rang again. Peter had forgotten something. She picked up the receiver but did not check the caller's ID.

"Anne Westin?" A woman's voice—tremulous and throaty—startled her.

It was a local number but appeared as "unknown," the kind of call she usually did not answer. She responded wearily, wishing she hadn't so rashly picked up. "Yes, this is Anne Westin."

"I've seen you...here." The voice, with its unfamiliar accent, paused.

"Please, I can't hear you," Anne said, aware that her mind was still a bit hazy from the long night on the couch. She massaged her temples, irritated. "Who is this?" she demanded.

"I can't talk long," came the guarded response. "Margaret's in trouble. I told her not to get mixed up in this."

"Margaret? What's wrong with Margaret?" Anne stammered, jolted wide awake, and saw that the clock on the wall was poised at 4:00 a.m.—the time the power must have resumed.

The voice became more urgent. "I have to go." A click and the connection was broken.

Who was this anonymous caller? A resident of Rutgers? What trouble could Margaret be in? Anne consulted her digital watch. What would prompt someone to call at 7:30 in the morning? And what had the woman meant about not getting mixed up in...in what? The caller kept her voice low as if afraid of being overheard.

She hesitated only a moment, her thoughts turning to frantic prayer, then punched in Lance's number. *Margaret!* How hard the world could be on the old and the very young—the vulnerable ones who couldn't fight for themselves. She waited. Four rings. Five.

"Leave a number; I'll return your call."

Was Lance still out looking for his nephew? Or had Jimmy been found? Perhaps the two were having a leisurely breakfast at a local pancake house. *Oh, God, let it be so.* But there was no time to deal with the doubt and guilt. She needed to talk about the woman's strange telephone call and thought of Lance immediately. But she'd have to handle this alone.

She quickly scanned her address book and found the number. The professional voice responded after two rings. "Rutgers Residence. How may I direct your call?"

"Margaret Morris, please. Room 204," Anne said confidently.

A pause followed, then a calm response. "I'm sorry. Miss Morris can't receive calls right now. Would you like to leave a message?"

Some invisible hammer tapped at Anne's temples. "No, I would like to speak to Miss Morris," she said, surprised by the granite edge in her voice. "Would you ring her room please?"

"I'm sorry. The order says she's not to be disturbed. I'll be happy to take a message."

"Let me speak to Helen Rutgers," Anne interrupted.

"I'm sorry. She won't be in until 9:00. Would you care to leave a message?"

Anne hit the disconnect button and cradled the receiver in both hands. She peered through the window into the sullen sky. What should she do? Something about that pause after she'd asked for Margaret bothered her. Or was it her imagination? She should have said it was important, that she'd received a phone call saying that Margaret might be in trouble. She began to redial and stopped.

Racing up the steps, she grabbed the first clothes that came to hand—gray wool slacks and a pink turtle neck sweater. She slipped them on quickly and ran a brush through her hair. She struggled into her boots and parka while dialing Lance's number again. Still the annoying answering machine. This time, she left word that she was on her way to Rutgers. Something had happened to Margaret. She paused and added breathlessly, "Please let me know if Jimmy's all right."

She forged her way down the unplowed driveway, marveling at her daring and praising her good sense in having installed snow tires. Giddily, she reached the road that had only moments ago been cleared. She pressed hard on the accelerator and headed into town.

Anne had planned to go directly to Margaret's room without preamble, but before she could move past the desk, a voice penetrated. "Excuse me. May I help you?" The woman with meticulously sculpted braids had a forthright manner and arresting dark eyes.

"I know it's early, but I must see Miss Morris." Anne stepped past the desk and prepared to head down the hall.

The receptionist rose and put out a restraining hand. "I'm sorry. The patients are being bathed and dressed right now. You will have to wait. Visiting hours begin at nine ... "

"But, it's important! I have to see her now." Anne smiled to soften the urgency in her voice. "You see, I received this call. I must know if Margaret's all right."

"Please, wait here a moment. Let me check."

Anne watched anxiously as the receptionist traced names on a piece of paper. "Morris," she repeated in a lilting Caribbean accent, her dark eyes sympathetic. "Miss Morris has been placed in an isolation room. That's why there's a no-visitors order. I'm sorry."

Anne stared into the compelling eyes. *How could that be? Margaret had been improving!* "What—what's wrong with her?"

"I'm sorry. I don't have that information," the receptionist answered, "but I can assure you it's not unusual. Infections can crop up very quickly. When they do, we must be very careful so that they do not spread to other patients." She gave a professional smile. "I'm sure it's nothing to be unduly concerned about."

"I see," Anne said, fighting rising panic. "I'd like to speak with the doctor then."

"Doctor won't be in until later. It is very early now."

"Ms. Rutgers then. Let me speak to her."

The attendant consulted a watch on her smooth brown wrist. "She should be along soon. Would you like to wait?" She pointed to a small waiting room near the entrance.

Anne felt the insistent pressure of the woman's hand on her arm and felt oddly violated. She hesitated, wondering if worry was causing her to overreact. "How long? How long has Margaret been in isolation?"

"Just since yesterday. I can assure you we're watching her very carefully." The innocent words took on sinister significance in Anne's bewildered mind. Margaret had been suspicious about her friends dying and about absent or belated obituaries. She had been watching the movements at Rutgers. Was she now the one being watched? But that was absurd, wasn't it?

Dazed, she allowed herself to be guided toward the waiting room. She prepared to sit when Helen Rutgers suddenly appeared at the end of the hall. She had obviously been in the building; she wasn't even carrying a coat. Anne watched her move slowly toward the nurses' station, her shoulders in an emerald-green suit slightly hunched as though she were very tired or anxious. Stray blond hairs escaped a chignon at the neckline of her jacket. Helen's face was white beneath a layer of powder, and two spots of blush hadn't been worked in properly. Large, round glasses in gaudy frames did not hide the dark circles under her eyes.

Anne watched, puzzled by the shapely, worldly-wise Helen who seemed so out of place in the small, unsophisticated town of Ladystone. Margaret had reported that she grew up here. *Her mother ran a local beauty shop, and we were never sure what business her father was in.*

Well, Margaret ought to know. She'd taught elementary school in Ladystone for more than 30 years, and Helen had been one of her students. Anne recalled Margaret saying that the girl had never been a good student, that at fourteen, she went to live with some aunt in Phoenix. That was terribly young to be separated from her parents, but, as Margaret had said, she'd returned looking very much the socialite and with enough gumption to get into the healthcare industry.

Anne moved out of the little ante-room, unable to wait any longer for Helen to complete her journey to the vestibule. Something had happened to Margaret, and she had to find out what it was. She brushed past the Caribbean receptionist and marched down the hall toward Helen.

"I understand my friend Margaret Morris is ill. I want to see her, please."

Helen adjusted her glasses and stared at Anne quizzically. She appeared confused and uncharacteristically rumpled. Perhaps the storm had kept her at the nursing home all night, or some difficult situation had ensued. She folded her arms and cleared her throat. "Miss Morris is in isolation. It's standard procedure when one of our patients comes down with an infection."

"What's wrong with her?" Anne countered.

Helen's remarkable eyes flashed green in the fluorescent light and darted back and forth behind Art Deco frames. "We don't know. We've phoned the doctor. I'm sure he'll order some tests. He may want to hospitalize her." Helen shifted her weight to her left foot and placed her right hand at her waist. Painted nails drummed nervously against her hip.

"I want to see her," Anne said abruptly.

"Sorry," Helen said, turning away. "That's against policy. Also, it's for your own protection as well as the protection of our patients. We'll advise you as soon as it's safe for her to have guests."

Anne felt pinpricks at her temples. Something was wrong. Isolation didn't mean a person couldn't visit. With proper precautions—a gown and a mask—one could at least see the patient. Besides, someone had called to say Margaret was in trouble. She started to share that fact with Helen but stopped. None of this made any sense. "I just want to see her. I won't even go near the bed," she appealed in her most conciliatory tone.

Helen whipped around then, both hands fixed impatiently on her hips. Her tapered nails made little scraping sounds against the fabric of her suit, but her voice remained steady. "We cannot endanger guests or further expose our patients to infection from the outside."

"Surely you have protective clothing," Anne said, equally undaunted. "I'll take responsibility. You know that Margaret has no family, but I am a close friend." She took a step closer. They were only inches apart, and they faced each other off in a silent duel.

Helen waited with tight lips for a few tense seconds. Then, an indulgent smile transformed her rigid features. "Very well," she said, removing the glittering spectacles. "Give me a minute, and I'll take you to her." She stepped to the desk and said something to the receptionist. She turned back to Anne. "Now, Mrs. Westin. If you'll follow me, please."

Anne followed Helen's high-heeled steps. Patients watched as they walked past. Some lingered in doorways, and others looked up from their beds. *Which one had called? Did anyone appear agitated? Did anyone look at her strangely?* Their faces revealed nothing.

"I'll pick up a couple of masks from supply," Helen said, ducking into a hall closet. In a moment, she returned with two blue gowns. Red fingernail polish had worn partially away, and two nails had been bitten to the quick. Helen tossed one of the gowns to Anne. She moved down the hall with squared shoulders.

They negotiated two more long hallways—past offices, exam rooms, bath and shower facilities, and closed doors bearing empty name plaques. Helen kept walking. They came to a section of the building where ceiling repairs were underway, and Helen stopped. Beads of sweat shone on her blonde upper lip.

Anne felt a small shiver race down her spine. Was it really necessary to move a patient so far from the others? Where was the nurses' station in this part of the building? She glanced around for monitoring devices, her mind whirling. This was no place for a sick patient!

"Here we are," Helen suddenly announced in a placating voice as though assuring a travel-weary child. She faced Anne and smiled. "Now we'll just don our glad rags."

Anne pushed her arms through the sleeves and secured the gown at her neck as Helen placed a mask across her own face. Her eyes were as green as her suit and strangely mesmerizing, her pupils enormous behind the glasses. *Magnifiers?*

"Now let me help you with yours." Helen pulled a second mask from her suit pocket and stepped behind Anne to tie it.

As the gauzy fabric closed over Anne's nose and mouth, she clenched her fists tightly at her sides and took a deep breath. She had never liked anything over her face. Once, when she was a child playing cowboys and Indians at her cousin's farm, a neighbor boy had gagged her. She'd had a cold and was sure she would be asphyxiated on the spot.

Now, she steeled herself against the rising panic as the mask tightened over her cheeks and ears. Helen turned her slowly. Anne stared into the eyes with their glittering magnetism and wondered if it really was possible to be hypnotized. She had never thought so. She felt lightheaded. It was strange that a childhood prank could cause such consternation at her age. Anne tried to reach up to touch the mask, but her fingers refused to move.

MARLENE CHASE

"There we are." Helen's voice was fluid like music. Anne felt the panic falling away. Yes, she felt much calmer now. The mask seemed to envelop her like a soft, billowy cloud, and she became aware of a sweet smell, even as the mask tightened against her head. Too tight.

"Please!" She tried to say, but the mask was too tight; she was having trouble talking. Strange. How odd to feel sleepy now.

The voice behind her drifted in a dreamlike cadence. Then she felt an arm around her waist, supporting, lifting. She had a sense of falling gently, slowly, and then, she felt nothing more at all.

Chapter 18

*D*avid drove toward Rutgers Care Home, half-formed thoughts tumbling over one another like frustrated hounds with no scent to follow. It was Sunday, and a sabbatical stillness spread across the landscape. A blinding sun shone on new snow as he prepared to make his rounds at the nursing home and, later, the hospital. It would be a day like any other. Routine, steady, normal. But none of those comforting attributes applied, he thought bitterly. He'd made an utter mess of things, and nothing would ever be right again.

He concentrated on maneuvering his car over snow-packed roads, which were less trafficked today than on weekday mornings. That might be cause for gratitude, but he felt no sense of well-being, only dread and defeat. He frowned at his reflection in the rear-view mirror, half expecting his hair to have turned white.

His journey had spanned continents and driven him from city to city, and now that the search was over—now that he had found out the truth about Victoria Grainger and the child she had borne, he had come to a dead end.

For ten years, he had looked for Victoria, moved from place to place, and dealt with the intricacies of immigration and medical licensing boards. But his time had run out. He had stayed in

Ladystone too long, and though the legal machinations in a small town such as the one in which he'd taken refuge ground more slowly than most, it couldn't be long until it was discovered that his work visa had expired. He no longer had legal authority to practice medicine there.

He should have moved on, but how could he leave without being sure Tess was the one? He'd suspected who Beatrice Popov really was, but not until last night had he taken the daring step that would bring his world crashing down. He half expected a thunderbolt to unleash an explosion, but all around him, the glittering white snow lay serene to the point of madness!

Victoria's child—his child— had been radiant at the theatre as she sat next to him, eyes beneath finely sculpted brows shining with sapphire brilliance. She had reveled in the poignant drama. She kept her expressive hands in her lap, except when joining the audience to clap in appreciation. She watched his hands and stopped when he did, a studied expression on her face. How odd to clap and hear nothing and how clever to find a way to join in without mistake. Ah, the cruel ironies of life. She had every right to be bitter, to curse the capricious fates for her silent world, but she did not.

He was filled with unaccustomed joy with her beside him, her amber hair swept up regally off delicate shoulders. What would it be like if her head should droop and touch his own? How would her silken hair feel against his cheek? If she knew how he longed to take her hands in his own, to protect her from harm! Only with supreme effort had he managed to pay some scant attention to what was happening on the stage when the action in his heart was larger than life and about to explode.

She was so like Victoria—the girl he had loved in the tender angst of his 18th year. The same delicate bones and translucent skin—like fine china, the same eyes blue as the Mediterranean and as changeable. He rubbed the ache settling in his left temple. They had met at the university, two European exchange students thousands of miles from their native land. In their desperate loneliness, they had clung to each other.

When she said it was over, he'd begged her to reconsider. Then, at the end of his term, he'd gone back to Russia, not knowing that new life stirred in her. He wouldn't know she was dead and that he had fathered a child until nearly a decade had passed.

"I didn't know," he whispered as he drove through the hushed countryside. It had been twenty years, but he was still haunted by the knowledge that somewhere, a child lived—a child for whom life had not been kind. Not only had she been born Deaf, but she'd been left an orphan in the care of old servants, one slow-minded and bitter, the other the only bright light in the child's life. And he was dead.

He thought about the day he had seen her in the hospital cafeteria. He had nearly dropped his tray. She was so like Victoria, with her queenly stature, gently rounded shoulders, and neck as fragile as a lily's stem. But it was her nose, slightly larger than the other features and with the little bump on its bridge, that spoke of his lineage. Was it possible he had found his child for whom he had searched so long?

He had to be sure. He'd taken her to the play and given her the necklace. Of course, he had known she would eventually open it. He'd kept her from examining it during the evening, clasping it around her lovely neck himself. It hadn't taken her long to find out that the pendant separated to hold a tiny, ancient photograph of her long-lost mother.

It was just after seven the next evening when, with no interest in food, he'd decided on coffee and three-day-old muffins for his supper. He'd been giving half-hearted attention to the news when she came to his condo. She stood in the open doorway, moonlight shining a ghostly blue on the snowy world behind her. Her violet eyes had pierced him with fiery clarity in the dim light as she held the necklace in a trembling hand.

How did you get this?

He had wanted to tell her that he had been searching for her in every young girl he met. He wanted her to know that he had never forgotten her mother, that nothing in his life had been more important than finding their child. But he hadn't been able to tell her.

What a cowardly, shocking way to reveal his identity. Well, he *was* a coward, he admitted to himself. And so, his mind a bewildering chaos, he had faced her in the eerie moonlight. His child! No longer a child but a woman. How could he explain his behavior toward her—dating his daughter?

The night of the blizzard, he insisted that she stay the night in his apartment. She had been angry when she left. Still, she had not refused his invitations for lunch, a play, or dinner. It was a dangerous game he was playing with her, a game that no one would win.

When she had confronted him with the necklace, He'd stammered like a tongue-tied child. *Beatrice ... please ...*

What were you doing with my mother's picture? Her lips quivered with the effort at pronunciation, but her jaw remained rigid. Icy air swept through the open door and ruffled the fire-lit hair beneath the loose hood of her green coat.

Please come inside. Let me explain.

What must she be thinking? He had deliberately given the appearance of the dashing ladies' man, the suave, mature doctor who dated every young attendant and nurse at the hospital. How else could he find the one young woman for whom he searched? Oh, it was crazy, bizarre. What must she think of him?

I don't want to come in. Her voice was sharp as honed steel. *And I don't want this!*

She dropped the necklace at his feet, and it sprang open on the hardwood floor. Victoria's sepia image looked up in silent accusation as the beautiful daughter, so like the mother, turned on her heel and left him standing in the doorway.

Now, he drove mindlessly toward the building that housed the old and sick and felt akin to them. Where would all this deception end?

The thing that lay between him and Beatrice was not the only burden weighing on his beleaguered mind as he approached Rutgers Nursing Home. There was the collusion with Helen. It was innocent enough in the beginning, but then there were questions and rumors of investigations. He had grown more and more suspicious that she was caught up in some dangerous game and had swept him into it.

Helen had smoothed things over for him with the authorities. He never asked how she managed it but had agreed to look after the medical needs of the patients and to leave the business to her. He told himself that the patients were cared for and that Helen was playing by the rules. But she had grown secretive, more and more possessive. Often, she would whip away documents he put his name on without giving him a chance to read them.

The threat hung unspoken in the air. Unless he agreed to her terms, she could ruin his chances to remain in the country. She would make it impossible to look for his daughter. He had been unable to think clearly about anything else.

Pain seared David's throat; his eyes stung as he steered through the snow. He must not lose her again! No matter what the consequences to his life and work, he could not let her go. It surprised him that there were still wells of anguish from which to generate tears. Cold fear gripped him. What did it mean for the residents of the care home? Had Helen snapped? What was she willing to do to keep what she had worked so hard for? Would she even endanger vulnerable old people she was pledged to care for?

I want Morris released by the end of the week. He recalled Helen's demand and his protest that the woman was not well enough to go home. Had Miss Morris learned something that threatened Helen's position? Was this woman who had befriended Victoria's child asking embarrassing questions?

An ironic smile tugged at his lips. Beatrice's grandmother had been clever. She had left an inheritance for Tess, and two women in the town had helped to protect it—Anne Westin and Margaret Morris. Gratitude sprang up in his heart, along with shame. They had done well. He, on the other hand, had failed his child and perhaps the patients who trusted him as well.

He gripped the steering wheel with painful force. There must be no more deception, no signing of papers he could not first authenticate. There could be no more hiding from Beatrice either, even though she surely despised him. He had been a coward, but no more! He found himself calling out to the God he'd been taught to believe did not exist. Next year he would be 40. A thousand regrets bore down on his shoulders.

The long brick structure with its terra cotta face came into view. Holly wreaths hung in each window of Rutgers Nursing Home. In the foyer beyond, he could see a tree sparkling with starry brilliance. Soon, the ailing residents would celebrate whatever magic Christmas might yet hold after centuries of mishap and mayhem.

He pulled into the reserved parking spot at Rutger's Nursing Home, knowing he could carry those regrets and secrets no longer. The coward's way had brought only pain to himself and others. He must find a way to make things right! Could they ever be right again?

He watched the movement of his bootless feet on the sidewalk. His steps in carefully polished black shoes propelled him with leaden slowness toward some dark end from which there would be no escape. He raised his head to the bleak landscape and was suddenly aware that he was not alone.

A large, shaggy dog leaped around from the rear of the building, followed by a small boy with bright red hair beneath a blue ski cap. The boy dropped to his knees and snapped a leash to the dog's collar. David had seen that dog. Margaret Morris's dog! The one Anne Westin had smuggled into the nursing home. The boy, with his impish face and spray of burgundy freckles, had been there too. He had heard Beatrice speak of him with a soft light in her eyes.

And suddenly, *she* stepped out from the side of the building. David's pulse raced, and his throat went dry. *His daughter!*

She was wearing a long dark skirt, high-top boots, and a white fur jacket. Around her head, a green scarf whipped in the wind like a brilliant flag. She saw him and quickly turned her head away, but she didn't move from the boy's side. What were they doing there? He walked faster, keeping pace with his quickened heartbeat.

"Hello!" he called.

He saw the dog bound toward him but couldn't take his eyes off his daughter's face. Even in profile, he could see that her features were clouded, worried, or ... what? Had Helen thrown the dog out again?

"What is happening?" he asked as he drew even with the little group on the sidewalk.

Beatrice moved past him as though she hadn't known he was speaking to her. He tried the odd, shortened version of her name. "Tess?" He sidestepped to face her and saw that there were tears in her eyes. He put a hand on her shoulder. "Please. Is something wrong?"

She stepped back as though his touch burned. "Jimmy and I have to go now," she said without looking at him, signing the words as she spoke. She sounded infinitely sad. "They won't let me see her anyway."

"You mean Miss Morris?" He knew she often stopped to visit the woman who had been her Uncle Alexei's close friend and ally.

She nodded briefly, and the tears in her eyes rendered her suddenly very young and vulnerable. A strand of auburn hair fell away from her green shawl and trembled uncertainly in the wind.

He put a hand on her arm and didn't let go even though she pulled back. "Why not? Why can you not see her?"

Looking from Tess to David with a puzzled expression, the boy spoke up. "They say she's too sick. She's got something catching, and we can't get near her."

Tess pulled away from David's grasp and tugged at the boy's hand. "Never mind, Jimmy, let's go." The garbled "l" sounded like a "w."

"Beatrice. Tess … please!" David took her by both shoulders and spun her around to face him. She must let him help her. He must make her understand how much he cared about her, how much he had loved her mother.

"Could we have some coffee or cocoa and talk?" he pleaded desperately. "We could go inside where it's warm and quiet. Please, I have so much I need to say to you."

Her hair whipped across her face like sails in a savage wind as she shook her head. Her eyes flashed with anger, and her lips trembled. "I don't want to talk to you," she said petulantly. "I don't want to see you!"

She jumped away from them both and raced away. Jimmy gave an apologetic glance over his shoulder and bounded after her, the dog close at his heels.

Chapter 19

"Annie! Wake up, Annie!" Someone shook her and called her name in short, hoarse whispers. Like a dream cadence, they floated around her.

She felt so tired. Surely, the pain in her head would explode if she opened her eyes. *Sleep. Sleep until this awful dream and its excruciating pain go away.*

"Annie!" The shaking grew more urgent, the familiar voice more intense.

She willed her eyelids to open. A field of multi-colored flowers blurred together, and some pungent aromas like peppermint or wintergreen evoked a puzzling nostalgia. She struggled against the euphoria, and when finally she was able to pierce the fog in her brain, she found two pale blue eyes looking into hers.

"Annie, dear. Are you all right?" Leaning over her, Margaret Morris shook her with soft, insistent pressure. Anne forced her eyes to focus. The field of flowers became a shower of tiny blooms in the blue folds of a cotton house coat.

She peered up into an anxious face surrounded by a halo of wild white hair. "Margaret?"

"Annie, what's happened? Oh, what have they done to you?" Margaret crooned as she stroked Anne's forehead and cheeks with fingers that fluttered over her like moth wings.

Anne blinked and closed her eyes as the fog descended again. Something sweet and spongy coated the inside of her mouth. She was desperately thirsty. "Margaret?"

Memories began to surface. Helen's green eyes over ornately framed glasses, the mask drawn tight against her temples, the sweet, enticing odor pushing her down into unconsciousness.

"It's all right," Margaret was saying. "You're going to be all right. I'm here. We're in a room in the old wing at Rutgers."

Anne focused on the watery blue gaze. "Why? What?" The sticky cobwebs in her brain clung tenaciously. She wondered if she was still dreaming.

"Helen found me going through her files; she put me in here." Margaret covered her eyes with her hands, then quickly withdrew them. "I've been trying to wake you for hours. Oh, Annie, are you all right?"

"Margaret?" Anne tried to lift her head. It felt like it weighed a hundred pounds. She clutched the older woman's cold hands. They were dry and trembling. *What was she doing in here? Why wasn't she in her bed, getting the care she needed? Why was it so cold?*

"You've been drugged, Annie," Margaret said as though she'd just then realized what was wrong. The words broke through the miasma in Anne's brain. "She must have done it because you came looking for me." Margaret's eyes widened. "I found the report about Erma. Her death has never been registered. I—I faced Helen about it, about the others whose checks continued to come. And when I did..." Margaret's explanation gave way to a long wheeze followed by a sputtering cough. She sat back heavily and leaned her head against the wall where they were huddled.

Anne winced. Her mind was growing clearer, and with the clarity came a strong sense of dread. Margaret had been taken from her cozy room and brought here. She, too, had been forced against her will to enter this place.

She looked around with growing despair. A high ceiling loomed above them. The walls were bare and peeling, and broken equipment was piled up at one end of the room. Old beds, tables without legs, and a few stained mattresses. A jumble of plastic tubs, urinals, and bedpans on sagging metal chests. A huge art print behind shattered glass leaned against a discarded wardrobe.

"This room is closed off from the rest of the place," Margaret whispered. "No one comes here." Her words ended in a shudder, and she covered her face with her hands.

They had been speaking in hushed tones, their whispers bouncing around them like tumbleweed. The aura of unreality persisted, and Anne wondered if she would once again drift into unconsciousness. She shook herself. "Helen did this?" She remembered the penetrating eyes above a mask and malevolent penciled brows.

Margaret's cough echoed eerily in the silence. She shivered in her summery housedress, inadequate against the damp chill of the room. She forced her eyes around the bleak, abandoned space. Surely there must be a blanket, a glass of water...something! She braced her palms on the brittle tile of the floor and pushed herself up.

How could anyone put a patient recovering from pneumonia in this barren place? Anne shook herself until she was fully alert. This was no dream; they were both in danger, and if Margaret didn't get out of the cold and the dampness soon, she could be in desperate trouble.

"Let me help you." She scrambled up and half-carried Margaret to the nearest mattress. She struggled out of her parka, which, thankfully, Helen had not taken before locking her away. She tugged it around Margaret. It would provide some small warmth until they found a way out. There had to be a way out!

Easing Margaret into a sitting position, she heaved a second mattress up onto the bed and propped it behind the elderly woman's shoulders and head. Though Margaret was slight, the strain of lifting her produced incredible fatigue, and Anne felt the muscles in her arms go slack from exertion. She rested briefly, then tucked her parka with its soft fleece lining more securely around Margaret's neck and shoulders. "I'm so sorry this is happening to you," she said, panting. "Try to rest."

She pulled herself up and hurried to the door. She shook it hard until it rattled in its frame. "Help. We're locked in. Please open the door!" Surely, someone would pass by and hear them. Someone would be looking for them, wouldn't they? Her voice returned to her weak and raspy. How long had she been here? Perhaps Peter had arrived at Grace Arbor and was waiting patiently for her return, not knowing his mother was in an unused, isolated wing of the nursing home. "Please! Somebody! Get us out!" But her voice came back a hollow echo.

Someone had to know where they were! Why, oh why, had she been so stubborn about buying a cell phone?

Lance, too, had chided her, insisting that a cell phone was not a luxury but a necessity. *A woman living alone in an immoderate climate is foolish not to get one.* And she'd enjoyed his irritation at her stubborn rebuttal.

Cell phones torment you; they interrupt your privacy. You can never get away from the jangling nuisance. They go off in the supermarket, the theater, and even in the middle of church. Of course, she knew the gismos had a "manner mode," and instead of the annoying ringtone, would merely buzz like angry hornets inside your purse or pocket. She regretted her naive refusal to join the 21st century. One call and the authorities could have been alerted.

But how could Helen know that she didn't have a cell phone? She hadn't taken her purse away from her before pushing her into the storeroom. She couldn't know. Maybe the woman would realize her foolish failure to check and come back. If Helen returned, would it mean more danger or a chance to talk sense to her? Whatever could have possessed the woman to do something so bizarre, so dangerous, so criminal?

She rifled through the contents of her purse and found a pair of tweezers. She pried the lock, praying hard as Margaret coughed and tossed on the makeshift bed. Her wordless prayer was perhaps the most eloquent anyone could pray—a simple one-word plea. *Help!*

Had Margaret fallen asleep? Worse, had she lost consciousness? Anne continued manipulating the unforgiving lock, fighting to make her stiff fingers work. Richard would make short work of a dilemma like this one, and she was overwhelmed once more by the thought of him. She fought against tears as the tweezers fell short of the mechanism that trapped them behind the door.

She couldn't tell how long she had worked and prayed but was heartened when she heard Margaret's weak voice. "Can you open it, Annie?"

She was still conscious, still okay. "I haven't got it yet, but don't worry," she said, reaching back under the parka to pat Margaret's hand. She dumped the remaining contents of her purse onto the floor, hoping to find something Margaret could eat. A foil-covered lump rolled out—the cinnamon roll she had saved from Hardy's! It was a habit her children had often scorned, but early years of deprivation were never far from the surface. "Waste not, want not," her mother had so often quoted.

She unwrapped the pastry with almost giddy happiness, broke off a small piece, and held it to Margaret's lips. "Here, eat this. You have to keep up your strength."

Margaret swallowed between wheezes and leaned back against the soiled mattress by the window. Anne secured the parka over her once more and peered through the smudged glass. The landscape beyond the pane was bleak, and it was growing dark.

Anne fumbled through a pile of junk in the corner and drew out an old lamp with no shade. The light bulb was intact. Joyously, she plugged the lamp into the nearest socket and heard her own mirthless laugh. There was no electricity in the abandoned wing.

She returned to work on the deadbolt with the tweezers, intermittently banging on the door and calling into the vacuum beyond. After a while, she rocked back on her heels and contemplated the unyielding door. She prayed desperately for calm. It was strange that such a sophisticated lock had been placed on the old door. It was so old that it even had an antique transom above the door. If only she were smaller and thinner, she might be able to crawl through. She could pile up the abandoned junk, stretch to her full height, and heave herself through it. Wrong! She'd never be able to reach it.

How long could Margaret go without her medicine? How much time had passed since she'd been put in this prison? She touched the elderly woman's shoulder. "Margaret, are you all right?"

She didn't answer but gave a feeble nod.

"See this window," Anne said, heartened. She indicated the smudged square of glass near Margaret's makeshift bed. "Maybe I can pry it open." She pressed her full weight into it, but it was nailed shut. Even if she could get it open, there was little hope of escape. It was too small to squeeze through, and the drop too far from the ground. But they had to do something!

"Margaret, I'm going to try to get the window open enough to throw something out. Maybe we can attract someone's attention." She continued to pray as she worked at the rusty nails, pausing now and then to listen for footfalls, but the only sound was Margaret's labored breathing. She peered through the darkness to the deserted west parking area beneath the window. Whatever she dropped to the ground would likely go unnoticed, perhaps for days.

Still, she pushed her weight against the frame, lifted the window with a mighty heave, and ushered in a blast of frigid, snow-swirled air. She grabbed a bedpan from the pile of junk and flung it through the opening. It fell with barely a sound to the ground below.

She glanced around for something else to throw. She spied a metal basin and heaved it through the opening, then a broken rail from a bed. With sudden inspiration, she picked up her empty purse from the floor and threw it out as well.

At the sound of renewed coughing, Anne closed the window and dropped down beside Margaret, offering her body heat. She repositioned the parka and stroked Margaret's forehead, pushing back wisps of damp hair from the pallid face.

"No one ever uses that parking lot, Annie," Margaret whispered. Her eyes glistened in the near darkness, and the spots on her cheeks brightened as she struggled to talk.

"Try to rest, Margaret. We'll think of something. We have to." Anne sat down on the bed and leaned her head against the mattress. "God will help us. He'll send someone." And surprising herself, she felt a strange sense of calm. She closed her eyes and waited, resting her head next to Margaret's.

"And He shall give His angels charge over thee, to keep thee." The words of Scripture leaped into her memory, and she whispered them over and over until she began to feel sleepy. Was it the after-effects of the drug Helen had used to incapacitate her? She mustn't fall asleep. She had to remain vigilant. But she was so tired!

Presently, she became aware of steps, a light footfall, and a scraping near the door as though someone waited on the other side. She stiffened. Was Helen coming back? What would she do with them?

She put a finger to her lips and gave Margaret a warning look. Edging off the mattress, she pressed herself against the wall.

The steps receded but, in seconds, returned. She waited, frozen, eyes glued to the oblong square of glass of the old-fashioned transom. Suddenly, two eyes peered directly into hers.

Wide, close-set eyes! Then, a shock of red hair. Jimmy? What was he doing here at the nursing home? Anne squeezed her eyes shut and opened them again to make sure she'd seen right. Was it really Lance's young nephew? It seemed a lifetime ago that he was eating pizza at Grace Arbor and laughing with Tess while their ski jackets dried on chairs in her kitchen.

She tried to smile, but her face felt frozen. Suddenly, the eyes disappeared, and she heard a light thud as though the boy had dropped lightly to the ground and run away. No, he mustn't run away.

"Jimmy!" she called with a sinking heart. He had seen her in the dark storeroom. Just her, the woman who had accused him of stealing and turned his uncle against him. Had there been anger, revenge in those eyes? She hadn't meant to accuse him. How could she have known that Vera had stolen her rings and hidden them under a laying hen? Jimmy had been completely innocent. Now, he had a chance to hurt her for her quick misjudgment.

Would he forgive her? Would Lance understand? Dear Lance, who had become such a part of her life. She couldn't bear to think of him angry with her. She longed to see his familiar angular face, the piercing gray eyes with their distinctive silver brows. She yearned to hear his soothing voice brushed with gentle irony. The sweetness of the moments when they put up the tree together came stealing over her with unutterable nostalgia.

She drew in a shallow breath, trembling fingertips poised against her lips. Jimmy knew where she was. It was only a matter of time before they were released, wasn't it?

Or would he leave and not tell anyone she was here? Leave them to freeze or waste away? He had only seen her. He didn't know his friend Miss Morris was there too, just beyond his line of sight. "Jimmy, please! We're locked in here." She struggled to call out against the constriction in her vocal cords. She pressed her palms against the door. "Margaret needs a doctor. She needs help. Jimmy?" But there was only silence.

"And He shall give His angels charge over thee to keep thee in all thy ways." But if angels were watching, they seemed as vaporous as Margaret's breath in the cold gloom.

Suddenly, she heard footsteps again—heavier, quicker. Over the rim of the transom, Jimmy's eyes returned. She held her breath as the boy scrambled lightly through the transom and dropped to the floor.

He stared in pale astonishment at Margaret Morris, at her, then back at the door where voices rose and fell with indiscernible words. Had Helen called her aides for assistance? Were they planning to aid or harm them?

"She's in here," Jimmy called in a high-pitched, squeaky voice to whoever was waiting behind the door. "Miss Morris is here too!"

Anne held out her arms to embrace him. "Oh, Jimmy, I'm so glad to see you."

He stepped back and looked down at his shoes.

"Jimmy, please forgive me," she said bleakly. "I know you didn't take the rings. I found them. I'm so sorry for blaming you."

There was no time to assess how he was taking her apology. The voices outside her door grew stronger. Panting and scuffling ensued until she recognized the mellow timbre of Tess's voice, the slightly muddled accents.

"Stand back!" came an order from another voice she didn't recognize. A deep, strident voice.

The door burst open, and in the glare of a flashlight, Dr. David Brevitz appeared—dark, disheveled, and larger than life. Grover leaped in, dancing and panting in a great rush of feet and fur, and nearly stumbled in his rush to get to Margaret's side. Behind David stood Tess, her eyes enormous in the dim light.

Anne's breath caught when she saw another familiar face. Two arms were flung around her. Fragrant, woodsy warmth enveloped her. "Lance, thank God!" she whispered.

Chapter 20

Encircled in Lance's arms, Anne was aware of little but bliss. His coat, rough and damp where the snow had melted on it, smelled of woods and windswept hills. A euphoric happiness transported her to some tranquil place where no terrors could emerge. Then suddenly, she remembered. She pulled back from his embrace. "Margaret. We have to help Margaret. Please..."

"It's all right, Anne. It's all right." He said it over and over, and her name on his lips sounded like music. "It's all right. The doctor's here. He's taking care of Margaret."

Dark overcoat flung back, David Brevitz bent his wild, tousled head to listen to the inert woman's heart. The long fingers he wrapped around Margaret's thin wrist were deeply tanned with large oval nails like finely crafted sculptures. Anne concentrated on the doctor's hands, fearful of Margaret's quick, raspy breathing. She leaned into Lance, suspended between comfort and dread.

"She'll be all right," Lance said quietly, pressing his fingers more deeply against her back as he held her.

Aware of the heady sense of happiness, she could have stayed there forever, wrapped in these arms and knowing that Margaret was all right. Suddenly, the door was flung wide, and a babble of voices and footsteps sounded in the outer hall.

Jimmy and Tess stood at the threshold of the abandoned storeroom, their grave faces like specters suspended in time. Tess held Grover's collar in a white-mittened hand, auburn hair spilling over the shoulders of her green coat. Her other hand was poised on Jimmy's shoulder.

Lance reached for Tess's arm as though to pull her into his embrace with Anne. "Are you all right?"

She nodded and quickly stepped further into the room just as a veritable fleet of people pushed past her. Nurses and attendants pressed in, one pushing a wheelchair and another rushing ahead of it with a grim expression on her face.

Two aides bent over Margaret, briskly professional, solicitous. One looped the plastic tubing of a portable oxygen tank over her ears and placed the cannula gently beneath her nostrils.

"We've called for the shuttle," one said, referring to the conveyance used to transport ill patients from nursing home to hospital. Another attendant hurried to speak to David, who was standing now, arms crossed over his open greatcoat as he peppered nurses and aids with a series of medical inquiries. One burly male attendant asked if Margaret was strong enough to be placed in a wheelchair.

"Yes, of course, I am," she rasped, as though offended that the question had been asked of a third party rather than herself. She pulled herself up on the tawdry mattress. A torrent of deep coughs belied her brave words and forced her to lie back and meekly accept the ministrations offered her. Two aides helped her into the wheelchair and began tucking blankets around her shoulders and legs.

"I will go with Miss Morris to the hospital," David said firmly, pulling the stethoscope from around his neck and stuffing it into the deep pocket of his coat. He turned to follow the cluster of support staff but paused at Anne's side on his way to the door. "Are you all right, Mrs. Westin?"

He looked old and worn, like a craggy mountain that had survived years of storms. There were dark circles under his eyes and rigid lines around his mouth. Gone was the suave, sure-of-himself ladies' man she had thought him to be. "Yes, yes, I'm fine. Take care of Margaret, please."

Tess swerved to avoid the rush of feet and arms as David and the nursing home staff prepared to usher Margaret from the room. Her brilliant hair tumbled about her shoulders, and her wide eyes were fixed on Margaret's pallid face. She seemed oblivious to the quick, penetrating glance of David Brevitz as he moved past her.

Standing beside Tess, Jimmy twisted his cap in small, chapped hands and shifted his weight from one sneakered foot to the other as she'd seen him do so often when he was nervous or troubled. She longed to convey her regret once more about the rings, but he wouldn't look her way.

"I'm going to drive to the hospital, too," Tess announced. "I'll take Jimmy. We want to be with Miss Morris."

"I'll meet you there," Lance said. "Try not to worry. Miss Morris is one feisty lady. She's going to be all right." But Tess had turned to follow the medical staff and likely hadn't caught Lance's attempt to allay her fears.

Someone stepped inside as the entourage, human and canine, departed. A large, dark-skinned woman in white approached Anne. "Mrs. Westin?"

"Yes," she responded, noting the aide's prominent badge announcing "Florence Brown." There were some initials after the name, which Anne couldn't interpret.

"We'll need you to sign a statement," she said. "Will you follow me, please?" Florence Brown nodded toward Lance, perhaps giving tacit approval for him to accompany them.

Anne took his arm, grateful for its comfort, and followed Ms. Brown, PRN or CRN, from the storeroom and into the breezy hall. Her mind spun as the events of the past few hours hovered, begging for reflection and understanding. What did the urgent phone call and the frustrating refusals to see Margaret mean? Why the isolation, the gowns, and the mask? The mask! She felt a quick renewal of panic and pressed closer to Lance so that she almost stumbled into him. The stultifying odor over her face must have been chloroform or ether. What did they use nowadays to render someone unconscious? "Helen? Where is Helen?"

Lance tugged Anne's parka more snugly around her shoulders as one might do to prepare a child for a romp in the snow. But he didn't break his stride as he shepherded her along the corridor with the strange parade. They were approaching the main wing. Patients peered around the doorways of their rooms. A group clustered near the receptionist's desk whispered excitedly among themselves. Some were being led back to their rooms.

Close to her ear, Lance said in a low voice, "Helen locked herself in her office. They had to break in."

"What has she done?" she stammered. "Why did she put us in that storage room? And how did you find us?" Anne's mind whirled with questions.

Lance guided her toward an alcove off the lobby and steered her inside. He told the aide that they would meet her at the desk in a few minutes to sign whatever needed to be signed but that right now, Mrs. Westin needed to rest. His calm manner clearly brooked no protest. "Please bring some coffee."

Staff members hurried to obey, confused and mollified by the presence of local officials. Lance led Anne to a low leather couch. They sat quietly until the click of nervous footsteps faded down the corridor. He raked his fingers through his silver hair, his anxious gaze fixed on her.

"I'm fine, really," she said tremulously. How good it was to have him near, to see his concern. But did he blame her for her quick reaction to the loss of her rings? He looked worn out. He must have been up all night looking for Jimmy in the storm, and now this.

She had to address the thing that lay unspoken between them, but would it end this closeness she felt with him now? She played with a stray thread on her burgundy blouse. "I was so worried about Jimmy, she said softly. "I could hardly believe it when I saw his head peek over the transom."

"He stayed the night with Tess," Lance said with a sigh. "I found him at her apartment." No longer watching her face, he stared absently toward the lobby. Had his manner changed? The timbre of his voice?

"Oh, Lance, I'm so sorry about blaming him. I didn't want to believe he took my rings, but I couldn't imagine who else could have. I found them in Vera's hen house! It was her all the time. I'm so sorry. I hope Jimmy will forgive me. And you—" She broke off, feeling tears rise.

"Anne, it's all right." He grasped both her hands in his. "We've all made mistakes in this, me not least of all. But Jimmy's fine. Actually, it was Jimmy and Tess who helped us find you. When they came to visit Margaret and were told they couldn't see her, they got help from David, who was coming on his regular rounds. He brought them inside and discovered what was going on."

"What *was* going on, Lance? What *is* going on?"

"Apparently, Helen has been falsifying documents. For how long, I don't know. She was accepting insurance payments for patients after they passed away. That's why there were no obituaries in the newspapers."

Anne gasped, remembering Erma's fearful declaration.

"Helen failed to file the death certificates with the proper authorities." Lance shook his head. "Margaret discovered it, and Helen got desperate."

"Oh, my Lord," Anne whispered, recalling Helen's crazed green eyes over the white mask. *They don't like us.* Erma had complained and worried that her friends' names were forgotten. Anne had dismissed the poor woman's protests, thinking them nothing more than a lonely woman's imaginings.

"We think there were only two violations—Loretta Jaynes and Pauline Hodges. Then, most recently, Erma Tanner. It was Erma's situation that got Margaret thinking. She started checking into things. You know how she is; nothing much gets by her." Lance grinned wryly and rubbed his jaw.

Erma. Dear Erma. Was it possible that her death was somehow tied into all this? Erma wouldn't have died from diabetes if her disease had been properly monitored. Was it deliberate neglect? When the aide came with coffee, Anne wrapped her hands around the cup's smooth contours, allowing its comfort to seep through her fingers. "You hear about these things, but you never think they'll happen to you or to someone you care about," she whispered.

"I know." He took a sip of his coffee. "When they broke into her office, Helen was just sitting there staring into space. Brevitz suspected something wrong was going on. He allowed Helen to sort of call the shots—handle all the business because she knew something about him..." He broke off and thrust a hand through his thick, silver hair.

Anne shuddered, unable to draw her eyes from his face.

"This is a shocker, Anne," he said. "Helen was effectively blackmailing the doctor." Lance drew in a quick breath and went on. "Helen knew why he came to Ladystone, and she held it over his head to keep him in the dark about what she was doing.

You see…" He thrust his hand through his hair again. "David Brevitz is Tess's biological father. She agreed to help him find his daughter as long as he left the nursing home business to her, including what he signed his name to."

Anne felt her knees grow weak. "Tess's father?"

"He's been looking for her for years. When he got here and learned about Elizabeth Grainger and how she'd died and left her granddaughter with the Popovs, well…" Lance shook his head as though overwhelmed by the complicated details.

"But I thought… We all thought…"

"I know. But we were all quite wrong. Brevitz dated a lot of young girls in town, especially at the hospital, because he was looking for his daughter. Then, when he met Tess…" His words fell away, and they gazed into each other's eyes as though all mysteries could be solved there. A moment or maybe an eternity passed, and there seemed to be nothing to say, nothing that would match the enormity of the discoveries this day had revealed.

"Mom?"

She became aware of Peter standing over her, looking down with intense, troubled eyes. She hadn't seen him or heard him coming. She had been expecting him at Grace Arbor, of course, but here he was beside her. How did he know to find her here?

"Peter!" she whispered.

He dropped down on the chair next to the sofa and studied her through luminous brown eyes. Gradually, the somber set of his mouth relaxed. He looked over at Lance and nodded, then returned his gaze to her. "He told me where you were. I was expecting you to be baking cookies, but instead…"

Anne reached up to touch his cheek to reassure herself that he was real. In moments, she and Lance filled him in on what had happened and what Helen had been doing. When she came to the part about Jimmy and Tess finding her in the storage room and bringing help, she paused. What would he think about the news that Dr. David Brevitz was really Tess's father? Anne knew he had been concerned, perhaps a little jealous, by the attention Tess was giving to the new town doctor.

"How is she? Tess—" Worry lines formed on Peter's forehead.

"Tess is fine, Peter. She's just fine. But if it hadn't been for her and Jimmy, I might still be growing icicles in that dark room."

Peter folded his left fist into his right hand and rubbed the knuckles thoughtfully. He searched their faces, eyes roaming from one to the other as though to work out a prickly mathematical problem. "I'm grateful to them and you, Lance," he said gravely.

A tender light shone in Lance's eyes. "Your mother is a remarkable woman. She faced up to Helen and demanded to see Margaret. Who knows what would have happened if she hadn't?"

Anne laughed lightly. "I didn't feel so brave when I woke up and found we were prisoners in that room. God was watching out for all of us, though," she said softly.

"He was at that, Mom," Peter said, still working the knuckles of his hands. "But then, you always taught us to trust Him."

Anne felt her heart leap. To hear her son speak this way after so many years of coldness when the subject of God came up nearly overwhelmed her. She put her hands together in her lap in a silent prayer of thanks. She looked up, feeling a love too big to contain. "He's been watching over all of us. Tess, too."

Anne drew in her breath. "Peter, something else has happened." The room grew still with tension. "You know the doctor who Tess has been ... " She couldn't quite complete what seemed now too ludicrous for words.

Peter's frown deepened with the silence.

"He knew her mother in Europe when they were just teen-agers," she continued. "They were in love, and well, apparently, they had a child." She paused, wondering if he would guess the truth. "He didn't learn that the child was his daughter for ten years. He spent those ten years looking for her."

The pupils of Peter's eyes darted back and forth. He said nothing for a long while. It was typical of him to think through a thing carefully and completely before offering an opinion of any sort. Presently, he stood, put his hands in his pockets, and walked the length of the room. He cleared his throat and asked quietly, "How does Tess feel about this?"

Anne hesitated, remembering the anxiety in David's eyes and the way Tess had walked past him without any sign of rec-ognition, as though he were a total stranger. Finding his daugh-ter was one thing; winning her love would be quite another. After all, in Tess's mind, her father had abandoned her and her mother.

"I don't know." She took a deep breath. "I don't know. At least we do know that he only appeared to be a Don Juan flirting with all those young women. All the time, he was looking for the girl he would learn was his daughter."

It was quiet in the nursing home lobby as the strange story unfolded, each absorbing it in their minds. Lance spoke first. "Maybe you should go home now, Anne. Peter or I could take you."

"No, please. I want to go to the hospital. I need to be sure Margaret's all right." She stood, and they quickly rose, too. She took Peter's arm on one side and Lance's on the other, feeling an incredible sense of well-being and peace. Peter had come a long way. His faith in life and its Creator seemed to be rekindling. He had been engrossed in the sciences as viewed by purely secular scholars who were convinced that life, like nature, was messy

and capricious and most certainly inscrutable. That was before
he had met beautiful, uncomplicated Tess, who heard, not with
her ears but with her soul. Dear Tess. How would she respond
now to the man who had abandoned her and had finally revealed
himself as her father?

Chapter 21

Beside the diminutive figure on the emergency room bed, garish monitors flashed their inscrutable secrets. Tess ignored them and took heart when she saw Miss Morris and smelled the familiar aromas of peppermint and lavender that always accompanied her.

"I'm so glad you're safe." Overcome, Tess could not utter the words, only sign them with trembling fingers.

"I'm all right," Margaret said huskily, fluttering her eyes in the bright light. "Please don't worry."

Tess swallowed, willing herself not to cry. Miss Morris was as close to a real grandmother as she'd ever known. In the last few months, she had come to love her, to cling ever more fiercely to her. They had both shared the love of Uncle Alexei. Both mourned him even now, six months since he'd left them. Tess shuddered, thinking if Miss Morris left her too, she couldn't bear it.

Locked in a cold storage room! How could anyone do such a thing? She touched Margaret's arm, the one without a tube trailing off in a long stream to the saline drip. Tess gently adjusted the blanket over Margaret's exposed arm. Uncle Alexei would be horrified. For the first time since he'd been found dead in Grace Arbor's woods, Tess was glad he wasn't there to see his dear Margaret like this.

The door opened, and David entered. Tess turned away angrily, her pulse beating hard and fast. He'd taken charge, ordering Miss Morris' transfer to the hospital, but she didn't want to look into his face and see those deceptive eyes.

She'd thrown the necklace at his feet when she realized who he was and what he'd done. She could still see the moonlight glistening on the oval locket that fell on his leather boot and broke open like an egg. She'd gone back to the nursing home and risked seeing him only because of Miss Morris.

He walked past her and directly to the bedside, where he bent over his patient and plied the stethoscope to her chest. She tore her eyes away, wanting to run from the room— from his lies! She hugged her arms across her stomach, feeling as though she'd been shaken and left to air like a beaten rug. He'd begged her to let him explain, but what was there to say? He had abandoned them, leaving an aged grandmother to find a home for them.

His features were plainly visible in profile—the prominent nose and dominant chin so like her own. Why had she not noticed before? The attraction she had felt hadn't been some romantic sensibility but a connection she hadn't understood. He had been laughing at her, pretending to court her, all the while keeping his secret joke.

She swallowed, feeling a hot flush rise to her neck. His deep-set eyes were fixed on Miss Morris's pallid face. She imagined a look of pity or pathos there. Pity for his patient? For her? For himself?

Suddenly, someone touched her shoulder. She was so engrossed that she couldn't feel the air moving when the door opened. Anne Westin hooked an arm through hers, the gesture soothing her rising panic. Tess leaned into her, drinking in the tenderness in her friend's hazel eyes.

"Tess, dear. Are you all right?"

She couldn't say anything or even find a sign to express herself. She gave a small nod and clung to the strength that Anne Westin's presence inspired.

"We're all so lucky that you came tonight and that you and Jimmy found us. Margaret's going to be all right, Tess. She will."

Tess swallowed as though to ingest the hope held out to her. Her heart was so full. Miss Morris was safe, and Mrs. Westin, who always seemed to be at the center of whatever crisis she faced, was there beside her. She always seemed to put things in perspective for her. But how would she ever make sense of what she'd learned?

"Tess," Mrs. Westin said softly, "Peter is here. He'll be coming up in a little while, and I know he wants to see you."

Tess felt her pulse quicken. Oh, yes, she wanted to see Peter. She wanted to look into those confident eyes, so richly brown and deep; she wanted to lose herself in them and banish the terrible truth she had learned. He'd have to know; perhaps he already knew. What would he think of her now? What could she possibly say to him? Everything was so mixed up.

"Why don't you look in on your Aunt Vera now?" Mrs. Westin said. She squeezed her hands gently and then released them, giving her the tiniest prod forward. "I think she needs you, Tess."

Aunt Vera needed her? That's what families did, wasn't it? The irony of her thoughts shocked her. The truth was she had no family, at least none that truly cared about her. Vera wasn't likely to want her around now any more than she had ever wanted her.

"She's bruised and sore after her fall," Mrs. Westin was saying, "but nothing's broken. She tore the cartilage in her right knee. They've immobilized it for a while, but she'll be back on her feet before long."

Tess smiled weakly. Could she do this? She lifted her chin. Peter wanted to see her. He would be expecting to see the brave young woman he thought her to be, not some trembling child afraid to speak her mind. Still, how could she tell him all that had been happening and how she felt when she didn't know herself? She turned away from Mrs. Westin and David Brevitz and fled from the room, her heart racing.

She found Vera lying with her right leg suspended in a sling-like contraption braced by metal bars and fastened to a swivel over the bed. How like a caricature she looked. Her considerable bulk formed an awkward mound under the blanket drawn up to her chin.

"Hello, Aunt Vera," she said softly, stopping a few feet from the bed.

Vera's dark hair splayed against the pillow as though electrified, and the birthmark on her left cheek stood out against the white sheet. Her lips formed a grim line above her double chin.

"How are you?" Tess asked, signing the question out of habit.

The eyes above the white sheet were flat and brown as old tree bark and traveled from ceiling to doorway before drifting toward her. Her hands fluttered nervously, then fell away. Something in the helplessness of that gesture touched Tess, and she stepped nearer.

Vera said nothing but watched her through eyes that seemed to grow gradually opaque. What went on behind that shield? Tess had often tried to penetrate those eyes and discern their secrets, but she'd been shut out. "I'm sorry about your accident," she signed. "Mrs. Westin says you'll be okay once your knee heals."

Vera shut her eyes slowly and opened them again. Tess felt a wave of longing or pity for the woman who had been the only mother she had known. She'd been an orphan too, she remembered, and she was startled by the sudden thought. An orphan like her. How did people learn to love without a mother or father to show them? Why had she never understood this about her aunt? "Mrs. Westin has been taking care of your chickens," she said.

"She is very mad?" Vera asked. She looked up at the ceiling, pouting like a child about to be punished.

"It was a foolish thing to do," Tess said gently, half amused at the bizarre role reversal that had so often been the case when she was growing up with her simple but remote aunt. "What you did got Jimmy in a lot of trouble. Everyone thought he was a thief."

Vera dropped her eyes. She clutched the sheet in both hands and pushed out her lower lip slowly. "That woman—she take Alexei away. Then she take you away!" Her eyes roved petulantly from her hands to the ceiling.

"That's crazy, Aunt Vera!" Tess said. "Uncle Alexei had a heart attack, and nobody sent me away. Don't you see?" She began to sign rapidly in her frustration. "Mrs. Westin bought Grace Arbor. She has every right to live there. And I'm grown up now. I have a life of my own and a job."

Vera turned her head like a stubborn child who refused to listen. Tess walked around the bed, commanding her attention. "You have to apologize to Mrs. Westin and Jimmy. It was very wrong of you."

Vera shut her eyes again and didn't open them for a long time. "I think you hate me too." Her lower lip protruded further in a childish pout.

Tess felt a strange need to laugh and released a long breath before saying, "Nobody hates you, but you act like you hate everybody." She walked around to the other side of the bed to quell some deep agitation building in her. The need to laugh was suddenly gone. "You pay more attention to those stupid chickens than you ever did to me." She hung her head, glad for the drape of hair that fell over her face, hiding her quick tears. "Didn't you know I just wanted you to like me?"

She had never spoken like this to her aunt, but now she had no patience for holding back. She would not give in to weakness, not anymore.

Tess watched Vera's little black eyes go shiny with tears. Her hands, folded over her stomach, fluttered like troubled birds without access to their nest.

"I am sorry," Vera said, signing as she seldom did.

Impulsively, Tess covered the rough hands with hers. Vera had never apologized for anything before. Tess felt her knees tremble. "Me too," she said. "Me too." And some subtle grace shone in the little space between them. Tess felt it covering them like an aura or a shield. She folded one of her aunt's dry hands in hers and held it beneath the sheet.

Like a child absolved, Vera grew sleepy. Tess sat with her, watching the rise and fall of her chest. They must have given her something to calm her; she would sleep now. She got up but stood looking down at her for a long while. Perhaps, after all, in her simple way, Aunt Vera had loved her.

She left her and wandered into the cafeteria. Despite a new sense of connectedness to the woman who had tried to care for her, a troubling loneliness persisted. She bought some hot tea that smelled of bitter coffee dregs and moved off to a deserted corner of the room. Why did people insist on brewing tea in the same pot used for coffee? She held her hands around the cup; she had no desire to taste the dark liquid.

She was glad it was late and that the cafeteria was all but deserted. She had no energy for the difficult art of conversation. She sat for a long time, piercing the Styrofoam cup over and over with her fingernail, thinking about everything and nothing, until she became aware that she was no longer alone in her corner. Her peripheral vision registered a man's approach.

She willed him to go away, but he proceeded toward her table, paused briefly, and sat down across from her. Her breath caught as a familiar scent wafted over her. She saw strong hands with clean, rounded nails. And she knew it was David. His lips were moving. She would not look; she would not listen!

"Beatrice—Tess."

If she looked into those dark eyes, the kindness in them would kill her. And she wanted to be angry. He had deceived them. She could feel her heart racing. She wanted to hate this man. He had no right to come back now. It was too late.

"Bea—Tess ... " He moved to touch her hand, but she pulled back and wrapped her arms over her chest, holding in the foment churning inside. She set her chin and met her father's penetrating gaze. Let him say what he must. He had a right to speak, but she would be fooled no longer. She was not a child, after all.

David opened his left hand to reveal the locket she had thrown at his feet. He pressed his thumbnail inside the delicate hinge and cupped her mother's image in his large palm. He coiled his fingers around the frame as though to caress the face that looked out from its enclosure. "I want to tell you about it—about us. Will you listen, Tess?"

She allowed herself to watch his lips, to read the story of young love, cherished and lost. She heard how the girl he had loved when he was merely a boy had gone away from the university and didn't want to see him anymore. She heard how he had buried himself in work.

"When I learned there was a child, I tried to find you," he said, closing his eyes and opening them again with an effort that seemed to pain him. "I tried for ten years. I'm sorry I didn't tell you earlier who I was, but I had to be sure. When I was sure, I couldn't find a way to tell you."

Even as she tried to disconnect herself from the story, she was moved with pity and squeezed her eyes tight against rising tears.

"I didn't know Helen was doing anything wrong, Tess," he said, looking down at his hands, curling them around the locket now closed in his fist. "I didn't know she was withholding reports and taking money for care that wasn't given." He shook his head as though trying to make sense of what he was saying. "I was afraid she would force me to leave before I found you." He paused, and she could see him swallowing against something in his throat. "There will be an investigation. I'll have to go away for a while."

"What do you mean?" she stammered, surprised by the anxiety threatening to choke her. She knew she was letting it happen, letting herself believe what he was telling her, caring about it, caring about him!

"My visa in this country has expired. I won't be able to continue practicing medicine here." He paused and ran a hand through hair that seemed to have grayed perceptibly in a matter of days. "I've told all this to the authorities." He broke off as though overwhelmed.

Impulsively, Tess touched the hand that held the locket. "Did Ms. Rutger put Mrs. Westin and Miss Morris in that room?" she asked.

He nodded. "Margaret found some damaging evidence about what Helen was doing. Helen had to stop her. I don't know what she would have done if Anne hadn't come looking for Margaret. We can only thank God that she did."

The memory chilled Tess—Jimmy climbing through the transom, Miss Morris on a bare mattress, and Mrs. Westin with her. Helen Rutger must have been desperate to do something so terrible. Perhaps her father, too, had been desperate. It surprised Tess that she had thought of him that way—her father.

She stood, backed up a little from the table where they had been sitting, but she couldn't tear her eyes away from the earnest face before her, the dark pools that reflected a world of pain. Eyes that begged her to understand, to forgive. She waited for him to speak again, afraid he might not.

"I had to find you, Tess," he said. "Please forgive me."

Tears stung her throat. She could feel them spilling over, blurring his face. He had risked everything to find her, and he would be torn away once more. She lifted a hand to her mouth, and in a second, he was at her side. She flung her arms around him, and this time, there was no holding back her sobs.

"Oh, my little Tess," he said with a tenderness that she thought would break her heart.

At last, she knew she belonged to someone who wanted her and had sacrificed so much to find her.

"There is so much I want to tell you, so much I want to learn about you," he said, drawing back a little but keeping her in the circle of his arms. "I am so proud of you."

She clung to him, drinking in his warmth. Had she the right to such happiness? Her heart filled with gratitude. "Thank God," she whispered against her father's chest. "Thank God."

Chapter 22

Miniature lights sparkled through evergreen garlands along Grace Arbor's deck rails. Anne stood listening. Just inside, the party she had planned in loving detail was underway. In the great room that shimmered with color and candlelight, early guests enjoyed a festive buffet. Others would join them soon, and the house would be ablaze with warmth and good cheer. It was what she had hoped for when she'd become the owner of Grace Arbor. Well almost.

She glanced across the adjoining property where Vera Popov's lone porch light shone again. She had come home from the hospital, her knee almost as good as new. But if there was light in her heart, it was indiscernible. Despite two invitations to the party, she had not shown up. Perhaps she would never accept her friendship.

Anne sighed and went inside, prepared to serve her guests, but she was caught by the shine of the moon on the snow. She lingered at the window, her heart full. How stunning the winter night, wrapped in ermine white and bejeweled with stars.

On a night like this, God had sent the bright morning Star to light the world's darkness. He spoke one single lovely Word and laid it in a manger.

Suddenly, a car door slammed, announcing the arrival of more guests. David Brevitz, with Tess on his arm, clambered from his car, carrying brightly wrapped packages. Snowflakes clung to David's dark coat and shimmered in Tess's auburn hair as they came up the walk, heads bent close together. Anne hurried to welcome them, these friends who had defied the odds and found each other.

They swept inside after their hostess, their faces rosy from wind or happiness. "Merry Christmas!" David said, offering Anne a tall gift bag with an enormous bow. "Romanian wassail," he said with an old-world bow, "a very fine vintage." A new light softened his rugged features and gentled the suave manner that had once been the talk of the hospital. He still retained the capacity to startle, to render her temporarily tongue-tied.

"Thank you," she stammered, marveling that she'd never noticed the strong resemblance between him and Tess before. She was copper-haired and willowy, and he was dark and swarthy, but something in the bearing and definitely in the aristocratic shape of their noses linked them. "I'm so glad you're here."

"Merry Christmas!" Tess's voice trilled with excitement, and her pronunciation was less guarded, but there was no hint of embarrassment in her shining eyes. She handed Anne a small silver box with a crimson bow. "For you," she said, dropping her eyes shyly.

"Thank you, both of you," Anne said, touched by their thoughtfulness and the wonder of their reunion that Tess had recounted. He came looking for her in the hospital coffee shop and told him everything that had happened to him and Tess's mother. "Come, let's join the others," she said, unable to stop smiling at the two of them. "Margaret has been waiting for you."

In a maroon suit with a ruffled collar of pale pink, Margaret Morris looked as regal as a queen. Her face, framed by snowy hair, was still pale but flushed by the fire's red glow. She'd been released only the day before. The party was her first outing after her ordeal. Lance had literally carried her from his car into the house where she'd been installed near the hearth, her portable oxygen tank close by. Her eyes lit up like blue sapphires when Tess came in.

"Are you all right?" Tess asked, kneeling beside her surrogate grandmother.

Margaret leaned forward to clasp her hand. "I've never felt better now that you're here," she said. "Besides, Annie here has been waiting on me hand and foot."

Anne waved her praise away and lifted a cup of hot cider from the serving table. "Come, David," she said, taking his arm. "I'll introduce you to some of our guests, but first…" She paused and guided him to a corner of the room. "Are *you* all right?"

He had been distraught over the discovery of fraudulent documents and delayed patient death reports. Anne shivered, realizing what might have happened if Helen hadn't been stopped.

The story would no doubt occupy the tongues of everyone in the small community for some months to come. David confessed that his visa had expired and was under review by licensing boards and other authorities.

"I am fine," he said, his eyes on Tess sitting on a low stool by Margaret's chair. "But I am so sorry, so ashamed, so…"

"These have been difficult days," she said softly. "I've been praying for you and Tess."

He touched the cider to his lips, and Anne saw that his dark eyes were moist. "They found Helen on her way to Florida," he said, his voice husky. "She was trying to find her mother." He shook his head as though dazed. "It was stupid of me not to see what was happening to her and the patients—everyone."

Anne nodded. Blinded by his longing to find his lost daughter, he had not seen the damage Helen's greed was causing her.

"It will be hard for Tess to say goodbye now that she's found you. What will happen now?"

David lowered his head, remorse plain in his chiseled face. "I don't know." He frowned into his cup of cider. "I will have to go back, at least for a while. I am grateful to you and to the others who have helped my daughter."

He seemed close to tears, and Anne's heart ached for him. Immigration authorities and licensing boards could be harsh, and Helen's violations would reflect badly on him. Still, he had not knowingly hurt anyone, and he had friends who would stand up for him. The hardest part would be leaving Tess. "We'll all watch out for her, David," she said softly. "And God will be with you too."

He held her gaze for a long moment. "I was not raised to believe, but I think it is as you say."

She covered his hand for a moment before stepping away. It was more than remarkable that he had found his daughter on the other side of the world. It was a miracle.

Anne joined Peter and Lance at the buffet table. They were engaged in conversation, Peter nudging his glasses up on his nose with the hand that held his fork. How she loved this man who amazed people with his acute mind but who would doubtless forever retain the "absent-minded professor syndrome."

She paused to listen to the sounds of laughter and animated conversation, the clink of glasses and silver. God had been faithful to them all. Anne caught sight of Jimmy standing near the piano, looking at the photos of her family and friends. She recalled his early attraction to them before—the time he had asked what it was like to be dead. She came alongside him and searched his face. "Jimmy, I'm sorry I blamed you for the rings."

He looked down and shrugged in that rolling gesture she had come to recognize as his signature. "It's okay," he said in a small voice.

"You were very brave, you know," she said. "Finding us there in that spooky old storeroom and bringing the others. If you hadn't come, well, who knows what would have happened to us?"

His face quickly colored from the collar of his shirt to his cheeks. Anne longed to put her arms around him and give him the love he had so long been denied. When Lance told her that he suspected Jimmy had endured abuse, she was stunned. It was unbelievable, outrageous! But she knew that there were virtually thousands of vulnerable children around the world who were victims of domestic violence. To think that Jimmy should have been hurt this way!

Jimmy left the piano and darted away to Margaret's chair, where Grover sat, wagging his tail. He slipped the dog a Ritz cracker generously spread with cheese. He would miss his furry pal. Lance was going back with Jimmy after the holidays to "sort things out and make sure he's okay." Now she regarded the strawberry blond head, which turned red as wine under the light of the chandelier, and had a hunch that when Lance returned to Ladystone, he wouldn't be alone.

As if her thoughts had summoned him, Lance came in from the kitchen bearing a replacement tray of fruit and rolled sandwiches. He had worked tirelessly with her, dragging chairs up from the basement, hanging greens from the high beams, and checking all the decorative lights for the party. In his royal blue sweater, he was singularly handsome.

His silvery head towered perilously close to the chandelier. He looked very much like a Viking fresh off the starboard deck. Anne's fingers brushed his as she took the tray from him and placed it on the nearby serving table.

"I've been thinking," Margaret's voice caught everyone's attention. She was looking from Lance to Jimmy to Grover with studied conspiracy and stroking one of the dog's silken ears. "I can't care for this mangy hound anymore."

The dog gave a low groan as though the insult had injured his canine pride. Jimmy hunched down beside him and murmured commiseration.

"Grover needs a strong, young owner to take care of him," Margaret continued solemnly. She fixed Jimmy with a level gaze. "I thought you might take him off my hands." She lifted a green olive from her plate and looked around at the guests as though calling them as witnesses.

Jimmy's mouth dropped open; his freckles blanched. "You mean it?" Then, as quickly, his brows drew together in a tight frown. He looked up at his uncle. "I can't. I mean..."

"Of course you can," Lance said. "I'll keep him for you temporarily."

The two looked at each other. Lance's love for the boy was written in 24-point type on his face. Anne saw him swallow and assume a sterner demeanor. "But I may charge a boarding fee if he gets to eating too much. I'm not made of money, you know." Lance laid a hand on the boy's shoulder. "Just say yes," he said gently.

"Yes. I mean... thanks. Oh, gosh, Grover!" Jimmy embraced the dog, nearly knocking over a huge poinsettia plant by Margaret's chair. Everyone applauded. Anne swallowed against a rush of emotion. The warmth and goodwill in the room was almost too much. Who would have thought that just a few days ago she and Margaret had been held captive in a frigid storeroom, Jimmy had run away, and Tess hadn't known she had a father who loved her.

Tears welled as she looked from one face to the next. These friends gathered together in her home had taught her trust, patience, and the importance of community. They had welcomed her, given their friendship, their love. Her eyes fell on the crèche, its white ceramic contours like gleaming pearls against a swirl of blue satin. It was so sad to realize that there were lonely people who couldn't or wouldn't embrace Christmas in their hearts.

A knock at the back door broke through her reverie and the chorus of voices. Everyone paused and looked toward the door—Jimmy with his hand on Grover's tawny head, Peter with an arm around Tess's waist, and Lance in mid-reach of a sugar cookie.

A solitary figure leaning heavily on a claw foot cane stood at the door. Vera Popov, hair drawn carefully back and wearing a frayed denim jacket over a long gray dress, frowned but raised hopeful eyebrows. The green brooch winked in the porch light.

"Vera! Anne put out both arms to draw her neighbor inside the fragrant kitchen.

"My shoes wet," she stammered in a voice creaky with disuse. She held her arms stiffly at her sides, and one chubby fist was tightly closed.

Anne caught the aroma of onions and detergent, Vera's signature fragrance, and found it oddly appealing. "Don't worry. This old rug by the door will soak it up before you can blink."

Vera looked up, then down again to her shoes. Hesitantly, she lifted her hand and opened her fingers.

Anne stared at the object—a familiar old-style key with a distinctive oval head. The key to Grace Arbor's rear door!

"I give it back," Vera said, tight-lipped and frowning.

So that was how she had gotten inside to steal her rings. When Anne discovered them in Vera's chicken coop, she wondered how to handle the situation. Should she notify the sheriff? Confront Vera? Then the black-out and getting imprisoned with Margaret had overtaken the drama of the rings. She decided to put off confronting the situation until Vera was well and Christmas was over.

"I...am sorry," she stammered through lips unaccustomed to apology. She stood still, her eyes a mask of hope and fear. "I got no right to come." She hugged herself as though she were cold or afraid. "I been mean to you."

"Vera," Anne said, her heart rising. "You are my guest, and I'm so pleased you came."

Tess froze when she saw Vera, but in seconds, a smile lit her violet eyes. She went to her and coiled an arm around her large waist. "Merry Christmas, Aunt Vera." Then, tugging her by the hand, she said in one joyous monosyllable, "Come." And Vera hobbled on her cane into the company of friends and neighbors.

Anne caught Lance's eye. After a momentary pause, he scooped up a tray, butler style, and held out a cup of cider to Vera. "Won't you join us, neighbor?" He gave a little bow and turned to the others with a wave of his hand as though to demand that the party resume. Immediately, laughter and chatter filled the room.

Lance moved to Anne's side. "Wonders never cease," he whispered.

Anne tucked her hand into the crook of his arm, euphoric as she watched Tess help Vera to a chair by the fireplace opposite Margaret. What grace had brought them all together, even this one who had been so full of bitterness and envy? Surely, the Christ whose birth they celebrated was among them, bringing His searching love to bear upon their secret sorrows and failures.

Lance's eyes were a mirror for her unspoken thoughts. She felt his lips brush hers. The pressure was so soft and quick that no one else had time to notice. She looked up, startled.

"Mistletoe," he whispered pointing. "You're standing under it."

She followed his gaze to the chandelier. "Oh," she said, nodding. "I see."

"I hope you do," he said tenderly. "I hope you see how glad I am that I am here with you."

She leaned into him and let her eyes speak for her heart. She was home. Yes, she was finally home to this house of grace where God's love dwelled.

About the Author

Marlene Chase is an ordained minister, serving as a Salvation Army officer for 43 years. She retired from her position as editor-in-chief and literary secretary for the Army's publications in the United States, having served in that capacity for 11 years. She traveled extensively in teaching/preaching ministries both in the U.S. and abroad. She holds a Bachelor of Arts degree in English from Mid-America Nazarene College and attended The Salvation Army College for Officer Training in Chicago, Illinois, and the International College for Officers in London. She has published 24 books and a host of articles, poetry, and internationally aired radio scripts. She continues to write both for the popular market and Salvation Army publications from her home in Rockford, Illinois.

More Books by Author

The Other Side of Silence, Barbour, Ulrichsville, O
This Trembling Cup, Barbour, Ulrichsville, O
A Seed in the Wind, The Salvation Army, Chicago, IL
Twenty-Five Years of CMI, The Salvation Army, Chicago, IL.
Our God Comes, Crest Books, Alexandria, VA.
Beside Still Waters, Crest Books, Alexandria, VA
Pictures from the Word, Crest Books, Alexandria, VA.
The Salvation Army, Crest Books, Alexandria, VA.
(Translations in Korean and Spanish)
Forever and a Day, Guideposts
The Greatest of These, Guideposts
Sapphire Secret, Guideposts
The Hidden Gate, Guideposts
Larceny and Old Lace, Annie's Mysteries
A Crime Well Versed, Annie's Mysteries
All That Glimmers, Annie's Mysteries
Deceptive Hearts, Annie's Mysteries

Acknowledgments

Grateful thanks to my family, especially my two daughters, Laurel and Evangeline, who have always encouraged their Mom's storytelling and provided many a stirring thought for a novel or poem.

It would not be possible to create enduring characters and scenes if it were not for The Salvation Army who allowed me a place to minister for 43 years. Its compassionate service to everyone, without discrimination, in the name of Christ has molded my thinking and given opportunity to develop my craft.

Thanks, once again, to Story Architect and Jill Kemerer at Books and Such, as well as my agent, Wendy Lawton, ever the staunch encourager and mistress of words.

To you, dear Reader, thank you for the investment of your valuable time. May it be well spent and bring joy to your heart.

Special thanks to Andrew and Kelleigh Miller of Oregon, IL for permission to use their lovely home on the cover of this book. "Pinehill," built in 1874 and added to the National Historic Register in 1978, is one of the largest, most ornate, and best preserved examples of Italianate Country Villa architecture in Illinois. The couple maintains the villa as a primary residence and opens the property to the public for philanthropic and private events.